"Hearing" With the Mind's Eye!
Can You *"SEE"*
What I Am *"SAYING?"*

FROM RESEARCH TO THEORY

Dr. Jean Pierre-Pipkin

EEUCbyPierre (R)
Beaumont, TX
Copyright 2009

Published by *EEUCbyPierre* © *2009*
Educational Equality in Urban Communities
3365 Blossom Drive
Beaumont, TX, 77705

Pierre-Pipkin, Jean © 2009
Hearing With the Mind's Eye: Can You "See"
What I Am "Saying?" From Research to Theory

This book was printed by
Xlibris Corporation, 2010
1663 Liberty Drive
Blooming, IN

Library of Congress Control Number: 2010904724
ISBN: Hardcover 978-1-4535-0547-2
Soft cover 978-1-4535-0546-5
To order in Print 978-1-4500-7611-1
Ebook orders:
www.eeucbypierre@sbcglobal.net
Ebook 978-1-4535-0548-9

79459

"Hearing" With the Mind's Eye!
Can You *"SEE"*
What I Am *"SAYING?"*

FROM RESEARCH TO THEORY

Dr. Jean Pierre-Pipkin

Ana Tra
Best Regards
from Pierre
Feb. 14, 2011

EEUCbyPierre (R)
Beaumont, TX
Copyright 2009

To my children and grandchildren—Darryl Joseph Pipkin, Alpha Lorraine Pipkin Guillory, and Lorenzo Pipkin, III; and their children—Laurent Michael Pipkin, Lorean Markus Pipkin, Doran Charles Guillory, Daniel Joseph Pipkin, and David Johnathan Pipkin.

May you have enough happiness to keep your days always sweet; enough trials to make you always strong; enough sorrow to keep you always human; and enough hope to make you always happy.

CONTENTS

PREFACE

When teachers reach out to understand the cultural worlds of diverse children, they touch their hearts, and subsequently touch their minds.   __ Jean Pierre-Pipkin

One of the greatest challenges confronting American's public schools is to critically, realistically and successfully address the complex issues that have purportedly created the miseducation and under achievement of African American and other marginalized children through poor quality education. In this regard, several essential issues need to be addressed: *Issue 1: The development of an effective educational delivery system that requires, as well as ensures, teaching methodologies and school practices that provide maximum opportunities for all children who are intellectually capable—regardless of their cultures and backgrounds—to learn the expected grade level academic content for the number of years of school attendance. Issue 2: Restructuring the manner of delivering instruction to ensure that African American and other marginalized children learn academic content with "understanding" within specific criterion referenced contexts, as opposed to teaching for testing. Issue 3: Establishing more effective methods of objectively measuring students' academic performance; and using assessment results diagnostically to improve classroom instruction; thereby eliminating the plethora of disadvantages placed on African American and other* *marginalized children in situations of paper-pencil "only" standardized test evaluations.*

A *critical* evaluation of how these issues are addressed requires educators to apply rational, methodical analysis to determine what practices are currently and consistently effective across the educational spectrum; and what practices, including federal, state, and local policies, currently and consistently fall short or fail to be effective in schooling and the teaching-learning process; especially for the significant numbers of African American and other marginalized children who are being *under-educated*.

This task may seem daunting, but it simply requires several factors: diagnostic analysis of what conditions propel student learning, and what factors present barriers; designing curriculum that considers the import of the cultural learning experiences of African American and other marginalized children; using relevant cultural themes in pedagogy; and a shift in attitudes that promote high expectations for this population of children. Moreover, in developing academic curriculums and delivering instruction, educators must implement *content* within *contexts* that consider different language patterns and word meanings that influence student discourse; and the sociocultural experiences that have shaped the learning styles of diverse students. The use of culturally relevant and culturally responsive instruction has proved an effective scaffolding practice that advances cognition and learning for diverse learners; especially when school discourse varies significantly from their cultural language experiences, learning patterns, and prior knowledge (Cole, et al., 1978; Delpit, 1995; Rogoff and Lave, 1999; Ackerman, 2003; Lee, 2005a).

An evaluation of the current process of public education must be *realistic* in the sense that schools must be viewed as part of the social context in which each school is situated. This requires a reflective understanding of the purposes and expectations of schooling for various cultural communities and groups—regardless of whether these purposes and expectations are self-imposed or result from socially imposed attitudes and traditions (Anderson, 1988; Crosby, 1999; Watkins, 2001a). *Realism* requires that where group or social constraints reduce or limit effective schooling for ethnic minority and/or poor urban children, educators must have a willingness to rise above such situations to deliver quality education. Finally, to *successfully* address these issues requires that educators consider the educational history, current social, political, and economic factors that impact equitable education of urban children. Other factors to consider include attitudes that reflect low expectations for urban children; and who dictates what will or will not be taught to *certain people's children* (Delpit, 1995; Kohn,

1998; Maeroff, 1988, 1998). Unless, or until educators give serious consideration to solving these issues, millions of African American and other marginalized children will continue to linger on the bottom rungs of the academic performance ladders in public schools throughout the country.

INTRODUCTION

If we spend too much time "fixing" how children talk, we won't hear what children say.   —Jean Pierre-Pipkin

---

Creating new paradigms for instructional effectiveness requires attitude changes of quantum proportions, primarily because the tasks of addressing and restructuring school practices present the greatest challenge in urban schools populated predominantly by African American and other marginalized children. This became especially apparent when urban districts shifted from schooling mainly middle-class, to poor and diverse student populations. Moreover, compared to suburban schools, urban schools continue to be unequal in access to quality instructional resources, teacher quality, and facilities; and data reflect that children in urban schools lag years behind suburban school children in academic performance and do less well than their suburban peers on tests of academic achievement (Tyack, 1974; Anderson, 1988; Kozol, 1991; Slavin, 1997; Helms, 1992; Hilliard, 1990 & 1996; Steele, 1992; Stiggins, 1999).

What perhaps has hindered the tasks of successfully educating African American and other marginalized children has been the 'blame game' where schools blame homes, homes blame schools, and communities blame both homes and schools; and unfortunately, children engender the most blame for poor academic performance (Pierre-Pipkin, 2004a; Scott,

1

2007). Moreover, the literature reflects that many teachers in urban schools have low expectations for diverse students' performance; project negative attitudes, and hold assumptions that poor performance is a consequence of social class and inabilities of the children (Shade, 1982; Gougis, 1986; Ashton & Esses, 1999; Cook-Gumprez, 2006). Consequently, the following questions should be addressed:

- How do we educate, and *objectively assess performance* of African American and other marginalized groups—to ensure that they perform academically as well as their suburban counterparts when measured by standardized tests?

- Should the definition of *Highly Qualified Teacher* be modified to include competence in knowing, respecting, and valuing African American and other marginalized students; having high student expectations; and the ability to make academic content *culturally relevant* through scaffolding methodologies to enhance student performance?

- How can schools identify and eliminate practices to reduce negative attitudes and social stigmas regarding ethnicity and being poor, which are embedded in the larger society and often carried into and reflected in both urban and suburban schools?

- How can we educate urban students for a global society given the state of urban schools that are poorly staffed and under-equipped; yet are expected to produce the same level of academic skills and marketplace readiness as high-wealth suburban students in well-staffed, highly-equipped schools? Should we be expected to do so?

- Finally, what is the most effective way of restructuring curriculum for diverse populations considering that most school curricula content, and assessment of academic performance mirror Eurocentric middle class lifestyles? (Helms, 1992; Maeroff, 1998; Kozol, 1991 & 2005)

It should be noted that while *unequal* educational resources and opportunities present significant barriers to quality education, *inequality* is not the sole cause of poor schooling and education in urban schools. Inequality and limited educational resources and opportunities have been with us for a long time. Moreover, for generations educators have overcome the barriers of inequalities in urban schools and have successfully educated urban school students (Sizemore, 1989; Pollard, 1989; Floyd, 1996; Slavin, 1997; Ancess, 2003). What successful educators of African American children did, and continue to do with limited resources, validate Ron Edmond's assertions on effective

3

schooling and education of poor children. Edmonds (1979 & 1986) concluded that, *educators have more than enough knowledge to successfully educate poor children.* However, Edmonds contended that *it takes a determined will to do so.*

The Focus of this Text

The focus of this text emphasizes the link between theory and practice, with particular emphasis on research and theories of *culturally influenced learning.* Further, much of the emphasis stresses the importance of ensuring that sound learning theory and field-tested practices are employed to guide curriculum design and inform instructional delivery; that pedagogy is theory-based, and not simply idealistic; but *realistically* related to the specific population of students being taught; and that content is relevantly contextualized to teach for *understanding,* as opposed to *memorization,* or teaching-to-test.

This text concurs with Edmonds' *Effective Schools Movement* (Ibid.) that identifies school practices found in successful schools. However, in addition to Edmonds' conclusion of *willingness*, this author posits that *specific,* not *extraordinary* teaching methodologies and school practices are needed for urban learners. The most critical of instructional practices include: first, recognizing the need to connect *content* with *contextual relevance* for urban learners; secondly, educators must provide varying

4

opportunities with actively engaged students, using scaffolding activities that consider their learning styles and cultural experiences to mediate understanding; and by establishing a nexus between in-school and out-of-school learning. Next, educators must create in-school climates that support and respect the cultural lifestyles of *all* students, making schools, in part, the extensions of their communities.

Moreover, it is critical for schools to be so structured that African American and other ethnic children feel *accepted* and *valued* every day throughout the year—not just in the month of February; or one May day devoted to *Cinco de Mayo;* thereby lessening the impact of the socially conceived stigmas associated with ethnicity and/or being poor. This means that students must be schooled in settings where significant credence is given to the import of society's influences on attitudes and expectations for poor or ethnic-minority children (Steele, 1992; Boykin, 2000 & 2004; Hale, 1986, 2001a, 2001b & 2003; Loury, 2002; Schultz & Hull, 2002). In schools where positive school climates prevail, studies reflect that social stigmas have little to no negative impact on students' self-esteem and their academic performances (Glick, 1985; Hoy & Feldman, 1987; Hoy & Tarter 1997; Pierre-Pipkin, 2001; Ancess, 2003). Urban students who attend such schools continue to overcome barriers of social inequities, indigent home and community environments and perform at age and grade expectancy. However, the realities of inequity, low expectations, and underachievement in poor or ethnic-minority schools continue to challenge educators in a majority of the nation's urban schools.

For the purpose of this text, the terms *urban poor, ethnic-minority,* or *other marginalized children* may be used interchangeable for brevity and collectively to reference *urban children (including African American children)* but the terms are not meant to be necessarily synonymous. Further, the term, *urban children,* is used as a collective reference because African American, poor, and other marginalized children make up the vast majority of students who populate urban schools. At issue, specifically, is the significant numbers of African American children being under-educated in public schools, and what can and should be done to address this disparity.

The Link Between Theory and Practice

Effective instruction begins and ends with a clear understanding of the link between sound learning theory and practice. Without such an understanding, the teaching-learning process becomes an a-b-c *"any road theorem"* which addresses the purpose of instruction as follows:

a) *Why the particular content?*
   ➢ Response: *It's what will be tested, and it fits into the timeline before testing.*

b) *How will content be delivered?*
   ➢ Response: *Via trail and error.*

6

c) *What are the expected outcomes?*

➤ Response: *Since we are not sure how learners develop cognitive skills, why we use particular methods, or what the expected outcomes should be; "any road" (i. e, content, method, or timeframe) will lead us somewhere.*

Regardless of the NCLB requirements, it is imperative that teachers, as well as school administrators, recognize the vast obligations school systems have to be knowledgeable in theories of *how people learn;* the sociocultural influences that shape learning patterns of diverse students; and to ensure that educational practices are grounded in empirically established and accepted theories regarding cognition and learning. In-depth knowledge of empirical research; and the subsequent data that validate accepted theories of cognition and learning should predicate all curriculum and instructional designs. Further, it is essential to incorporate theories of *culturally influenced learning* in theory-based classroom activities to strengthen pedagogy as learning theories apply specifically to African American and other marginalized children.

The design of the pedagogy postulated in this text and companion text--*Teaching Learners to See What You Are Saying: from Theory to Practice*-- integrates various tenets and postulates of empirically proved and generally accepted theories of cognitive development, including theories that address the influences of environment, language, and culture in shaping cognition. The goal of this approach is to present an alternative paradigm supported by learning theory of cognitive development, to advance learning; specifically culturally influenced learning in educational settings. It is argued that an effective paradigm for educating diverse learners must be a delivery system that creates a nexus between students' in-school learning and their out-of-school cultural experiences. This can be done through pedagogy that incorporates students' prior knowledge and learning styles in a multi-sensory teaching-learning framework; thereby providing a broad range of opportunities for all students to process information in a manner that they *"mentally see"* concepts (gain insight) in order to *"learn with understanding."*

Auditory Situated Field

The paradigm for this text coins the term *Auditory Situated Field (ASF)* to augment the explanation of what it means for learners to *"see"* what is *"said." Auditory Situated Field* implies that people think in terms of *pictures* or *images* (Gough, 1975; Joynt, 1975); that all auditory sensory input requires the hearer to *situate* what is heard within a conceptually relevant context—both internally and externally. The explanation is this: When someone hears words or interprets language, concepts are figuratively *pictured* or *visualized (visual imagery), recalled, mentally cued,* or *referenced* based on *encoded* prior knowledge or experiences. It is posited that sensory perception and multi-modal sensory processing are essential to cognition; that is, all learning depends on the interpretation of sensory information that is processed "within the mind" using interdependent multiple senses (Eisner, 1994; Lindsay & Norman, 1977; Pierre-Pipkin, 2003).

Oral speech and language are the main modalities of non-disabled communication regarding learning in educational settings; thus the focus here is on spoken language and understanding. Learners of all ages interpret or attempt to understand oral language using more than one sensory modality; and while the main channel of auditory information is in hearing sounds, words, or sentences; learners employ prior visual sensory input that augmented or established the original conceptual understanding. For example, when a young person first heard the word, *chair,* and visually looked at the three-dimensional object, both auditory and visual senses were used to learn the concept of "chair." This simply means, that all learning is related to a learner's prior knowledge or experiences; and how the information was processed through multi-sensory input, and coded for mental storage (Crowder, 1972; Pierre-Pierre, 2003). This does not imply that individual experiences are "wired" into the brain and stored separately (Byrnes 2001); but rather, according to schemata theory, each experience creates a mental representation that is stored in common categories, along with similar experiences. For example, "chair" is similar to "sofa" and share *common* elements; thus both might be stored in the same memory. Byrnes explains: "Creating categories makes for a more efficient use of . . . memory capacity than storing each individual experience . . . as a separate memory" (p. 23).

Input received through all senses requires a learner to attach meaning based on prior learning or experiences. For instance, a very young learner may need literal concrete sensory stimuli, or a direct experience to understand and interpret new information in order to develop conceptual understanding. Thus, in classroom activities, a young learner may initially require concrete referents, other person mediation, or *repeated interaction* to derive meaning. An older learner would not depend on concrete stimuli, direct experiences, or symbolic referents to understand new information; but would use *mental cues* stored in *memory* to instantaneously interpret sensory input, or new information. Neural processing creates or modifies mental structures within the brain to encode, interpret, or to store the information in memory for retrieval when needed. Subsequently, through experience or maturation, learners exhibit understanding mainly through articulation, other language modes, or demonstrated behaviors (Lindsay & Norman, 1977; Strachan, 2000; Pierre-Pipkin, 2003).

For the purpose of this text, it is posited that the *Auditory Situated Field* is a "situation" where *content* and *context* work interdependently. This means that the "content" of what *heard,* derives meaning from the "specific context" of the moment, or the *situatededness* of the auditory stimuli. However, auditory input must be associated with prior *multi-sensory processes (i.e., visual imagery; auditory memory);* or other *sense processes (tactile, etc.)* within the *mind;* cross-modally *encoded,* and retrieved for comprehension. Auditory stimuli is always conditioned by how the prior information needed for encoding "new input" was stored "in the brain;" referred to as either memory, or experience.

Bransford and colleagues (2000) illustrated the role of experience as a condition of "how" a brain was "wired." In the example of "wiring of the brain," the authors explain: "(An) eye (that was) . . . incapable of seeing at a very early age;" and the vision was later corrected, "the afflicted eye still could not see" (p. 117). The conclusion is that both experience and neural activity are needed for brain development. They conclude that ". . . the quality of information to which one is exposed and the amount of information one acquires is reflected throughout one's life in the structure of the brain" (p. 118).

In essence, the *eye* is the "conduit" or "extension" of the brain; the organ that assists in understanding the external world. In the example of a young person's first experience of internalizing the concept of "chair" (the three-dimensional object); the *eye* acted interdependently with *auditory reception* of the word, "chair," and *wired the brain* to understand the word. Thereafter, when the child hears the word "chair," her ears not only *"hear"* the word, but her *"mind sees"* the originally encoded concept, in an *ear-eye function* (Kavanagh & Mattingly, 1972; Pierre-Pipkin, 2003).

The instantaneous process of hearing and associating input with prior knowledge or experiences is an example of the *Auditory Situated Field.* This text argues that much of what is processed related to language has been *wired* in the brain mainly through *visual* experiences that originally internalized concepts. Thus understanding much of "what is heard" depends on the human ability of visual imagery; and retrieval of prior information or experiences to "contextualize" what is "heard" (Pierre-Pipkin, 2007). Auditory comprehension is therefore a mental process of *sight* "inside the head." What is heard is "contextualized" in the *Auditory Situated Field* in two ways: First, *externally,* by connecting new acoustic information to previously stored visual input; and second, *internally,* through the ability to "make sense of" what is heard. This process explains *"How the Mind's Eye Hears."*

The significance of *ASF* in the teaching learning process is for teachers to understand the importance of knowing what prior knowledge and language meanings, created by experiences students may or may not have related to the content under discussion. Teachers must consider that all students bring to the classroom, varying levels of receptiveness for understanding "what is heard." In situations where students have no prior experiences or knowledge with concepts being presented; it is critical that teachers "create" the necessary *contexts* or *conditions,* beyond verbal explanations, for subject content to be understood. Teachers must create a "nexus" between students' current understanding and how they process information, to the content knowledge they are expected to learn (Pierre-Pipkin, 2004a & 2007).

Factors that Impact Achievement of African American and Other Marginalized Children

Were absolute *equality of educational opportunity* provided for every child in American schools, would *all* children subsequently perform equally as well in all areas as any of their counterparts within a school district, regardless of the school—urban or suburban; teacher expectations, the socio-economic status of students and communities, or the ethnic composition of the student population? If this indeed were the case, there would not be a need to develop alternatives to traditional curriculums or employ special pedagogies to ensure that no student is *left behind*—particularly African American and other marginalized children. In reality, however, simply equalizing opportunities, including facilities, teaching staffs and curriculums would not be sufficient to predict, ensure, or even expect that all children would learn and perform equally as well as their age and grade peers within a school district, school, or classroom. Another way to consider this question is, if all things were equal, and educational systems existed in a utopian society, the answer to the question would be an unequivocal, *yes*. Of course this is not the case, even though studies have shown many instances where urban school children can perform and have performed equally as well— in some cases better than—children in suburban, private or parochial schools (Sizemore, 1985 & 1989; Goycochea, 1998; Ancess, 2003). Unfortunately, such cases are the exceptions, not the rule; because in addition to the historical educational inequalities that left generations of urban students behind, significant numbers of urban school children have various out-of-school social needs and barriers that have a negative impact on their school performance.

However, regardless of historical patterns, limited human and physical resources or social factors—without question—urban school educators are expected to employ school practices that deliver effective instruction. Teachers in urban schools must establish alternatives to traditional practices by delivering criterion-referenced instruction to ensure the success of urban poor and ethnic-minority children. The expectations for urban student performance should be essentially the same as for suburban and other school children—to perform at age-grade levels *(e.g., demonstrated knowledge of content expected for the number of years of school attendance).* Effective schooling of urban children requires "alternatively specific pedagogies" that focus particularly on the learning styles of the diverse students being served. This text, along with the companion text previous referenced, offers such an alternative means of accomplishing this goal.

An Alternative Approach to Traditional Instruction of Urban School Children

Establishing effective instructional delivery systems for urban students can be accomplished by utilizing *specific instructional methodologies* of culturally relevant contexts—discourse and situations that are familiar to urban children—that create scaffolds in advancing conceptual understanding to enhance academic performance. It has been asserted that people do not think in *words* (Gough, 1975; Joynt, 1975). However, traditional curriculum and instructional designs and pedagogy place primary emphasis on *word* meanings and discourse based on Anglo middle-class lifestyles. Moreover, classroom instruction employing Euro-American mainstream and academic language often varies from language and word meanings for diverse student populations (Labov, 1989; Heath, 2006). Thus from a perspective that people think and conceptualize in terms of *visual imagery* (Gough and Joynt, 1975; Labov, 1989; Heath, 2006), many African American and other marginalized children are placed at disadvantages in classrooms situations where the academic language of instruction is discernibly different from the language styles formed by their cultural experiences. Therefore fundamental changes must be made in the way curriculum is developed, and how instruction is delivered; not to lower academic standards, but to employ scaffolding activities that augment and maximize opportunities for diverse student populations to succeed.

It is posited that learning occurs when learners can *"see what is said."* This requires specific pedagogy that considers the diverse linguistic styles of ethnic minority learners, and provides opportunities for students to *"make sense of"* content knowledge. This is done by assisting learners to increase abilities of conceptualization, and by making connections between new information and concepts, and their prior knowledge and experiences (Hale, 1986; Delpit, 1995; Delpit & Dowdy, 2002; Pierre-Pipkin, 2004a & 2007).

Fundamental changes require a re-definition of the term *Highly Qualified Teacher* to extend beyond simply having competence in the subject discipline being taught. An adequate definition includes competence in *knowing* and *understanding culturally diverse children*; demonstrating the ability to effectively *teach culturally responsive* content; and as important, the ability to design and administer objective subject content *assessments.*

Additionally, effective instructional practices for urban classrooms entail self-evaluations by teachers to scrutinize their attitudes about students to determine whether they hold stereotypical opinions and low expectations for diverse student populations; and the impact that their attitudes and modeling behaviors may have on student underperformance. Successful instruction therefore necessitates an understanding of the learning styles of the students being taught; knowing at all times *what content* students know; *when* students obtain or do not obtain content knowledge and skills; and how to identify the *specific conditions* under which students succeed or fail.

The Rationale for an Instructional Alternative

Instructional effectiveness for urban students requires *pedagogy* that delivers sequentially contextualized instruction based on learning theory such as *concrete, semi-concrete* and *abstract* cognitive development, and how these theories relate to instructional content for the age and grade level of the students being taught. Where teachers understand and incorporate sound learning theories into instructional designs and practices, students are provided significantly better quality instruction and opportunities for success. Knowledge of child development applied to sequentially delivered instruction advances learners from *concept formation*, to *demonstrating* the degree to which information and concepts are understood; and to levels of *transfer* and *application of content knowledge* (Pierre-Pipkin, 2004a & 2007).

Curriculum development and instructional designs must also provide opportunities for students to be actively engaged in reciprocal instruction to learn *with understanding*; as opposed to being inactive in *spectator-type* lecture instruction that promotes committing isolated information to memory mainly for testing purposes. Additionally, instructional designs should incorporate culturally responsive learning activities as mediating tools to facilitate and enhance learning for diverse students (Olson, 1972; Falk, 1996; Kozulin, et al., 2006). Culturally relevant instruction extends beyond textbooks that depict people and lifestyles similar to those of diverse learners; rather, use of *culturally relevant instructional themes, activities, materials* and *human resources* provide augmented opportunities for success by creating a nexus between students' prior knowledge and experiences in a manner that respects and values their cultures and learning styles; and in raising the self-esteem of urban students (Shade, 1982; Huber, et al., 1997; Cochran & Smith, 1996, 2000; Stokes, 2001; Spencer, et al., 1991).

Cultural Contexts and
Criterion-Reference Instruction

The theoretical instructional delivery paradigm postulated by this text and the companion instructional text, *Teaching Learners to See What You Are Saying: From Theory to Practice,* is based in part, on an adaptation of Mager's (1975) theory of *Criterion-Referenced Instruction.* Both texts hypothesize that the application of *Criterion-Referenced Instruction (CRI)* delivered within *culturally relevant formats* is a more effective instructional pedagogy compared to traditional pre-test—lecture—post-test pedagogies. Simply stated, *Criterion-Reference Instruction (CRI)* tells the *content* as well as the *context* of the instruction and the *criteria for success*—the proposed learner outcomes or the degree to which learners are expected to master content and skills at specific points in a lesson cycle; regardless of the socio-economic status of the school or the cultural environment of the learners.

CRI states at all times, specifically *what* content learners are expected to know; the *context (i.e., format)* for instructional activities for both teacher and learners; and

19

the *timeframe* in which learners are expected to know the content. Additionally, *CRI* informs the teacher whether or not to continue, expand, or change the lesson content or instructional methodologies. Both texts propose the use of *cultural contexts* in content delivery to provide scaffolding and mediating factors to increase opportunities for learners to develop conceptual understanding, applications, and other higher level thinking skills.

Also, both texts emphasize the importance of understanding the interdependent nature of *content* and *context* in the delivery of instruction; that the effectiveness of *what* is taught is dependent on *how* content is taught. This emphasis varies from traditional pedagogy structured as lecture-test-lecture-retest; that uses "only" lecture formats; and evaluation of achievement based mainly on commercial textbook quizzes, and standardized or other norm-referenced tests. Traditional pedagogy and evaluation are usually based on experiences; or obtained from school practices applicable to non-minority students in middle or high-income suburban schools; and often have little to no fair nexus or contextual relevance for most urban school children. Since urban students are expected to perform as successfully within the same age-grade curriculums as suburban middle and high wealth school students, the use of instructional practices of *CRI* provides a broader framework for this to happen. Teaching and learning objectives are criteria-based that obligate teachers to structure content delivery to provide multiple opportunities for learners to "demonstrate" *understanding* rather than simply *recalling* isolated information that is assessed solely by paper-pencil tests.

The Rationale for Criterion Referenced Assessment

In the recent past instructional objectives and goals for student performance were mainly non-measurable statements such as: *The student (or students) will perform to the maximum extent of her/his (their) potential;* or *The purpose of this lesson is to teach percentages.* Such nebulous phrases regarding student performance proved to be a major part of the problem in teaching, evaluating and/or correcting urban students' underachievement. First, because the stated objectives and goals were not measurable; and as the objectives were stated, exit evaluations simply determined whether or not the "teacher taught;" and not whether the "students learned" (Beauchamp, 1956; Pierre-Pipkin, 2007). Second, periodic intervening checkpoints of formative assessment and mid-cycle corrections of student progress were not apparent or required. Teachers seldom, if ever, used the learning styles or lived experiences of students as scaffolds to assist their understanding of new concepts and information. Further, globally stated, unclear, or non-measurable goals failed to connect the delivery of content to expected student performance outcomes. Thus, student progress or failure was evaluated only at the end of the lesson cycle or instructional unit. Moreover, except for teacher-constructed (mainly "true-false"), and textbook unit tests, student exit level assessments were crouched in "norm-referenced" processes, included content that was not completely understood, but memorized; and subsequently not recognized in the contexts of assessment. The results were generally low student performance and subsequently low expectations, especially for urban children (Russell, et al., 1994).

Assessment of student performance has shifted from non-measurable phrases and globally stated goals, to objectives that are measurable; however, similar to the language of subject content, tests are standardized based on language meanings, concepts, discourse, and life experiences of the dominant group's *cultural ways of knowing*; thus presents performance barriers for culturally diverse students, and limits their abilities to perform with acceptable levels of proficiency. Despite the validity of commercially produced subject tests, urban teachers must understand the importance of content relevance for diverse students; and the importance of creating a nexus between subject content and the students' prior in-school, and out-of-school knowledge and cultural experiences. The use of multiple formative and summative assessments to guide instruction allows a broader range of methods and perspectives for appropriately and accurately evaluating student progress.

It is therefore important to *restructure* how student performance is assessed. This process begins with teachers ensuring that "maximum opportunities" to learn the content have been provided for all students; including opportunities for demonstrated benchmark progress through formative evaluations that allow mid-course corrections of both instruction and learning (Pierre-Pipkin, 2007). An effective paradigm for student assessment is one that shifts to *diagnostic use* of achievement tests, combined with observations, and learner portfolios that document progress. This structure provides multiple assessment formats, rather than penalizing students by relying solely on paper-pencil assessments that are primarily multiple-choice that assess students' abilities of rote memory; and elicit only factual, declarative information.

This text recommends an instructional design of *Criterion Referenced Assessment* for evaluating academic performance of urban students. *Criterion Referenced Assessment* places reciprocal accountability within a framework for both teachers and learners to evaluate when learning has or has not occurred. Teachers are responsible for providing extensive opportunities for learners to

23

demonstrate progress and levels of knowledge, by utilizing their learning styles, prior knowledge and experiences. This structure ensures that assessment is objectively measured based on previously stated criteria. In turn, students share the responsibility for knowing at all times their expected levels of engagement in content activities; their expected performance levels within a lesson cycle; the timeframe for lesson completion; and the criteria for demonstrated mastery of knowledge and skills.

A Transformative Design for Alternative Student Assessment

Effective evaluations of student performance and classroom instruction require teachers to have a complete theoretical understanding of how students acquire knowledge; how they demonstrate understandings; and how students make applications of academic skills in the transfer of knowledge to new situations. Secondly, teachers must clearly and succinctly articulate instructional purposes, goals, and performance expectations to students. Next, an evaluation of urban student performance is equitable only when instructional objectives have been stated in measurable terms, and when students have been provided many opportunities to learn content referenced by the objectives, including activities of culturally related content in various contexts. A clear distinction must be made between subjective *non-measurable performance goals* regarding learner performance; and criterion-referenced *objectively measurable* learner goals and expected performance outcomes. This means that instruction should proceed as stated by all givens of *what* content will be taught, *how* the content will be taught (the *context),* the *timeline* for completion, and the *criteria* for mastery of knowledge and skills. Formative and summative assessments are criterion-referenced (i.e., evaluated by stated criteria and timelines); and reflect the degree to which individual learners, as well as the percent of all learners, are expected to "demonstrate" knowledge and skills as specified by the learning objectives. The "effectiveness" of instruction is determined by the degree to which objectives are met.

Standard vs. Academic English

A factor often overlooked when evaluating low test performance is the element of the language-gap between students' culturally influenced language and academic discourse in classroom instruction. Difficulties experienced during classroom learning present the same or similar barriers in written assessments. This discrepancy should be considered, not only during instruction, but in designing and analyzing paper-pencil assessments as well.

Research reveals that language discourse in classroom settings varies from the cultural contexts and everyday language and understanding for significant numbers of African American and other marginalized children (Shade, 1982; Hilliard, 1992; Labov, 1986; Delpit & Dowdy, 2002; Heath, 2000 & 2006; Gee, 2004; Maiga, 2005). Consequently, many urban children are penalized by having to learn English language concepts, expressions, vocabularies, and nuances that are foreign to their cultural backgrounds; presented by teachers who often have limited or no experience with their out-of-school lives. It is therefore essential that scaffolding is included in instructional activities to mediate or transition students' understanding of language-based academic content. Scaffolding removes the element of *double jeopardy* that causes students to struggle with unfamiliar language and syntax, and unfamiliar discourse while simultaneously struggling to *grasp* the knowledge of the academic content. While studies reveal that urban students can and are able to shift between home and classroom language, quite often many students do so by subjugating their individual language discourse to the expected school and social forms of Euro-American mainstream language. DuBois refers to this as the "two-ness" of their lives (Labov, 1986; Bigelow, et al., 2001; Hale, 2001b).

In situations where variances between academic and cultural language present barriers to understanding content, another problem exist. When urban children are compared to mainstream learners or their peers in high-wealth schools, their academic difficulties are attributed to *inabilities* in learning academic subjects, or interpreted as limited or lack of mental capabilities. Thus many of these children are referred to special education programs. Hilliard (1995, 1992 & 2001) contends that urban children learn *all of their home language,* and can successfully negotiate their environments and cultures; however, it is in school settings where they experience terminologies and written or spoken expressions foreign to their backgrounds and cultures that prevent or delay their achievement. Consequently, significant numbers of urban children under perform in both academic areas and on standardized achievement tests.

Many African American students are academically successful, despite the language gap or other factors; but are often marked by some of their peers as *acting white* (Fordham & Ogbu, 1986; Kohl, 1994; Steinberg, 2007). Their desire to *belong* to their group often outweighs their need to succeed; thus, many of these children physically or mentally disengage from learning or under perform. Teachers must be sensitive to such situations, and intervene through encouragement, sensitivity discussions, and modeling behaviors. Further, teachers must understand the cultural context of why this happens; the impact on classroom learning and assessment of performance; and avoid assumptions about students' lack of motivation or abilities.

An Alternative Pedagogy

The recommended pedagogy presented in this text, and the companion text, advocates the use of Criterion-Referenced Instruction (CRI) to eliminate or lessen the impact of the school-culture language gap, and other sociocultural factors that impact African American and other marginalized students' classroom performance. Learners are more likely to grasp and learn concepts presented in culturally responsive formats that allow use of their learning styles in scaffolding activities that assist them in understanding subject concepts (Vygotsky, 1978; Kozulin, A., 2006; Delpit, 1995; Falk, 1996; Beach, 1998). The instructional format of CRI does not depend on a strict adherence to academic language, but allows learners to "demonstrate" their understanding of knowledge and skills in various modes using their learning styles; and through various contexts that have relevance to their prior in-school and out-of-school knowledge. Moreover, CRI requires learners to *demonstrate* understanding of content knowledge and skills based on specifically stated givens, reciprocal instruction, interactive modeling, and learner practice.

It is clear that students are expected to learn and understand academic language, however, scaffolding and culturally responsive instruction provide a basis for formative evaluation without penalizing students whose cultural ways of knowing and understanding vary from classroom discourse; and culturally responsive pedagogical practices facilitate higher levels of performance (King, et al., 1997; Gay, 2002). It is also emphasized that CRI does not suggest *"dummying down"* the academic content in instructional delivery; but provides an alternative instructional framework that employs mediating factors to assist transitions in learning that do not depend on a strict adherence to mainstream discourse. This simply means that teachers must understand the role that culture plays in creating word meanings; how culture shapes learning styles and students' preparedness and receptiveness to instruction; and to use this understanding to mediate and guide instruction. Further, teachers are encouraged to "listen" to urban children; learn to understand their expressions, analyze their paraphrases to determine if concepts are grasped, in order to know what they understand or have learned.

While teaching academic English is required and expected, assisting diverse learners to distinguish the

29

difference, as well as similarities, between cultural language use and language used to negotiate school, the workplace and general society; instruction must be delivered in a manner that models respect for students' use of their out-of-school language. A means of walking this balancing beam is allowing students to demonstrate and apply skills and concepts immediately after lesson content has been introduced and modeled; and to use their demonstrated skills and knowledge for evaluative purposes. Further, teachers must provide activities that ensure students are able to recognize differences of when everyday language expressions are appropriate, and when academic language is required for the subject under discussion. A CRI design provides opportunities for scaffolding between these discourses in content activities; and provides contexts for scaffolding that incorporate cultural themes of students' cultural knowledge and experiences.

Understanding what is important to students at home and in their communities is a basis for creating effective scaffolding between academic language and students' everyday language. Moreover, using students' out-of-school experiences provides relevant contextual referents for cultural themes to introduce new concepts in classroom discussions. Effective teachers of culturally diverse students exert much effort in building repertoires of knowledge of the out-of–school *environments* that shape students' learning styles. This is done by establishing relationships with the parents of students and visiting the communities where children live. Often teachers at the secondary level think of these outreach activities having relevance only to elementary and lower grade children. However, there must be a seamless path between homes and schools in both directions at all grade levels—schools a part of communities; classrooms that reflect communities of all of the students; and homes an intricate part of the teaching-learning process. All teachers must demonstrate the same level of competence in *knowing the children* and their lifestyles as demonstrated in knowing subject content (King, et al., 1997; Darling-Hammond & Bransford, 2005; Ladson-Billings, 1995; Darling-Hammond, 1997a).

Chapter One of this text presents three discussions: First, a brief perspective of traditional theories of cognition, followed by current research in this area. Next, is a discussion that focuses on the neurological basis for human learning, and theories of cognitive development related to learning. A third discussion analyzes the structure of language related to developmental aspects of cognition, language development, and culturally influenced learning.

Chapter Two—How the Mind's Eye Hears, continues the discussion of learning theories outlined in the first chapter by focusing on three constructs: *concrete, semi-concrete* and *abstract learning;* and the relationship of these constructs to *sensory perception, concept formation; demonstrated understanding, transfer,* and *application of knowledge and skills.* The second discussion considers the importance of understanding culturally influenced learning, and related pedagogical practices for culturally diverse students, with specific emphasis on theory-based instructional designs.

The focus of *Chapter Three* is based on a commonly held belief that schools are cosmic reflections of the larger society, and as such, factors and influences from communities do not stop at the schoolhouse door, but impact school expectations for urban students. A discussion addresses an often-overlooked question in evaluating student performance in low wealth community settings by addressing the question: *How do schools function as governmental agencies in providing fair and equitable education to urban school children?* Similarities and differences of delivery systems in urban and suburban schools are discussed, including school and community socio-economic environments; school expectations, staffing, and facilities. Also, the attitudes of school personnel—who may or may not reside in the school's community; and how various negative attitudes and presumptions of teachers impact urban students' performance, commonly known as the *self-fulfilling prophecy.*

Chapter Four discusses standardized tests as measures of achievement. The discussions examine the continued inequities of norm-referenced standardized tests as assessment relates to urban and ethnic minority school children; and an alternative paradigm for criterion referenced instruction and assessment. A discussion analyzes the impact of *No Child Left Behind* requirements on classroom learning; and a suggested re-definition of the term, *Highly Qualified Teacher.*

An analysis of the impact of school and classroom climates on the academic performance of students is the focus of *Chapter Five.* The discussions emphasize the importance of employing culturally responsive theory to establish conditions for teaching African American and other marginalized children; and how school and classroom climates evolve and can be improved to support student academic success. A discussion of group dynamics in the classroom emphasizes the import of out-of-school learner experiences on in-school learning; and how teachers can use group dynamics, real life experiences, and situational teaching to increase students' academic performance.

Chapter Six is a concluding summary and challenge to educators to "reframe" the delivery of instruction for African American and other urban children; also, the need to redefine teacher qualities to include *cultural competence* and abilities to deliver culturally responsive instruction. The final points review the issue of teachers' understanding the connections between research and theory; how educational theory should underscore teaching and assessment practices; and recommendations for college and university teacher training programs.

CHAPTER ONE

Theories of Cognitive Development and Learning

According to the laws of aerodynamics, the bumblebee is not supposed to fly, because its body is too heavy, and its wings are too light—but no one told the bumblebee!

_Jean Pierre-Pipkin

INTRODUCTION

How people *come to know* has long been a question posed by neuroscientists, psychologists, researchers, theorists, and educators. Theories infer anatomical explanations of learning from a neuroscientific perspective; hypothesize knowing as conceptual schemata from biological and mental perspectives; and others theorize that cognition develops through perceptual experiences and associations in the world (Bransford, et al., 1998; Bransford, et al., 2000; Byrnes, 2001; Kozulin, et al., 2006; Lave and Wenger, 2003; Donovan, et al., 2005). The various theories that address *knowing* from each perspective appear to have consensus on at least one factor, that *cognition is developmental.*

This text posits that cognitive development occurs or can be explained by a combination of factors found among various theories regarding learning; but the main focus of the text is an emphasis on the *relationship* between research and theory; how research *links* theory to practice; and the relevance of this link to effective instruction. Note that *research* is placed here in a first position, rather than the traditional manner posed by a problem or situation that seeks to solve an issue by first, posing a *theory*, followed by the *research* to establish validity of the hypothesis.

The rationale for the perspective of considering *research* first to address educational issues is mainly because of the abundance of empirically valid and accepted cognitive theory available; and the belief that additional research is not necessarily required; but rather, that educators should use current research and theory in a more thoughtful and efficient manner to support effective school practices. Therefore, the structure of the discussions places emphasis on *how* research *forms* theory generally accepted in explaining cognition as it applies to learning; and *how* sound theory supports effective teaching practices—specifically for African American and other marginalized children in all school settings. Further, in addition to a review to the literature on learning theory, this text discusses other learning-related topics that support the pedagogical design of the instructional companion text, *Teaching Learners to See What You are Saying: From Theory to Practice.*

The plethora of empirical research in the literature is too vast and varied to address but a small fraction of the available data in this text. Therefore this text presents a brief historical perspective of learning theory from traditional theories to current research. The conjectural positions in this text are limited to several theories that support neurological conceptions of cognition; the impact of language in cognitive development; and theories of culturally influenced learning regarding the instruction of African American, and other marginalized children (Shade, 1982). The approach in this text combines elements of several theories to posit that *people come to know* by *"hearing with the mind's eye."*

The Neurological Basis of Cognitive Development

A significant body of research exists that supports the anatomical or neurological basis of human learning; that human cognitive development is grounded in biological and biochemical maturation of the brain and nervous system (Critchley, 1975; Gough, 1975; Joynt, 1975; Bigge and Shermis, 1999; Bransford, et al., 2000; Strachan, 2000; Byrnes, 2001; Donovan, et al., 2005).

Critchley (1975) argues that human cognition is influenced by "genetic make-up . . . that guides and limits the development of . . . biological, behavioral and psychological characteristics . . . within the context of opportunities and constraints provided by . . . the environment" (p. 14). Critchley theorizes from a biological perspective, that the physiological make up of the brain and nervous system consists of various neurons, circuits, synapses, and the complex integration of these processes in receiving sensory information or exhibiting behavior.

However the problem of accuracy or absolute knowledge of how these systems function in cognitive development is still elusive, as Joynt (1975) concludes; because so little is known about the mechanism of the human brain, and this is due in part to the "discrepancy between our knowledge of neuroanatomy and our knowledge of behavior" . . . (p. 43). Joynt points out that much of what is known about the anatomical structure of the brain result from brain injuries of patients. For example, damage to certain areas of the brain produces language dysfunctions; and where damage to the left side of the brain occurred, speech subsequently developed in the right hemisphere of the brain (Ibid., p. 47).

The theory posited by Demetriou & Kyriakides (2006) support the concept that various domains interact dynamically during cognitive development. They argue that first order reasoning factors of *categorical, quantitative, causal, spatial* and *propositional thought* function independently, but work interactively. Changes in the thought domains are age-related that extend beyond simple processing. "Specifically . . . change from the ability to solve intuitively facilitated problems to the ability to solve problems requiring the integration of multiple structures . . . implies . . . that with development thinkers (become better able to analyze and synthesize component parts of situations in problem solving.) . . ." (p. 236).

Other advances have been made in the study of cognition through neuroscience; specifically, non-invasive imaging technology that allows researchers to observe structural changes in the brain during learning. Bransford and colleagues (2000) found that electro-physiological recordings confirm that learning creates new patterns of organization of the brain cells; and activity of the nervous system during learning causes nerve cells to produce or modify synapses, a process driven by experiences (Ibid., p. 115). The authors present a comprehensive analysis of how the brain works from a neuroscientific perspective that focuses on stages in cognitive development; how information is encoded, and how experience affects the brain. Their discussion explains the processes of neurons that guide synapse production, reduction, and conduction to produce human behavior. They conclude that the brain functions in coordination with the environment; and that brain development uses visual information entering from the outside to become more precisely organized than could be possible with intrinsic molecular mechanism alone (Ibid., p. 118).

In a point of departure from focusing on neurology as the primary basis of human cognition, this text agrees with Bransford and colleagues in addressing a *chicken or egg* type question of what plays the greater role in cognition, genes or environment. Bransford and colleagues conclude that the question is moot because "brain development and psychological development involve continuous interaction between a child and the external environment . . ." (p. 115). Their analogy reasons that the question is similar to determining which has the greater impact on the area of a rectangle, the height or the width.

This author uses the analogy; *I never placed my foot twice in the same river,* to explain the theory of the dynamic nature of knowing postulated in this text (and companion text previously referenced). A body of flowing river water passes a particular location only once; and the same body of water— in essence—does not exist from one moment to the next. The original flowing body of water may return to the same spot, but it has deposited or picked up various elements along the way and has been, in part, either purified or contaminated; and is not the same water that went before. A similar situation applies to cognitive development; whether *knowing* is thought to originate through biological maturation, ecological influences, or the interaction of both factors, human cognition is not static, but is in a dynamic state of change. At all times, the brain and nervous system continuously change through nerve cell production, restructuring and reorganizing; and through synaptic interaction with sensory information gathering input from the environment (Critchley, 1975; Gough, 1975; Bransford, et al., 2000). This dynamic state of human cognition is reflected by data from advances in neuroscience, technical imaging, and research in human cognition that have given new directions in understandings of how the brain and nervous system function; and the influences of the external environment on maturation and cognition (Bransford, et al., 2000).

Studies of human learning and cognitive development have evolved over many centuries and include studies of craniology to quantified intelligence quotients (Gould, 1996); but the voluminous literature that addresses the historical development is beyond the intent or scope of this text. The studies discussed represent relatively recent biological or environmental theories of cognitive development; serve as foundational to an understanding of the link between research and theory regarding learning in school settings; and support the postulates of *how people learn* argued in this text.

The intent is to emphasize that it is incumbent on educators to have an in-depth understanding of theory as it applies to learning, from both a historical and contemporary perspective; thereby to understand *how children learn,* and factors that impact classroom learning. There is much to learn about the nature of knowledge acquisition and the relationship of learning and brain functions. Whether or not there is an absolute method of defining which has the greater affect on human cognition, biology or ecology, research seems to suggest that cognition begins from a neurological base and is modified, influenced, or shaped by environmental experiences.

Traditional Theories of Cognitive Development and Learning

Traditional concepts of human intelligence theorized cognition as a construct that defines differences between individuals; that intelligence could be identified and measured by standardized tests, and quantified from numerical data. However, because the differences were markedly negative when various marginalized racial groups were compared to mainstream populations, legal challenges to intelligence testing shifted the focus of human cognition from tests of intelligence to approaches of neuroscientific, ecological, sociocultural, and other theories of cognitive development (Johnson, 1989; Shade, 1982; Fan, et al, 1996; Kluger, 1997). Lohman (1989) posits that new methods in the study of human cognition have been applied to old tests and theories of individual differences. He summarized three traditional theories of human intelligence: *trait theories* that emphasized fluid and crystallized abilities; *information processing theories* of intelligence explained by abilities of mental speed, verbal-crystallized abilities, fluid reasoning, and spatial-visualization; and third, *general theories of thinking* that attempted to move beyond measuring individual differences to new methods that focused on "particular processes or knowledge structure hypothesized by these theories" (p. 337).

Briefly, Lohman explained that *trait theories* sought to define human intelligence as having two general factors: fluid intelligence indexed as *Gf*—a reasoning ability of discriminating and perceiving relations between any fundamentals, new or old; thought of as a physiologically determined *process* which persists and increases though adolescence. The second factor, crystallized intelligence, indexed as *Gc* explains cognition of adult intellectual thinking whereby knowledge or habits developed in earlier years crystallize and no longer require perceptual insightfulness, but patterns of speed and power thought of as *product;* and thereby environmentally determined. *Information processing theory* extends the concepts of fluid and crystallized abilities with second-order factors arrayed along a continuum which progresses from surface, or infancy, to deep processing, or adulthood, and include m*ental speed*—a construct that considers rate of thinking or response time in individual problem solving. V*erbal crystallized abilities* are knowledge intensive that relate to encoding, and hold a prominent place in all theories of intelligence regarding how knowledge is stored in memory. *Fluid reasoning* involves abilities to solve problems in novel situations. *Spatial visualization* is process intensive and focuses on "how" individuals exhibit thinking relating to spatial and figural tasks. *General theories of thinking* pose an integrative approach to understanding human cognition that removes definitions from a vacuum based solely on theory, to a broader perspective within a collection of independent systems including biological and psychological capacities and abilities influenced by sociological and ecological factors (Ibid., p. 339).

Research in cognitive development has shifted back and forth between a focus on individual intellectual differences and modular systems, distinguished respectively, by theories of intelligence as a construct; and definitions of cognition as a developmental process. These theories have been augured, accepted, or rejected relative to the time period in which each is defined. Therefore, current and future directions for research in human cognition should recognize the merit found in theories of individual differences in knowledge acquisition and cognitive development measured through assessment, as well as giving credence to what can be ascribed in understanding the correlation between "processes used to solve both test problems and school learning tasks" (Lohman, 1989; p. 361).

The Swiss psychologist, Jean Piaget (1896-1980), holds a prominent place among traditional theorists, and elements of his concepts regarding cognitive development are in current practice by theorists, educators and Neo-Piagetian movements. Piaget theorized a genetic epistemology of knowledge acquisition in studies of innate developmental stages of children. He posited that psychological functioning is structurally or biologically based; and surmised social influences as peripheral in cognitive development. Piaget conceptualized learning as biological maturation or an unfolding of various age-related stages referred to as *schemes.* These stages progress from sensorimotor development in infancy, and egocentric thought at pre-school ages, to symbolic and concrete operations that evolve into abstract and formal thinking in adolescents and adults (Furth, 1970; Bigge and Shermis, 1999; Byrnes, 2001; Bransford, et al., 2000).

Similar to Piaget, Vygotsky's theory of learning is explained as developmental, but cognition is viewed as mediated and sociologically specific. According to Vygotsky, mediators of cognitive development are language used as a tool, and a learner's interpersonal relations with experts. Vygotsky posited a *zone of proximal development (ZPD)* to reference a *metaphorical space* between where a learner is able to function independently, and where a learner functions with the assistance of an instructor. Further, Vygotsky reasoned that cognition develops through qualitative transformations; "marked by periods of stability transitioning into qualitative transformations . . . of mental functions and structures" (Kozulin, et al., 2006, p. 5). In this respect, his view differed from Piaget's position that through maturation, new or reformed structures of mental capacities *replace* old structures or mental schemes through assimilation and accommodation; and environment plays a secondary role in cognition.

Vygotsky posited that new knowledge *does not replace* prior knowledge, but *coexists* and explains new forms of understanding (Lidz & Gindis, 2006; Byrnes, 2001; Bransford, et al., 2000). Vygotsky sought to find a comprehensive approach that would describe and explain higher psychological functions in scientific terms; and questioned a direct relation between the brain mechanisms underlying particular function of simple and complex forms of the same behavior (Cole, et al., 1978). In identifying behavior, Vygotsky felt it important to specify the social context in which the behavior developed, and consequently stressed the social origins of language and thinking. Moreover, Vygotsky was the first modern psychologist to suggest the mechanisms by which culture becomes a part of a person's nature (Ibid.). Renewed interest in both

Piaget and Vygotsky's theories places their theories in a new framework that has relevance to current research and classroom practice.

Harris (n.d.; Article 00559) presented a brief historical review of the development of theories that address the relationship between language and cognition. In the late 1950's into the 1960's traditional theories generally focused on innate abilities as conceived by the linguist, Chromsky. This period included investigating artificial intelligence (AI) using a computer metaphor in explaining how the mind processes information. By the 1970's and 1980's theory focused on cognitive science where the attention of linguists and psychologists focused on differences and similarities between language and cognition. A growing consensus among current research appears to reflect an interdisciplinary approach to understanding cognition influenced by perspectives of a cognitive neuroscience movement.

The shift from viewing intelligence as a construct to contemporary explanations of *how people come to know* covers a wide spectrum among theories. The perspectives discussed in the following section will be limited to a few of the theories, several of which are incorporated into the conceptual positions of this text and a companion text referenced in a prior section.

Learning Theory in Contemporary and Current Research

Byrnes (2001) discussed cognitive development by posing questions that linked theories directly to instruction. His analysis was limited to several theories that have influenced research based on two main requirements: that the theories are educationally relevant; and currently driving research. The author sort answers of whether the theories addressed educationally related issues and provide answers to the following issues:

- the nature and growth of knowledge;
- whether the theory addressed self-regulation in learning;
- the educational application; and
- the relevance to the field of neuroscience.

The summarized theories are presented from a historical perspective and viewed as instrumental in shaping contemporary research regarding academic subject disciplines. Byrnes emphasized two central constructs: *The meaning of cognitive development;* and *cognitive development in instructional contexts.* Byrnes hypothesized that cognitive development involves mental processes of thinking, remembering, problem solving; and positive changes that occur with age and experiences; including factors and mechanisms that produce changes. The following discussions will focus on three of the issues identified by Byrnes (Ibid., p. 9) as having relevance to current research:

- *how knowledge is acquired,*
- the *application of the specific theory to learning;* and
- *the relation of the theory to cognitive neuroscience.*

Current Research Theories

Information-processing theory evolved in the mid 1970's and addressed the form and nature of knowledge, positing two main knowledge structures: *declarative knowledge* that consists of facts; and *procedural knowledge* that means knowing "how" to do something. Marzano & Costa (1987) explain *factual* or *declarative knowledge* as knowing *who, what, where, and when;* for instance, *understanding concepts of numbers;* and *procedural knowledge* as the process of demonstrating the *how* of knowledge—*how* to divide numbers. Byrnes (Ibid.) contends that application of information-processing theory in learning requires presenting information is small segments with sufficient time, exposure and activities as needed. Regarding neuroscience, this theory compared cognition to artificial intelligence contending that the brain is analogous to a computer, and the mind is the software

Bloom's hierarchy model of educational objectives is viewed as theory (Byrnes, 2001), and implies that specific levels of knowledge have logical prerequisites to others; that complex thinking is not attainable until more simple forms of knowledge have been mastered. The application to instruction lies in teaching through a hierarchical structure that progresses from lower to higher levels of cognition: knowledge of rote information, understanding and comprehending, to demonstrated application, analysis, synthesis and evaluation. There is no specific implication to neuroscience in the Bloom's model (Ibid., p. 76).

Vygotsky's theory advanced in the 1920's in Germany, gained popularity in America in the 1960's and is still vibrant in current thinking regarding cognition (Cole, et al., 1978; Brynes, 2001; Kozulin, A., 2006). Vygotsky identified two kinds of cognition: *concepts* and *functions*. Concepts are developed through abilities to define a set of criteria that may be pseudo or spontaneous concepts—information not fully understood; and scientific concepts that occur when information is fully comprehended. Functions are combinations of mental processes of perception, attention, language, thinking and memory. Knowledge is thus acquired through interaction of functions. The relation to instruction is to change spontaneous concepts to scientific concepts that require time and adult intervention (Byrnes, 2001, p. 37). Similar to Bloom's theory,

Vygotsky conceptualized thought as higher order thinking; that children progress from lower forms of thought to higher forms of thought and cognitive development. The application to instruction requires social interaction of the learner and use of symbolic tools that mediate cognitive activity. Interaction includes modeling, reciprocal teaching, small group activities, feedback and fading by the teacher; and learner mastery. No specific connection to neuroscience is inferred in Vygotsky's theory of cognitive development (Ibid.).

Trends in Current Theory

Current research on cognitive development reflects trends of understanding the influence of sociocultural factors on learning. One approach in this direction is led by neo-Vygotskian theorists who analyze the meaning of Vygotsky's views on *mediating tools*—mainly language and human relationships that are critical in cognitive development. These theorists suggest that children acquire knowledge through interpersonal communications with adults in the context of human and social society, referred to as the external world (Karpov, 2006a & 2006b). Further, in Vygotsky's view, cognition extends beyond thought and language in that the social situation in which children grow forms their personalities and behaviors. Thus, Vygotsky posited that human cognition is predicated on development in the context of social and cultural situations, as opposed to being strictly individual abilities (Bodrova & Leong, 2003; Kozulin, et al., 2006).

Theories of *Culturally Influenced Cognition* give new meaning to understanding individual differences as determined by traditional test assessments and academic performances among diverse learners in classroom settings. A sociocultural consideration of cognitive development and individual differences allows insight into various factors that illuminate why differences are present. Hilliard (1991; 1992; 1995) wrote extensively on the role of language in learning, and how language styles, in syntax and meaning, differ among various cultural groups. Hilliard argued that views of language as abstract and disconnected from a particular cultural context carries the assumption of a standard language of convenience that does not consider that learners may have another language shaped by their cultures and world experiences. He concluded that since culture cannot be ignored as influencing cognition and behavioral styles, cognition and language are functions of culture, and critical aspects in learning.

Shade (1982) examined differences in academic achievement of African American children from the perspective of culturally specific factors that influence achievement rather than individual abilities of learners. Shade posits that differences found in tasks and achievement result from "culturally induced *psychological, cognitive,* and *behavioral* strategies rather than ability differences" (p. 219—italics added); and it appears that interpersonal relations and situational cultural contexts are two major factors that influence cognitive style. Regarding interpersonal relations, the author's findings inferred that African American learners are accustomed to affection; that attentiveness focuses on cues from people; and language use and understanding involve subjective nuances of word meanings. Further, meanings are also derived from perceptual problem solving strategies gathered from the social environment. In this sense, students' conceptual or cognitive style is *field dependent;* and may be at variance with other views of non-contextualized cognitive styles that typically form the contexts of classroom discourse.

Current research on the *cultural nature of knowing* includes an Ecological theory espoused by Barab & Roth (2006). The authors argue that an ecological theory of what it means to know recognizes engaged participation over knowledge acquisition; and cognition and meaning are considered socially and culturally constructed. From an ecological perspective, learning is not solely an individual phenomenon of progressive adaptations, but is a process of contextualized participation in cognitive development. The central tenets of the theory include: knowing is an activity; is always contextualized; and is reciprocal between an individual and the environment. Additionally, an ecological theory of knowing proposes two concepts: First, *Affordance Networks,* interpreted as interaction between an individual and the environment—materially and socially—that *extend* opportunities to increase cognition and participation. Networks *(i.e., culturally determined opportunities)* exist naturally, and others are created intentionally. The second concept, *Life-Worlds,* found in other theories, refers to the material world of an individual. "Different individuals relate to the same material environment in different ways because prior actions and past experiences form an individual's life-world" (p. 7). This means that the individual, as an organism, couples with his or her life-world and theoretically neither entity is functionally independent of the other. The authors theorize knowing as a *process* of enlisting affordance networks in terms of an individual's life-world to actualize various goals.

Situated Learning

Rogoff and Lave (2003) find that increasingly, studies of cognitive development interpret learning as a function of specific situations, and "skills are limited in their generality" (p. 1). Thus, a critical aspect of cognition is the role of context, including the physical and conceptual structures, as well as the social milieu. Their findings are the summarized outcome of a conference of interdisciplinary fields that focused on the development of cognition in everyday and social contexts. In their discussions, culture and context are used interchangeably. Consensus from the conference centered on defining human development in terms of cultural participation; and performance depends in large part on the circumstances that are routine in the community and cultural practices of individuals. Cognitive development is explained as more than acquisition of knowledge; and consists of a change in how an individual perceives, thinks, understands, remembers or reflects on situations. Additionally, cognitive development occurs through individual participation in sociologically situated activities.

Situated cognition theory posited by Lave and Wenger (2003), also reflects a growing body of research and cognitive science that explores the situated character of how individuals acquire knowledge. However, the concept departs from emphasis on learning in terms of the conceptual processes involved in cognition. The focus is on " . . . what kinds of social engagements provide the proper context for learning to take place" (Ibid., Hanks, p. 14). This perspective implies a social practice theory. Further, the concept is that learning occurs through frameworks of co-participation in communities of practice where an individual functions first, as an apprentice who is a *legitimate peripheral participant* engaged with experts, or *masters;* and eventually progresses to a level of full participation and expertness. The concept also denotes *communities of practice* and unequal power relations of master-apprentice. Newcomers are peripheral observers; and become full participants through progressive stages of apprenticeship. Lave and Wenger emphasize that peripheral participation is a *viewpoint* of understanding circumstances in which learning occurs; that the process of learning is not dependent on instruction, but learning occurs where there is teaching. Their viewpoint extends beyond the context of schooling by contending that individuals learn as participants in a social process in any context.

The theories we have discussed are presented for two reasons. First, to focus attention on the significance of understanding *how people come to know,* and the nexus between understanding cognitive development and the application of theory to teaching and learning. Second, to emphasize positions arguing it cannot be assumed that all learners have been exposed to the same social experiences; and teachers must consider the issue of learners' prior experiences, backgrounds, and cultural ways of knowing, as critical factors that impact in-school learning. Consequently, it is important to find more effective ways of instructing students, giving consideration to factors of culturally influenced learning; and understanding the import of these factors should inform curriculum design and instructional delivery.

Language Use and Cognitive Development

A summary of the 1974 World Congress on Dyslexia focused on studies of disabilities, specifically reading. Findings reflected a consensus that reading is part of the language process correlated in general and in particular with perception and memory. The symposium's focus on variances of what is considered normative functioning in the process of reading gave insight to when, how, and the extent inabilities can be identified through objective data. Symposium participants agreed that of necessity, data is multifaceted and must be derived from interdisciplinary studies including cultural, cross-cultural, neurology relating to the roles of maturation and memory; and studies of visual and auditory perception (Duane & Rawson, 1975). For example, an array of symposium papers was drawn from a broad interdisciplinary field.

Gough posited that knowledge of the language is crucial for the reading process, and that understanding the *nature of language* enhances the efforts in teaching language. Calfee focused on the impact of memory regarding aspects of cognition and learning; and emphasized *the role of memory* in the acquisition of reading using an information-processing approach to find ways a learner thinks. Other symposium papers included the role of *auditory perception* discussed by

Schubert; *Cross-modal cognition* presented by Bryant; and a *visual perceptual* focus by Turvey. While the symposium focused mainly on "inabilities" compared to normative functioning; lessons are provided from other collective studies in education. Similar multi-theoretical symposiums have considered the nature of learning and the complexities involved in how best to utilize what is known about cognitive development regarding normative functioning, as well. The following discussions analyze cognitive development and the critical role language plays in learning (Gough, 1975; Cole, et al., 1978; Blake, 1994; Mehler, et al., 1995; Heath, 2002).

A cursory review of factors hypothesized as having the greatest impact on cognition points in several directions; however, it is argued that language in general, and language use, in specific, appear to be the major underpinning elements associated with cognitive development. Recent advances in cognitive science and cognitive neuroscience have expanded the body of knowledge on learning, in part, because interdisciplinary perspectives present convincing evidence that supports the relevance of how language functions relate to cognition, neurological, sociological, and biochemical factors associated with mental processing abilities (Gough, 1975; Critchley, 1975; Cole & Scribner, 1978; Winograd, 1980; Strachan, 2000; Heath, 2002; Litz & Gindis, 2006; Mehler, et al., 1995). This multi-theoretical approach in explaining cognitive development provides a broader field for more in-depth analyses, as well as a framework for consensus in identifying critical factors related to cognition. While increased attention to culturally responsive school practices is relatively recent regarding culturally influenced theories of language learning; the relation of culture to learning has been the focus of research for some time; most seriously considered, it appears, during the time period from Vygotsky's theory to the present intensified focus on the relationship of culture, language and learning.

The Structure and Foundations of Language

Gough (1975) contends that there is a need for a better understanding of the nature of language, and argues that since language is seldom absent in humans, that its presence is taken for granted; thus the *meaning* of language is not overtly considered. The author explains the structure of language, identifying three parts: sounds, words and sentences. He contends that language is abstract and few referents to words exist that can be reduced to single perceptual images because most words are interpreted through a multi-sensory process. Thus, language and meanings are "within the head" (p. 15). Gough posits that the relationship between language and cognition is explained in understanding that words and sentences in the lexicon of a language are mentally conceptualized, therefore there is an interdependence of cognition and language development; and neither of the abilities exists without the other. Gough concludes:

> Someone who knows a language knows the sentences of that language. He can tell you whether one of the sentences is meaningful . . . consistent . . . or contradictory. He can . . . answer questions about (the language) . . . and most importantly he can understand (the language.) (p.28)

Similar to Gough, Joynt (1975) describes the relationship between language and cognition and the placement of thought within the brain. The author points out that absolute knowledge of language functions remains obscure with no universal agreement of how functions operate. Therefore, Joynt argues, it would be more productive to focus on what is historically known about the structure and functions of language, the role of speech, and the development of thought. Joynt suggests a biological basis of human language; but explains that an understanding of "the mechanism of human language by certain unique structures of the . . . brain is not possible because we have limited knowledge of both neuroanatomy and knowledge of behavior . . ." Also, more is known about what disturbs language than what constitutes the neural basis for language (pp. 39-43). Examples are revealed in situations where the right brain hemisphere has compensated for structural damage of the left brain hemisphere.

Other research examined the nervous system and the biochemical nature of maturation of the brain. Critchley (1975) investigated the relation between language and cognition and posited that maturation of the brain depends on biochemical functions and partly upon appropriately timed myelination of the nerve fibers and the structure of the nerve cells. Further, that "human genetic makeup . . . guides and limits the development of biological, behavioral and psychological characteristics within the context of opportunities and constraints provided by the physical and social conditions of . . . environments . . ." (p. 14). In this sense, Critchley conceives an interdependent relationship between language and cognition.

Cole and Scribner's (1978) analysis of Vygotsky's theory also reflects a structural conception of brain mechanisms and underlying functions. The authors looked at two scientific terms: "simple and complex forms of what appeared to be the same behaviors" (p. 6). This infers that maturation alone does not account for higher order mental processes; that processes do not lie dormant in children waiting to be used in the adult brain. They agree with the position of Vygotsky that stressed the importance of social context in which behavior develops, including language use in social intercourse, and language use as a mediating agent in the development of higher mental processes.

Mehler, Pallier & Chistopher (1995) investigated cortical representation of speech from brain imaging data of bilinguals where second language activities revealed higher levels of variability of the neural structure. They contend that contrary to Piaget's position regarding *critical periods* of neural maturation, Vygotsky's position of plasticity appears to be more representative of language related mental processes. They pointed out that learning allows the cortical regions of the brain to reorganize throughout one's life. Further, that mental faculty is biologically determined, but is shaped by the environment. They too, use the example of left-right hemisphere functions of the brain using data that showed where patients suffered damage or removal of the left hemisphere associated with language, speech functions were subsequently acquired in the right hemisphere. The authors conclude that considering the universality of language grammar in all adult communities where individuals have been exposed to varying different sentences, "anything that differs between languages has to be learned by children from . . . (their environments)" (p. 2).

The discussion by Harris (n.d., Article 00559) presents a different perspective of the relationship of language and learning. Rather than looking at the interdependence of the two factors, Harris sought to answer whether a certain level of cognition is required for language acquisition; and whether language abilities are the same or different from other mental abilities. The author considered two ways of conceptualizing mental abilities—general purpose, which is foundational for all human ability; and modularity of distinct mental domains. In addressing the questions the author points to a growing consensus that language and cognition are both similar and different; and both develop as a function of biology and ecology (p. 5). Harris surmises that the relation between language and cognition appears to be co-dependent; thus, research is mutually informing in both areas.

Artificial intelligence (AI) is often overlooked as an area that could illuminate or explain cognition. Winograd (1980) addressed issues of determining whether language and cognition are similar or different, and what it means to understand language. He sought to create a computer design that could understand language by comparing human and artificial intelligence. The researcher made several assumptions about language and representation. First, sentences of language correspond to facts about the world. Next, it is possible to design a formal system that is representative of the relevant facts of the world. Finally, there is a way of correlating language sentences directly to a representational system that can accurately reason about the world. From the results, however, the author's attempt to create such a design left many questions unanswered, and a different issue to be addressed—whether human knowledge can be represented in formal structures.

Cultural Factors of Language and Cognition

A significant body of research exists that addresses the integral relations of language, cognition, and culture (Geetz, 1973; Hale, 1986; Giglioli, 1986; Heath, 2004, 2006; Greenfield & Cocking, 1994; Hilliard, 1992; Delpit, 2002; Maiga, 2005; Lave & Wenger, 2003; Lidz & Gindis, 2003). Many linguists support the view that language develops in cultural contexts, but is acquired by cognitive abilities that operate as functions of mental faculties. Theorists and researchers who view language and cognition as mutually dependent in cognitive development propose a social-cultural theory of an interactive relationship between individual biological make-up and culturally influenced environments. A cursory review of several culturally related perspectives reveals that regardless of the specific theory, there is consensus on the related role that culture plays in language development and in learning.

Emphasis on culturally related behaviors has filtered through conceptualizations of Piaget and Neo-Piagetian views of the secondary role of culture; to the primary role of culture of Vygotsky and Neo-Vygotskian movements, through contemporary theories and research. While the *chicken or egg* relationship remains elusive regarding which factor is dominant in cognitive development—nature or nurture—we are better informed through an *analysis* of perspectives among various theories that give insight into specific factors and practices that provide realistic utility and application in addressing learning. *Cultural influences* on cognition appear to be at the forefront of theories for such analysis.

The Social Context of Language Development

Our discussion turns now to consider two other perspectives of the relationship of culture and language. First, we address how language develops within social contexts; and second the influence of culture on learning. The purpose is to analyze generally accepted views regarding the relations of language, culture, and cognition; and whether a theory of culturally influenced learning needs more articulation or in-depth study regarding the relevance of culture specifically related to classroom learning for diverse students.

Giglioli, et al., (1986) explored aspects of the social construction of language. The authors sought to answer the question, "Who speaks what language to whom on what occasion?" (p. 11). The analyses focused on theoretical contributions of speech to other social and psychological disciplines, such as face-to-face interactive speech; the relationships between social and cultural structures of speech; social knowledge and social change; and the social reality of various kinds of speech. Their multidisciplinary analysis of language attempted to find a theory relevant to various approaches of language in social contexts. The authors observed that speech and meaning are embedded in social contexts; and speech is "understandable only in connection with social interaction" (Ibid.). Moreover, language meaning is either reflective, meaning to refer to a common stock of knowledge; or language is indexical— interpreted as the degree to which speech is context free, or completely context bound. They argue that it is vital to distinguish between language and speech. Agreeing with (and quoting) Bernstein is the basis of their reasoning:

> The type of social relations does not directly influence linguistic codes but exert certain constraints on speech; in turn, the type of speech used reinforces the selective perception of the speaker, shaping his apprehension of social reality. Thus in the process of socialization, the child learns . . . the requirements of a certain social structure (p. 14).

The cultural context of language and learning is the focus of situated learning. Lave & Wenger, (2003) and others explain situated learning as the relationship between learning and the social situation in which learning occurs. The authors suggest that learning is more than the acquisition of knowledge, and agree with Hanks (2003) who urges that instead of query regarding the cognitive processes involved in learning, the issue to address is finding the ". . . kinds of social engagements (that) provide the proper contexts for learning to take place . . . (because) learning is a process that takes place in a participation framework, not in an individual mind" (Ibid., p. 15). Further, persons who engage in learning contexts, *learn* through such participation (Italics added). This theory contrasts with conceptions of the cerebral nature of learning which primarily involves internalization of knowledge. Situated learning theory posits that increased co-participation and sociocultural practices in community create situations for learning to occur. Thus, meaning, understanding and learning are defined relative to situational contexts.

Hilliard (1995) found that much of what is assumed about language acquisition and meaning emanates from a dominant cultural perspective. This means that language use, vocabulary and meaning in mainstream America assume an approach that all language should conform to a single linguistic structure or standard. Hilliard argues that such an assumption indicates ". . . not only is there a standard language of convenience, but that there is a 'standard' language, meaning superior language to which all citizens must conform" (p. 43). In cultures where discourse differs by having other languages, members are thought to be "unintelligent;" therefore, misunderstanding of cultural behavior styles leads to erroneous estimates of the mental abilities of individuals. Hilliard suggests that there is a need to understand the nature of socially constructed language and argues: "Culture provides group members a deep sense of belonging and often a strong preference for behaving in certain ways" (p. 170). While learning theory infers that style is learned and such patterns can be either changed or augmented, cultural style cannot be ignored and behavioral style (including language) is a function (i.e. aspect) of culture (p. 172).

Culturally Influenced Learning

Heath (2006) investigated cultural ways of language use between two different working class community groups, one black and one white. The study sought to determine the effects of preschool home and community environments on learning, language structures, and uses needed in school and in job settings. Her findings showed that most people in the study, black and white, could shift among various language usages across and within groups or regions. Heath found that while the "world of learning is very different from that of school classrooms . . . (in both schools and workplaces) mainstream language values and skills were the expected norm . . ." (p. 4). Heath also found that people in the study used their everyday languages, values and skills in both settings. The author suggests that the focus of research should look at the everyday language learning environments of children; ". . . their ways of living, eating, sleeping, worshipping, using space, and filling time" (p. 3).

An understanding of the influence of culture on language and learning is critical to the discussions of this text, because of general misconceptions based on diverse language use in classrooms and in the larger society; particularly regarding abilities of ethnic minority children whose language differs significantly from mainstream discourse. Understanding culturally influenced language and learning is germane to any discussion regarding fair and equitable education, particularly considering the focus and dependence on *standardized testing* that purports to evaluate student performance; but results of which perpetuate the misconceptions (Cochran-Smith, 1996 & 2000; Steinberg, 1996; Ashton, 1999; Loury, 2002; Lynch, 2006; Au, et al., 2007). When language use among ethnic minority groups is compared to mainstream Euro-American language, any variances in language from a supposed *standard* language is generalized to questions of mental abilities of ethnic minority groups.

Blake (1994) contends that much of the research on the role of language in performance of African American children focuses on the form of language rather than how language is acquired and used within specific cultures. Blake sought to explain structural differences between the language behaviors of African American children and mainstream Euro-American children. Findings revealed that many researchers emphasized a deficit theory of language used by African American children that was learned from adults in their environment; and the remedy for this deficiency was to have these children immersed in mainstream Euro-American language experiences. Blake argued that this approach failed to explain why differences exist; that the deficiency view infers that Euro-American language is the standard "against which all others are judged." Further, since language develops in cultural contexts, ". . . differences cannot be understood or reconciled for improving performance if the differences cannot be described or the importance cannot be explained" (p. 168).

Labov (1986) notes that researchers who advocate a *standard language* perspective consider the variances of language as "verbal deprivation," or a deficit theory of learning directly attributable to minority cultures that do not provide the proper models or interactive communication skills needed to acquire *standard* language. Labov argues that the concept of "verbal deprivation" has no basis in reality because advocates of the concept have limited knowledge about either the reference group of children or their social lives. Moreover, contrary to the deficiency theory these reference groups of children receive extensive verbal stimulation from their environments; they "participate in a highly verbal culture . . . possess the same capacity for conceptual learning and use the same logic as anyone else who learns to speak and understand English" (p. 179).

Delpit (2002) makes a similar argument that African American vernacular compared to mainstream language leads to misinterpretation of African American capabilities. Delpit states:

> . . . (I)n our stratified society . . . appearance can serve to create an expectation of success or failure, of brilliance or stupidity, of power or impotence . . . our language "skin" provides an even more precise mechanism for determining status (p. xvii-xviii).

Kohl (1994), and Howard (1999a & 1999b) are among many educators and researchers who advocate that non-minority teachers, especially, need to understand the cultural languages and experiences of diverse children. Kohl points out that many children choose "not" to learn for various reasons. Often the cause is the mismatch between their language and language used in schools and the disparity between their experiences and those pre-supposed by their texts and teachers. He concludes: "The reasons for failure may be personal, social, or cultural, but whatever they are, the results of failure are most often a loss of self-confidence accompanied by a sense of inferiority and inadequacy" (1999a, pp 6-7). Howard points out:

> Diversity is not a choice, but . . . responses to it certainly are . . . In the face of a teacher population that is primarily White and culturally isolated, a student population increasingly diverse, and outcomes that reflect persistent inequalities across racial differences . . . (there needs to be a) search for a deeper understanding of the personal and social dynamics that have made the process . . . (of teaching) so difficult (Ibid., pp. 2-3).

In summary, theory of cognitive development in general and in specific, emphasizes the link between mental processes and linguistic ability often concluding that language, itself, is a mental process of cognitive development (Bransford, et al., 2000 & 2005). Consequently the relationship between language and cognition is intrinsically linked; and seldom are these factors considered distinctly separate. The influence of culture on learning is often conveyed through spoken language; and where language use of a cultural group is recognizably different from mainstream discourse, many people form misconceptions regarding the intellectual abilities of individual members, as well as the cultural group; ascribing "inferiority" generalized from language that is considered *non-standard*. Whether theorists conclude that language acquisition is predicated on mental abilities, or that language is a domain specific mental ability, in Vygotskian thought, language is a critical mediating tool in cognitive development and learning; and the impact of culture on learning must be given substantial weight in examining learning theories. This is particularly relevant regarding implications for educating diverse students in general; and in specific, in curriculum design, instructions, and classroom activities.

CHAPTER TWO

How the Mind's Eye Hears— Implications for Instruction

The reasonable man adapts himself to the world; the unreasonable one persists in trying to adapt the world to himself. Therefore all progress depends on the unreasonable man.
— George Bernard Shaw

INTRODUCTION

In chapter one the discussions focused on cognitive development from various theoretical perspectives that included biological, ecological, sociological, and neurological conceptions of learning. Much of the discussions analyzed factors hypothesized as foundational for human learning. We also looked at the relationship between language and learning; specifically, how language functions as a mediating tool in cognitive development and the subsequent impact of culture as it affects and shapes language use and understanding.

This chapter revisits theories that support the postulates of cognitive development of this text: that learning occurs when the *mind's eye* processes perceptual information. If we begin from a premise that cognition is dependent first, on an *established* biological structure and neural readiness that process sensory input, we surmise that cognition develops as a function of internalizing the outside world. However, if our assumption is that sensory input is processed, acted upon, or interacts in modifying biological structures and neural processes, we then conclude that the *situated place*

74

of an individual in the external world is the critical element necessary for cognition to develop. This *either-or* analysis returns us to the *chicken-egg* argument that seldom, if ever, establishes general consensus or extends an understanding of cognitive development. The position of this text argues that *nature* and *nurture* are interactively co-dependent; and a focus on which element has the greater impact is counterintuitive and counterproductive in solving critical educational issues.

The goal of this text is to present a framework that integrates concepts of sound theories that have consistently proved to enhance opportunities for cognitive development and higher levels of learning from both perspectives—*nature* and *nurture;* including theories of culturally related learning. This text theorizes cognition as a mental function involving multi-sensory processing mainly through language. This position agrees with Bryant (1975) that individuals perceive sensory input simultaneously though more than one sense; and connections are made between the modalities of visual and auditory perception (p. 195). It is posited that cognition develops through dynamic interactive sensory input within individuals, regardless of age or circumstances, and co-exists within *situated contexts.* Bransford, et al. (2000) explain, ". . . (E)ven infants are active learners . . . (that) an infant's brain gives precedence to certain kinds of information: language, basic concepts of number . . . and movement" (p. 10).

Regarding learning in educational settings, this text further agrees with a Vygotskian perspective, that language is a mediating tool in comprehension and cognitive development (Cole, et al. 1978; Kozulin, et al., 2006). It is argued that language plays a major role in cross-modal processing of information received through sensory input in specific situations. The term coined for this concept is *Auditory Situated Field (ASF)* that explains how individuals understand auditory information through functions of language. It is posited that internal neural processing co-exists with encoded knowledge, and auditory information is understood in *situated contexts*. This means that multi-modal sensory processing of information in specific situations is a necessary condition for individuals to make sense of the world (LaBerge, 1972; Bryant, 1975; Gough, 1975; Schubert, 1975; Eisner, 1994; Lindsay & Norman, 1977). This text posits that the mind has an *"ear-eye"* function critical to cognitive development (Kavanagh & Mattingly, 1972). This *"ear-eye"* function interprets auditory information based on previously stored visual input. In turn, the *mind* "cross-modally" decodes, and encodes auditory input by referencing previously stored visual-auditory "mental cues" or concepts.

The important point emphasized by the *"ear-eye"* function theory is that instruction should employ multiple approaches, especially in the delivery of introductory information in varying similar and different contexts that build upon learners' prior knowledge, experiences, and language use. This provides opportunities for learners to make connections between mentally stored psychological, physical, concrete or abstract references, and new information. Such opportunities allow learners to interpret information and content from a perspective of relevancy and prior experiences in order to learn with understanding. In essence, learners must understand what is *heard* figuratively through the *mind's eye—i.e.,* to reference visual imagery and concepts of prior knowledge or experiences to understand auditory input in current situated contexts.

In an earlier work (Pierre-Pipkin, 2003), the author explored areas of significance in cognitive development and *how people come to know* mainly through language; that various cultural influences shape the lexicon of language concepts, syntax, and meanings. A question posed was: "When someone is talking to you, do you literally *form pictures* in your mind?" (p. 13). The question produced a *yes* and a *no* response regarding both younger and older learners. The answer is *no* for older learners where concepts are understood based on past experiences; but possibly *yes,* in situations involving unknown concepts. Older learners might *figuratively "picture"* concepts of what is heard *(i.e.,* referred to as employing *mental imaging)* to encode or process unknown information. This occurs by associating new input with prior knowledge stored in, and retrieved from a language memory bank. For younger learners, *yes,* when information is completely novel; and possibly *yes,* if information requires functions beyond simple recall or recognition. Young learners may need many interactive experiences with the unknown and opportunities for transition from concrete levels to abstract levels of thought in order to associate and immediately retrieve meaning through perceptual and conceptual processes. Once sensory information has been encoded at a conceptual level, the answer would be *no;* because young learners would then understand related, or variations of information based on prior knowledge or experiences. The following discussion emphasizes how individuals form concepts through sensory perceptual input.

Understanding Perceptual and Conceptual Cognition

Three critical elements are identified as foundational in learning: *percept, concept,* and the *role of memory* in perceptual and conceptual functioning. From a basic dictionary perspective, the word *percept* simply means acuity, to distinguish, to see, to observe, to recognize, to discern. *Concept* is defined as a belief, a theory, an idea, impression, hypothesis, to comprehend, understand, or to grasp. The difference between the two terms relates to the level of mental processing needed for cognition. A distinction is made between the physical acts of seeing and hearing (*acuity*), and the processes of visual and auditory perception. Thus, *perception* involves a basic level of mentally processing sensory input; *i.e.,* to interpret visual or acoustical stimuli; to recognize, to recall. *Conceptualization* is also a mental process, but extends beyond basic perception by attaching categorical meaning to sensory input through associations and contextualizing; *i.e.*, to understand meaning, application, to see differences or similarities, etc. Both processes function interdependently to make sense of the environment (Turvey, 1979; Eisner, 1994; Lindsay & Norman, 1977).

The *role of memory* in processing sensory information will be discussed in detail later in this section; but briefly, memory implies an ability to sustain sensory input long enough for interpretation or to derive meaning. Calfee (1975) contends that memory is comprised of interrelated psychological processes for encoding, storing, and retrieving information; and argues, ". . . you can't remember what you didn't process" (p. 62). This suggests that learning begins with the functions of perception and conceptualization that require employing short-term memory. Therefore an understanding of how perceptual and conceptual functions coalesce with memory provides clarity to how tasks are handled, or what to do when difficulty occurs.

Conditions for Learning

The concept of *conditions for learning* posited in this text, including the phrase, *how people come to know,* is synonymous with Gagne's (1967) definition of learning as "... a *change in human disposition or capability, which can be retained, and is not simply ascribable to the process of growth*" (p. 5). Gagne explored critical elements of learning situations by identifying various kinds of learning beginning first with stimuli received through the senses. Gagne posited that the conditions for learning to occur involve an individual's senses and nervous system—specifically the brain. Other elements include output that can be indirectly observed when individuals demonstrate increased capability through eight types of learning including attention, discrimination, verbal association and problem solving. This text incorporates Gagne's *concept learning* that involves neural abilities and classification in concept development. According to Gagne, learning a concept depends on neural processes of *representation* for its existence (p. 47). This means that concept learning is a process of internalizing the environment. Gagne posits:

> Learning a concept means learning to respond
> to stimuli in terms of abstracted properties . . .
> as opposed to concrete physical properties . . .
> (For example,) a child may learn to call a two-
> inch cube a "block" and also apply this name

to other objects that differ from it . . . in size
and shape . . . Later, he learns the concept of
cube, and by so doing is able to identify a class of
objects that differ from each other physically . . .
A cube may be represented concretely by objects
made of wood, glass, (or) wire . . . (Eventually the
child) identifies a cube "intuitively" . . . on the
basis of an internalized representation that does
not employ the words of the geometer's definition
(pp. 47-48).

This perspective generally accepted in the literature
is explained in Norman's (1972) discussion that conceptual
processing is an internal mental function of the *role of
memory*; and "what is necessary in the processing of incoming
language-based sensory materials . . ." (p. 280). Norman
contends that "seeing and hearing enter the information
sequence as sensory-oriented signals . . . (thus) the internal
processing of language is organized around representation
as acoustical, articulation and/or abstraction . . ." (Ibid.).
Similarly, Lindsay and Norman (1977) explain how external
signals arriving at the sense organs are fed to the brain and
converted into meaningful perceptual experiences. This is
accomplished when incoming information is matched with
previous experiences, referred to as an internal template.
The authors argue that through the manipulation of mental
imagery, sensory input is interpreted to a degree sufficient
for understanding (p. 414).

Memory in Perceptual and Conceptual Development

A brief review of the literature regarding the role of memory in processing sensory input reflects a plethora of terms that identify various types of memory including: short-term or primary memory; long-term or secondary memory; perceptual, sensory, visual, or auditory memory; verbal memory; and information processing memory. Some theorists argue separate isolated memory stores for each modality; other views theorize two basic categories of short-term and long-term memory of visual and auditory sensory input. There is general agreement among theories that memory is critical in both perception and conception (Kintsch, 1970; Bower, 1972).

The role of memory in perceptual and conceptual functioning focuses primarily on short-term and long-term memory; and the consensus is that short-term memory appears to be the primary receptor for processing sensory input (Kintsch, 1970; Wood, 1972; Crowder, 1972; Norman, 1972; Lindsay & Norman, 1977; Bransford, et al., 2000; Byrnes, 2001). Lindsay and Norman (Ibid.) describe the structure of concepts with emphasis on how concepts are represented in human memory. They find three properties essential in the development of concepts: receiving sensory input; interrelating input to other information; and accessing information from memory. The authors suggest that memory involves *mental imaging*—that *pictures* are not literally *formed* or *stored* in the head; rather, the processing of information indicates that perception of images might be similar to perception of reality. Further, representations of perceptual experiences are stored in a manner that mental images can be used when needed. According to Rumelhart, et al., (1972), concepts refer to ideas in the memory system, and "three types of functional relations are of primary importance . . . classes to which a concept belongs; characteristics which define it as a member of that class; and the examples of the concepts . . . (Further) most concepts have no simple natural language equivalent" (p. 203).

Crowder (1972) finds that auditory memory appears to be superior to visual memory because acoustical stimuli has direct access to an auditory store, while visual input has to be processed and translated into auditory form. The inference is that "seeing or reading memory stimulus is an indirect way of hearing them" (p. 270). Schubert (1975) however, contends that initially the auditory system depends heavily on other sensory modalities for establishing associations; and once connections are made, the auditory system is able to function unassisted. LaBerge (1972) explains the functions of visual and auditory perception as cross-modal processing of information. Visual and auditory inputs enter on parallel channels, and converge with a memory system.

This means that there is a crossover from visual processing stages (particularly in reading) to an auditory path prior to entering the memory system at a level where sounds are coded into speech, and output from the visual system enters the auditory system. This may seem perplexing, because we do not know with complete accuracy *how* these neural processes function, and can only theorize indirectly from an individual's demonstrated behavior. For example, Winograd (1972) explains that children understand spoken language before they learn to read; thereby demonstrating that reading takes place by mentally translating printed words into spoken sounds.

Norman (1972) contends that awareness of the many varied memory systems is not as critical as having an understanding of "what is necessary to process incoming language-based sensory materials" (p. 280), because information is not understood by separate word units; but language input is temporarily held in short-term memory until conceptual meaning is accomplished. These postulates and others reflect the significant role that memory plays in processing information; and the implications for instruction and learning.

How the Mind's Eye Hears

Several commonly accepted learning theories are integrated in the hypothesis that the *"mind"* has an *"eye"* that *"hears;"* referred to as "insight" that is a critical and necessary function in cognitive development, processing language-based information, and in higher order thinking. Some of the theories discussed in *Chapter One* are combined to support this hypothesis:

- *Information-processing theory* that explains how cognition develops along a continuum from surface to deep process learning (Lohman, 1989);
- *Vygotsky's Theory* of language mediated learning in cognitive development, and the *zone of proximal development (ZPD)* that explore language as a critical tool and mediator in learning (Kozulin, et al., 2006);
- *Bloom's Hierarchy of Educational Objectives: The Cognitive Domain* that established an instructional taxonomy that is congruent with conceptual development (Byrnes, 2001);
- *Culturally Influenced Learning* that explores an ecological theory of engagement in socially and culturally constructed contexts (Barab & Roth, 2006); and
- *Situated Cognition Theory* that examines learning through participation in socially situated activities (Rogoff & Lave, 2003; Lave & Wenger, 2003).

The theory advanced by this text is to emphasize the importance of understanding what is known or theorized about how sensory perceptual and neural processes function in concept development; and to illuminate what specific elements create the conditions for cognitive development and higher order thinking in instructional contexts, in order to answer: *How* do we get from *there,* which is *theory* (e.g., how people come to know); to *here,* which is *practice* (e.g., successful instructional design and delivery)?

The answer, in part, lies first, in an understanding of how people learn—in this text referenced as, how the *mind's eye hears.* The concept is supported by a consensus that sensory perceptual abilities, neural processing, and mental imagery co-exist and act interdependently in cross-modal sensory activities in an *"ear-eye"* function. This permits reception; storage in memory; association for meaning; and retrieval of language-based information beyond acuity and perceptual processing. Understanding the *"ear-eye"* function is necessary for evaluating if students are *demonstrating* cognitive development, acquisition of knowledge, and increased cognition and content capabilities.

Learning Theory and the Teaching-Learning Process

An analysis of how learning theory is linked to instruction requires identifying basic steps that make the connections between *processes* of perceptual and the conceptual functions in cognitive development; and how *conditions for learning* can *be created* to provide opportunities for learners to demonstrate that learning is occurring. How can this be done? Since theories infer and identify specific behaviors that are exhibited when *an individual is learning,* a logical first step would be to design activities—based on learning theories—whereby learners consistently exhibit behaviors of growth in knowledge and skills. This means, what is perceived and mentally processed in concept formation is clearly understood by learners to the extent that new knowledge is overtly and consistently demonstrated, as determined by application, transfer in problem solving; and increased capabilities in the subject content under discussion.

Because learning is defined in terms of *insight,* meaning *within; internalizing the environment; or to see relationships,* it is crucial that teachers provide many and differently varying opportunities for learners to develop *insight* to increase knowledge and skills. Various activities and opportunities beyond generic style teaching formats, such as lecture-only methods, provide conditions for learners to develop "insight;" i.e., to *"see"* with their *mind's eye.* Enhanced learning conditions are created when learners engage in activities that require "mental imaging" in information processing abilities; use of prior knowledge, cultural experiences; and individual learning styles in understanding subject content. Teachers must be sensitive to the "ah, ha!" or "eureka" moments of expressions students display non-verbally; or the verbal, "Oh, I see!" exclamations. These are opportunities to indirectly observe that learners figuratively use their *minds' eyes* in *seeing what is said* (Pierre-Pipkin, 2007).

Designing learning formats that are theory-based can be accomplished by employing concepts of *concrete, semi-concrete,* and *abstract* teaching and learning in instructional formats and activities appropriate for the age, grade, and abilities of students in scope and sequence of knowledge and skills students are expected to learn. Young learners may need many *concrete* activities; while symbolic, representational or mediated activities for older learners establish foundational basis for understanding. The use of age-appropriate scaffolding activities, also, augments instruction; and allows opportunities to incorporate cultural themes and concepts of students' prior out-of-school experiences to mediate understanding for diverse learners. Scaffolding also provides opportunities for students to advance to higher levels of functioning.

The important point being stressed is twofold: first, teachers must be purposefully aware that effective instructional practices must be grounded in learning theory; and second, teachers must understand the significance of culturally-influenced learning when designing responsive practices; and know when to adjust curriculum delivery and instructional activities to reach diverse students (Hale, 1986, 2001a, 2001b; Delpit, 1996; Falk, 1996). Consequently, it is critical for teachers to be constantly aware that culture influences the *mindset* of diverse students based on experiences that may be *different* from discourse in classroom settings; and to note that the *"mind's eyes"* of students may *"hear"* from completely different *auditory situated field*s than the intended emphasis of instruction. Thus, multiple formats (contexts) and activities should be provided to ensure that content is "understood" at a level to accurately demonstrate knowledge and skills. An instructional design that integrates multiple learning theories of *concrete, semi-concrete,* and *abstract learning* in pedagogy is the most effective means of creating learning conditions, frameworks, and taxonomic learning structures to ensure that teaching and learning, *with understanding,* occur intentionally and sequentially appropriate for all age and grade levels of diverse cultural groups; in all instructional settings.

Concrete, Semi-Concrete, and Abstract Learning

A substantial body of data support learning as being developmental from lower to higher forms of cognition: either biologically, neurologically mental, or through mediated situated conditions (Lindsay & Norman, 1977; Cole, et al., 1978; Byrnes, 2001; Bransford, et al., 2000; Donovan, et al., 2005; Konsulin, et al., 2006; Lave and Wenger, 2003; Rogoff, 2003). This text posits that cognitive development and conceptualization occur at three distinct levels: *concrete, semi-concrete* and *abstract* levels of learning.

The terms, *concrete* and *semi-concrete learning* appear to be oxymoronic if *learning,* in essence, is viewed in terms of neural processing of sensory input; i.e., mental functions that occur within the mind, and clearly not directly observable. Therefore, the term *abstract learning* seems to more accurately define *all types* of learning. Perhaps an appropriate explanation of *concrete* and *semi-concrete learning* is to note that many theories infer that all learning develops progressively from tangible or actual experiences that act as *conduits* in the development of conceptual *abstractness* (Bransford, et al., 2000; Brynes, 2001). *Concreteness* thus is something three-dimensional, material, or perceived though the senses—visual, acoustical, tactile, etc.; and *semi-concreteness*, lies somewhere between the concrete and the abstract; and is classified as *symbolic* or *representative* of the concrete as well as the abstract. For example, a *picture* can be symbolic of a physical object, or a concept. Consequently, the terms *concrete* and *semi-concrete learning* are used to identify conditions though which learning is mediated and can be indirectly observed. Additionally, symbols augment learning as representations of actual objects, knowledge, or experiences in the real-world, and provide mediating transitions from concrete learning stages to abstract learning during the process of conceptual development (Pierre-Pipkin, 2003; 2007). The theories of *concrete, semi-concrete,* and *abstract* learning support and encourage mediated, transformative, and culturally responsive teaching practices.

Concrete Learning

To articulate *how people come to know*, it is necessary to identify a point at which cognition begins. It is theorized that cognition begins at a *concrete* or direct experience level when the unknown is encountered; or at a level of sensory input (Eisner, 1994). Further, with continual exposure to information, or interaction in mediated activities, an individual is able to process sensory input into meaningful and relevant conceptual understanding, thereby beginning the process of *knowing*. According to Bloom (Byrnes, 2001), simple recognition or recall is considered lower level thinking in cognitive development. This means that this level of perceptual processing of sensory input does not constitute complete or thorough conceptualization at an *abstract* level for application and transfer. Rather, lower levels of learning are considered the use of *memory* in *rote* learning. This is interpreted as abilities at a *concrete* or basic level that are prerequisite for higher forms of thinking. Similarly, Byrnes explains Piaget's theory of *knowing*. Piaget contended that to ultimately acquire abilities of *abstract reasoning* "children need to interact with objects or actual content" (Ibid. p. 73). For example, to understand the concept of "three-ness," children must count actual sets of objects containing three things to comprehend the symbol "3." Therefore, thought develops from lower forms of thinking to higher forms that are mediated through experiences. Vygotsky also conceived learning as development that progresses from lower to higher levels of thought. Learning originates in social contexts, but is centered on cognitive activities and is either "other-regulated," which means mediated through other persons, or the environment; or learning is "self-regulated" and not dependent on others or the environment, but eventually shifts completely to the individual (Ibid. p. 75). Further, according to Vygotsky, young children transfer "general representations of the world based on recall of concrete instances that do not yet represent the character of an abstraction" (Cole, et al., 1978, p. 50).

A *concrete stage* of cognition is considered the basic starting point in learning and is a lower form of thought that requires direct contact, content, and/or experience in the real-world for perceptual and conceptual processing. This lower level is referred to as a *Basic Level* of teaching and learning in an instructional design, and the necessary prerequisite for encoding sensory perceptions into *symbolic representations* for comprehension at an *intermediate stage*—which is the next step in the developmental process of learning.

Semi-concrete Learning

Semi-concrete learning is an *Intermediate Level* between concrete and abstract learning and is termed a *Representative Level* in teaching and learning. This means that information is not completely *abstract*, yet is removed from *concreteness.* For example, numerical symbols as "2 or 3" may represent the physical objects that compose sets of items at a concrete level. The words, "two or three" would be language symbols representative of an abstract conceptual level of "two-ness" or "three-ness." Both *numbers* and *words* then are *semi-concrete symbols* that *mediate* or *augment* comprehension. This intermediate step between concrete and abstract learning requires *mediated* support of others; symbolic representations; or situations within the environment to make transitions from *concrete* to *abstract* conceptual development. Thus, in explaining subject content, a teacher may employ *language* that is humorous, as *tools* to explain concepts; or utilize symbolic representations of real-world referents, as discussed above regarding numbers "2" or "3", and the words, "two" or "three;" or provide activities for students to create, *situational contexts* as scaffolding activities to model concepts contained within content discussions (Pierre-Pipkin, 2007). These are conditions referred to as *mediating points* or *semi-concrete* between understanding at a basic, or *concrete* level; and conceptualizing at an *abstract level* where mediation or representational tools are not required for understanding.

Vygotsky's intermediate point in learning is the use of language and other persons, as *tools* to mediate learning. Vygotsky refers to this stage as the *Zone of Proximal Development (ZPD)*—a metaphorical space between where children function independently in cognitive activities, and the level at which they need the assistance of a teacher or others. Thus mediated social interaction is necessary before skills are internalized and consciously mastered.

An intermediate step of learning in Bloom's hierarchy is not as definitive in specifying a transition from lower to higher levels as other theories discussed here. However, Bloom's Taxonomy involves progression from rote learning at lower levels to deeper understanding at higher levels. For the purpose of this text, Bloom's *Level Three—Application* is surmised as an intermediate step in cognition; albeit Bloom considered "application" as higher order thinking. *Application* falls into a symbolic or representative level because it involves indirect observations of demonstrated understanding of basic knowledge and skills. *Application* of knowledge and skills requires an individual to exhibit internalized comprehension of knowledge in transfer of skills above rote recall or recognition, yet is not reflective of deep understanding as *analysis, synthesis,* or *evaluation* which, according to Bloom, are considered *abstract*

94

levels of cognitive skills. Therefore, *Application* is considered the intermediate step (*why, how,* or *when application* is made) between lower levels of basic *knowledge understanding,* and *abstract* higher order thinking.

Abstract Learning

Higher order functioning, or an *abstract level* of cognition is considered an independent or mastery stage within the theories discussed, and is referred to in this text as a *Conceptual Level* in learning. Piaget posited higher order thinking as less tied to perception and concrete thought, as both *abstract* and *logical,* and acquired developmentally with biological readiness (Cole, et al., 1978; Byrnes, 2001; Bransford, et al., 2000). Bloom's Hierarchy identifies three other levels beyond *application* in higher order thinking as: abilities of finding relationships through *analysis*; restructuring information through *synthesis*; and making judgments or explaining information based on criteria of *evaluative thinking.*

Similar to Piaget's and Bloom's conceptions of abstract thinking, Vygotsky contended that higher order thinking is demonstrated when children consciously master cognitive tasks through self-regulated thought. Unlike Piaget, however, Vygotsky refutes that cognition represents mere unfolding of an individual's organically predetermined system; rather, higher psychological functioning or higher order thinking is the internal reconstruction of external forms of activity, including cultural forms that are mediated by the learner's experience and environment. Further, all higher functioning originates at two levels: *interpersonal*—between the learner and others; and *intrapersonal*—*inside the learner.* Vygotsky explained the instruction from simple to complex forms of conceptual processing as initially having *spontaneous* concepts attained through everyday experiences that provide the foundation for more complex forms of what appears to be the same behavior. More complex forms of thinking are defined as *scientific* concepts which are thought to be taxonomic and *abstract*; and this level of internalized, self-regulated activity is considered higher psychological functioning (Byrnes, 2001; Bransford, et al., 2000; Cole, et al., 1978; Kozulin, et al., 2006).

In a previous discussion we looked at Gagne's analysis of conditions required for learning. This text agrees with his theory of *learning* and *conceptual development* being dependent on representation and internalizing the environment. In this context, *abstract learning* is explained as an independent *conceptual level* where guided instruction may support learning, but is not a required condition for learning. Learning is indirectly observed when a learner is able to function independently, demonstrating increased understanding and by exhibiting specific behaviors that reflect increased *abstract* cognitive capabilities.

The critical issue in the discussions of *concrete, semi-concrete,* and *abstract* learning—adapted in this text based on *information processing theory*—is that cognition and concept development progress from surface learning to deep processing abilities; thus, teachers must understand the developmental nature of learning. Moreover, regardless of the age of the learner, or the content of the knowledge and skills, information must first be understood at a *basic level* before learners can internalize novel information and progress to higher levels of cognition and thinking. For younger learners, first-step activities may involve real-world concrete, symbolic, or direct experiences; while older learners may require only reflection of prior knowledge or experiences; or the use of modeling and situational contexts to establish a foundation for new learning.

It is important to have theoretical clarity in articulating and understanding the relationship between cognitive development and learning; and to distinguish the difference. While the terms are often used interchangeably, the concepts are not necessarily synonymous. Theories of learning previously discussed, support the proposition that cognitive development relates to the anatomical and neural structural processes necessary for learning to occur (Critchley, 1975; Gough, 1975; Joynt, 1975; Bigge and Shermis, 1999; Bransford, et al., 2000; Byrnes, 2001; Bransford, et al., 2005). This means that a learner has biological, neurological, and mental abilities to process external sensory stimuli at a specific level of perception and conceptualization. Learning is perceived as the "use" of anatomical and neural processing to build upon previously formed concepts in acquiring knowledge for application or to interpret the world. The difference in these terms is subtle, but critical in understanding learning theory. It is often said that learning is as natural for humans, as flying is for birds. Thus, learning occurs with or without instructional intervention (Lave and Wenger, 2003); thereby instruction serves the purpose of mediating cognition by structuring and creating conditions for "accurate' and "precise" learning to occur (Gagne, 1967). Teachers must understand that the individual mind of a learner determines preparedness and receptiveness for learning. This means to be continuously aware of "where" students function cognitively—in "reality"—not in the teacher's "presumptions;" and to design instructional activities that "create conditions" for students to develop insight in order to learn with understanding. Therefore, effective application of learning theory depends on ensuring that learners come to know the correct information, "correctly."

At issue then is how to connect research to practice. Wiske (1998) pointed out that *teaching for understanding* is a complex process that cannot be explained as simply using one's knowledge in novel situations; but an explanation extends to include other elements teachers must know: "How can we foster understanding? How can we tell what students understand?" (p. 61). This is answered, in part, by understanding the goals; observing their demonstrated performance; and through ongoing assessment. Wiske posits that teachers must define and articulate explicitly what students are expected to eventually understand; provide multiple, ongoing assessments in the early guided inquiry stage of instructions; and to eventually assess performance through more formal feedback, sampling, and cumulative performance.

Culturally Influenced Learning

An example often used to show how different individuals interpret their world space at a particular moment are the descriptions given at the scene of an accident. A group of people who witnesses the same accident at the same moment in time may render several quite different versions of that same situation. Why? Because each person approaches the external world from his or her particular perspective; and each perspective is conditioned and influenced by the individual person's worldview. Moreover, each person articulates his or her particular *mindset* based on prior knowledge, experiences, suppositions, judgments, expectations, and a plethora of other factors that may render each description of the accident distinctly different from others.

A similar situation exists in classrooms where the same instructional conditions are provided to individuals who compose a classroom group. Instruction is delivered within a specific context to learners, whose *mindsets, experiences* and *backgrounds* represent differing levels of readiness or prior knowledge bases, thereby rendering many distinct learner *perspectives.* Regardless of the homogeneous or heterogeneous makeup of the classroom group, the import of prior in-school and out-of-school knowledge, experiences—particularly *cultural experiences*—often dictate a challenging and an almost untenable situation for ensuring that all learners acquire the approximate same level of knowledge and skills, at the approximate same time. Unlike witnessing an accident, however, the forgiving nature of instruction is that it is amendable to *re-creation:* we get to *re-design curriculum; re-do instruction; make mid-cycle instructional corrections;* and *provide enhanced learning activities* to mediate correct interpretations and understanding of subject content. Unfortunately, in most of the initial instructional delivery or the *re-doing,* a critical element is often neglected—a consideration of the import of *cultural factors* that influence in-school learning (Hale, 1986; Giglioli, 1986; Greenfield and Cocking, 1994; Delpit, 1995 Delpit & Dowdy, 2002; Rogoff, 2003; Cook-Gumperz; Kozulin, et al., 2006; Heath, 2006). This neglect is reflected in a thought advanced by Shujaa (1998) who states:

In societies where multiple cultures exist and where the power relations among them are unequal, the existence of a politically dominant cultural group ensures that schooling and education cannot be assumed to be overlapping social processes (p.11).

Culturally acquired behaviors, particularly communication patterns, impact learning across all social situations—in and out-of-school; yet in educational settings it is simply assumed that the dominant cultural group's socialization is the *sole* standard through which education must be delivered, and diverse learner populations must suppress the influences that have shaped their social realities (Heath, 2006). Moreover, language use, including meaning utilized in classrooms, is often diametrically different from the thought patterns of diverse learners; thus much of their school learning is unnatural. It seems to make sense, that since school systems are not likely to change the out-of-school *cultures* of diverse learners that educators adapt curriculum and in-school practices to the cultural learning patterns of the learners. The point is reiterated, that adapting culturally *inclusive school practices* does not reduce standards or diminish knowledge and learning expectations; instead, incorporating culturally responsive scaffolding in pedagogy enhances opportunities for students and schools to meet standards; and for students to learn the expected knowledge; rather than "memorizing" declarative information for testing purposes (Pierre-Pipkin, 2008).

Giglioli (1986) notes the difference between linguistic views that posit society shapes language, and the view of *linguistic relativity* advanced by Whorf, who asserts ". . . it is the structure of language which determines ways of thought and cultural patterns, thereby influencing social structures as well" (p. 13). The influence of culture on "ways of thought" in learning is most prevalent in school settings, which is the focus of the following discussions. Let's briefly review several theories that argue, advocate, or support the importance of understanding the import of culture; particularly language factors that impact classroom learning.

Learning in Cultural Contexts

We begin with Vygotsky's interpretation of culturally influenced learning. An important tenet of Vygotsky's theory is that children develop culturally and acquire knowledge through social interaction; and every function in cultural development appears first on a social level between children and people; and second, inside the child on an intrapersonal level. Vygotsky argued that language use in cultural contexts is a tool that mediates progression from *spontaneous* to *scientific* concepts, the necessary progression from lower to higher forms of thought (Kozulin, et al., 2006). According to Brynes (2001), Vygotsky contended that adult modeling within a culture symbolically mediates learning and is a necessary scaffold in cognitive development; and without mediation in social situations—including instructional settings—children's thinking would remain in a lower-level state.

Ecological Theory explains how culture contextualizes human activity. In a previous discussion of this theory analyzed by Barab and Roth (2006), the emphasis focused on cognitive development. Ecological theory also explains how social contexts impact learning, whether in-school or out-of-school. According to Barab and Roth, human learning depends on inter-active engagement with the environment and the subsequent culturally determined *networks* that evolve. *Networks* are composed of people, situations, social behaviors, language use and meanings and operate in all social settings, including learning in school contexts.

Sociolinguistic and Social Learning Theory

Strikingly similar to cultural theories are concepts of *Sociolinguistic Theory* (Giglioli, 1986; Cook-Gumperz, 2006) and *Social Learning Theory* (Hale, 1986; Greenfield and Cocking, 1994; Rogoff, 1999; Scribner, 1999; White and Seigel, 1999;

Delpit, 2002). Sociolinguistic and Social Learning Theory can be summed up in the position of White and Siegel (Ibid.).

> The contexts in which children live are, with minor exceptions, social contexts. Children . . . are not engaged in solitary achievement. They are working with other humans. To abstract the cognitive part of a social encounter imperils the texture and meaning of the cognitive phenomena. (Further, cognition must be viewed across) time and space as deeply embedded in a social world (p. 239).

Sociolinguistic Theory implies that speech represents "replicable accounts of concrete social events within specific cultures . . . (the) ethnography of speaking . . . (and) is understandable in connection with social interaction . . ." (Giglioli, 1986, pp. 10 & 13). Since the social function of language serves to define the communication systems among various social groups, language use and meaning must be analyzed within the speech community of those various cultural groups. Similarly, Cook-Gumperz (2006) contends that literacy takes place in many different settings; and what is spoken, written, or understood is "situated, context-embedded practices" (p. 3).

Research reveals that the discontinuity between language use in diverse cultural communities and language use in classrooms disadvantages urban school children, mainly because their language is viewed as impoverished (Hale, 1986; Rogoff, 1999; Scribner, 1999; White & Seigel, 1999; Delpit, & Dowdy, 2002). Subsequently, such attitudes have widespread negative influences on how urban children are perceived in schools; primarily that they have limited mental abilities; and as a result, significant numbers are relegated to special situations and marginalized spaces in schools. However, as Labov (1986) states: "The concept of verbal deprivation has no basis in social reality . . ." (p. 179).

Heath (2006) pursued the issue of patterns of language socialization of preschool home and community environments, compared to language structures needed in classrooms and job settings. Findings indicated that the "kind" of talk, not the "quantity" of talk establishes the foundational readiness for school children. Also, some children enter school with specific ways of understanding words "out of context"; while low-wealth children generally are conditioned to understand "context-bound" communication, and encounter cultural shock when expected to lift items and events out of context. In the majority of American schools—urban and suburban—minority children's language use is thought to be the major cause of learning problems. However, Delpit (2002) argues that language does not exist apart from cultural context; thus language, *per se* is not the problem; rather, the educational system's response to language as demonstrated by the fact that teachers do not know how to deal with diversity in classrooms. In this regard, Delpit cites Michael Stubbs: "(I)f school considers someone's language inadequate, they'll probably fail" (p. xvii).

Social Theory illuminates the problem that communication differences exist among various social groups; and it is generally agreed that the family interactions transmit values and skills that influence learning and cognitive development in young children (Greenfield and Cocking, 1994). However, solutions for school learning are less apparent. Greenfield and Cocking argue that research does not inform us of the reasons these differences exist; and does not address "the interactive role of language and cultural experiences of the groups" (p. 168). The authors agree with the position they cite by Feagan and Fannan that since minority group language is viewed from a deficit perspective, what is lost is "the recognition that language is learned within a cultural context and that its most useful, and hence valuable form and manner of use are those most effective within that cultural context" (Ibid.).

Situated Learning Theory advanced by Lave & Wenger (2003) is classified as a social practice theory of learning. However, the postulates include culture and school learning only by reference as social settings. The primary emphasis of situated learning is the participatory dynamics. Neither culture nor school instruction is necessarily pivotal to acquire learning; but learning is acquired in those social activities.

Learning is distributed among members of a group and the activities are defined as specific kinds of social engagement that constitute conditions for learning to occur.

Hale (1986) proposes that a solution for understanding the influences of cultural learning in school contexts for Black children, and argues the need for a social-psychological theory in education to illuminate aspects of their learning styles. In such a theory, the social, historical, and cultural factors that affect, form, and maintain their development and learning styles must be defined (p. 5). The important factor of Hale's theory is to understand that it is unwise to expect learners to succeed in school learning if they are separated from the cultural language and experiences that shaped their learning styles.

To use a metaphor: Asking diverse learners to suppress the influences that have conditioned their language and thinking processes, and engage attentively and successfully in instruction, would be similar to asking them to leave their shoes on the school house doorsteps; to put on shoes provided by the school, *that do not fit*; and despite the discomfort, to glide easily through daily activities with the expectation that eventually their feet will become accustomed to *walking in someone else's shoes*. To add insult to injury, at the end of each day, students would return home in their own shoes. This is an extreme example of the significant disconnect between homes and most urban public schools. It is therefore incumbent on educational systems to understand the import of cultural factors; and to create the critical nexuses between in and out of school language, knowledge, and experiences that impact classroom learning. This has to happen if we are to reclaim thousands of urban children from school failures, disengagement in classrooms, or ultimately disengaging completely from schooling.

Taxonomies: Lineal and Horizontal Patterns of Learning

This section will outline and discuss theoretical support for a pedagogy designed specifically to address the learning styles of African American and other marginalized children who *live culturally* in urban communities and attend public schools. The bi-dimensional matrix design for teaching and learning is presented in a companion text, *Teaching Learners to See What You Are Saying: From Theory to Practice;* and in a *Chapter 7* supplement—*Instructional Application of The Pierre Pedagogy (2007).* The underlying tenets for the pedagogy are predicated on conceptual adaptations of Bloom's *Taxonomy of Educational Objectives* (Bloom, et al., 1956); and Mager's (1975) *Preparing Instructional Objectives,* for the vertical formats of teaching and learning; and on theories of *information processing;* and *concrete, semi-concrete,* and *abstract* learning for the horizontal formats of the design. The specific relation of the design to the learning styles of African American and other marginalized children is the incorporation of formats that require criterion-referenced instructional objectives to address culturally relevant themes for diverse students; that the teaching-learning process is reciprocal with actively engaged students; and that teaching and learning meet a concept of *goodness-of-fit* for both cultural activities and the subject content under discussion. This means that instructional activities are realistic, and age-appropriate regarding students' cultural backgrounds. Further, activities provide relevance for students regarding the subject being taught and learned; with culturally responsive activities that create *nexuses* between in-school and out-of-school learning.

The major hypothesis of the pedagogy is that this design would lift instruction and learning out of the traditional nineteenth century *straightjacket* that confines schooling to boring lecture-only formats, disengaged students, paper-pencil only evaluations, and activities that often have no resemblance to the real world outside of schools. Superior academic standards, time-tested effective instructional delivery, and excellence in academic performance are attainable, and more likely to occur, if schools were structured as places where *all* learners *want to be;* and if they perceive schools as extensions of their normal everyday lives; rather than places to be until 12th grade, memorizing bits and pieces of information to pass standardized tests.

Bloom's Hierarchy of Educational Objectives: The Cognitive Domain

The tenets of the Cognitive Domain of Bloom's Taxonomy are integrated with other learning theories as foundational to the instructional design of the *Pierre Pedagogy* that is briefly discussed in this text, and comprehensively presented in the companion texts (previously referenced). There have been revised and new taxonomies since the Bloom, et al. publication in 1956 (Marzano and Kendall, 2007); and this text does not attempt a revision, rather, an *adaptation* of the basic concepts of the original taxonomy, using the hierarchy as *levels of teaching and learning* for instructional objectives and evaluation.

Lower Levels of Learning

According to Bloom (1956), *Level I: Knowledge* and *Level II: Comprehension* are lower levels of conceptualization whereby individuals exhibit abilities that require simple rote memory for recall, identification, and understanding basic knowledge and skills; but not necessarily abilities of *abstract* higher order thinking. In addition to Bloom's hierarchy, theories of cognition at lower levels can be identified in traditional learning theory by the concept of *fluid intelligence (Gf),* that is the ability to discriminate; by the concept of schema at *preoperational* and *concrete operation* levels of cognition proposed by Piaget; and the concept of *spontaneous* thinking advocated by Vygotsky; a

110

level where information is not fully understood, and mediation is needed to advance to higher order *scientific* thinking (Lohman, 1989; Byrnes, 2001; Kozulin, et al., 2006). The design of this text uses these constructs to posit that lower levels of thinking are considered *concrete levels,* or the introductory levels for both *teaching* and *learning.* Based on these time-tested theories, acquisition of knowledge begins with lower levels of perceptual and conceptual understanding that predicate higher levels of thinking and cognition.

Higher Levels of Learning

Level III: Application, Level IV: Analysis, Level V: Synthesis; and *Level VI: Evaluation* in Bloom's hierarchy are posited as levels of higher order cognition and thinking. However, in *The Pierre-Pedagogy, Application,* which is *Level III* in Bloom's Taxonomy, is adapted to identify a "mid-point" between lower and higher order thinking and abilities (i.e., between *concrete* and *abstract* processes*).* This text places *Application* at a level above basic *Knowledge* and *Comprehension,* but not necessarily, at a level of *abstract* higher order thinking. Thus *Application* is adapted to mean a *semi-concrete*—symbolic or representative level for both teaching and learning. Theories that support a *semi-concrete* or "mid-point" level in cognition include: Vygotsky's *ZPD;* which is a "transition" or "mediating" stage between dependent and independent capabilities; and mediating *tools* of language, a teacher, or the environment act as transitions between *spontaneous* and *scientific* thought. Similarly, Piaget's maturational stages of *symbolic* and *concrete operations* are transitional, prerequisite to *formal thinking* in adolescents and adults.

Among Gagne's (1967) eight *conditions for learning,* no specific *level* is identified as a "mid-point." However, a brief review of Gagne's concept of *learning conditions* reveals one factor that reflects transition from lower to higher levels. This factor is Gagne's concept of an *Application* level in learning. *Application* can be the simple transfer of rote learning or modeling of a process. This position is based on Gagne's assertion that, "the presence of performance does not make it possible to conclude that learning has occurred" (p. 20). Gagne contends that a "learning situation" is the point *before* and *after* learning has occurred; the point between *prior* capability and *required* capability to demonstrate learning. In other words, the "learning situation" is the *condition,* or "mid-point" between *prerequisite* knowledge and *mastery.*

Gagne points out distinctions among various forms of learning; and notes that the use of instructional media; symbolic representations of concepts; and prerequisite knowledge, are identified as *chaining. Chaining* augments students' capabilities by providing activities that *show changes* in behavior and performance. It should be noted that Gagne contends *Application* is determined by the use of information in novel situations, meaning *transfer*. This text adds that mere *transfer,* like *performance* discussed above, does not imply complete conceptualization at a level for *analysis, synthesis* or *evaluation*—the mental processes categorized by Bloom as higher order *abstract* cognition and thinking.

In traditional learning theory, *abstract* cognition has been defined as *crystallized intelligence,* indexed as *Gc;* a level of adult thinking where intelligence or thinking does not require concrete, perceptual, or augmented processing; rather is an independent conceptual level of cognition and thinking that requires speed and power. Piaget defines *abstract* cognition as *formal operations*; and Vygotsky posits that *scientific concepts* depict levels of higher order and abstract cognition. The postulates of this text place *analysis, synthesis* and *evaluation* of Bloom's taxonomy at a *mastery* level of learning, indexed on an instructional matrix (*LTLMC*) as an *abstract* level in teaching and learning.

Robert Mager's Criterion Referenced Instruction (CRI)

Mager (1975) posits that it is possible to measure an individual's level of mastery of knowledge and skills through programmed instruction when learning tasks are hierarchically structured. Further, that specifically stated, well-defined objectives provide measurable criteria for evaluating performance and mastery. Basic elements of Mager's modular framework include stated goals of content to be learned; how the content will be learned; the expected learner outcomes; and criterion referenced assessment. Mager's framework emphasizes self-paced programmed instruction for use mainly in training programs; modules can be learned out of order, but advancement requires that prerequisite tasks for a specific module must be mastered.

The adaptations of Mager's framework for *The Pierre Pedagogy* include the titles, *Criterion Referenced Instruction (CRI)*, and *Criterion Referenced Assessment (CRA);* however, other adaptations are primarily conceptual. This text does not advocate adherence to programmed, modular, or self-paced learning as the basic delivery system of classroom pedagogy; rather, teachers might choose to incorporate aspects of these methodologies in various delivery formats in supplemental classroom activities as applicable or appropriate.

The basic adaptations of Mager's framework include criterion referenced objectives that:

- specify what is to be taught and learned, referenced in this text as the *content*;

- specify *how* the content will be taught and learned, defined in this text as the *context;* and

- the learner outcomes.

This text maintains use of the term *outcomes* for expected learner performance as well as for instructional effectiveness. Theory-based criterion referenced instructional objectives are stated for each vertical format of *content, context,* and *outcomes* (See Appendix A; and the *Levels of Teaching and Learning Master Chart (LTLMC);* and in the companion texts referenced above.)

Vertical and Horizontal Patterns of Learning

Content: *Concrete, Semi-concrete,* and *Abstract*

The matrix of *The Pierre Pedagogy* positions *content* on a *vertical* plane with three categories extended on a *horizontal* plane for three formats: *concrete, semi-concrete* and *abstract* teaching and learning.

Criterion referenced instructional objectives are stated for each of the horizontal formats for the *content* to be "taught" and "learned" within each category. Classroom activities for each of the three formats are based on the following theoretical concepts:

- First, instruction addresses the capabilities and readiness of students to receive content, including prerequisite knowledge;

- Second, that sufficient time is allowed for modeling by the teacher; reciprocal interaction between the teacher and students; formative assessments and mid-course corrections; and

- Third, the appropriateness of instructional content regarding the age and grade of the learners.

Context*: Concrete, Semi-concrete,* and *Abstract*

Context is positioned second on the vertical plane of the matrix, also with three categories extended on a *horizontal* plane for formats of *concrete, semi-concrete* and *abstract* teaching and learning. Criterion referenced *context* objectives are stated for each of the horizontal categories of *concrete, semi-concrete* and *abstract* teaching and learning. Criterion objectives are all the *givens* that specify *how* the teacher and learners are to engage in content activities: the structure of the classroom; the levels of learner involvement; and the materials and resources to be used. The theoretical consideration is appropriateness of instructional *context,* including *culturally relevant themes,* regarding the age and grade of the learners.

Outcomes: *Concrete, Semi-concrete,* and *Abstract*

Outcomes identify the expected levels of learner performance, as well as, instructional effectiveness. The *outcome* format is positioned last on the vertical plane of the matrix, with three categories extended on a *horizontal* plane for formats of *concrete, semi-concrete,* and *abstract* teaching and learning. Criterion referenced assessment objectives reflect the previously stated expected learner performance levels for formative and summative assessments. Results are used diagnostically to correct instruction; and to determine the degree and levels of learners' demonstrated skills and knowledge.

CHAPTER THREE

The Urban School in a Governmental Context

> Education has as its objective,
> the formation of character.
> __ Herbert Spencer

INTRODUCTION

The purpose of this text is to explore theories that explain and support tenets of *how people learn*; and to present a paradigm that integrates several learning theories into a framework for delivering effective instruction to African American and other marginalized children—collectively referenced in this text as *urban children.* Chapters one and two focused mainly on specific learning theories. This chapter will identify and analyze other issues that bear directly on *school learning*—specifically sociopolitical and historical factors that impact learning in urban schools. Other issues considered include governmental structures, legislation, community input, and who controls, influences, or determines how education is delivered in urban school settings.

Since the educational system is a part of the governmental structure, educators, policymakers, and other stakeholders must understand the significance of legislated policies and how political factors impact school learning for "all" children— positively, as well as *negatively*. This includes issues that underlie school reform; the level of government from which

118

reforms emanate; implementation of reforms; and subsequent outcomes for various diverse groups of children. Substantial consideration must be given to whether or not diverse student groups have had "the opportunities to learn" knowledge that is required in meeting mandated standards. These issues influence the degree to which equitable education is provided for urban school children. The discussions that follow include a brief review of the literature that addresses these issues.

The Legal Context for
Public Education

The roles of the several levels of government—federal, state, and local—provide the legal structure for education in American society; a process that has been framed and reframed over several centuries; and evolved into schooling that often has been, and in many cases continues to be *separate* and *unequal* for various cultural and ethnic groups (Bowles, 1968; Anderson, 1988; Hacker, 1992; Kretovics & Nussel, 1994; Watkins, 2001; Kozol, 2005). At the federal level, it is clear that the Constitution makes no specific mention of education. Thus, the federal government does not possess any inherent powers for education; and such powers at the federal level are those enumerated, delegated, or implied by some clause or a combination of clauses within the Constitution. The *General Welfare Clause* has been interpreted by the Supreme Court to *imply* that education is in the best interest and *general welfare* of the United States; thus the Congress has the power to tax and spend for the purpose of education, and as such may have control, as well (Garber & Edwards, 1970; Reutter, Jr., & Hamilton, 1976; 1979; Zirkel, 1978).

State governments have plenary powers for education determined by the Tenth Amendment of the Constitution that states: *The powers not delegated to the United States by the Constitution, nor prohibited by it to the states, are reserved to the states respectively, or to the people.* Thus, individual states do not have to consult the federal government to structure public education. State legislatures have considerable powers to develop educational policy, determine patterns of school and district organizations; abolish local school units and redistrict; determine the ends to be achieved, and the means to be employed; define the content of curriculum; and the qualifications of teachers. However, the Constitution of the United States places certain limitations that affect state policies; particularly state powers that infringe upon the First Amendment, or the *Establishment Clause,* regarding establishment of, or prohibiting religion; and the Fourteenth Amendment regarding *due process.* Further, courts have the power to invalidate state legislative ACTS found to be arbitrary or unreasonable (Ibid.).

120

Local governing bodies of public education are agents of the state with the responsibility to carry out an exclusive state purpose—educating the children within its jurisdiction. Because education is a state and not a local function, the main responsibility rests with *boards of education* as agents of the state. As agents, local boards of education, as well as school administrators, have the authority to adopt and enforce reasonable rules and regulations as deemed necessary to advance educational goals; but such rules are subject to state statue and constitutional limitations (Garber & Edwards, 1970).

Where a municipality and a school district comprise the exact same territory, the state intends that the functions of education rest with the school boards, and the municipality has no authority regarding local education. In cases where a state has conferred the power of education to a city and has established a department of education, the municipality cannot use its funds to support education unless such authority is clearly stated in its charter or statutes; as such, a state has the right to abolish the local school board. However, with regards to interpreting charters and statues, courts have generally held that where there may be conflict between local school districts and municipalities, the dispute will be resolved in favor of the local school board (Ibid).

Federal and State Legislatures

Adler (1987) and others see the development of American education as evolving congruently with the development of the nation and the tenets of the Constitution that delineate the responsibilities for citizenship. Further, the original purpose of public schooling was to understand the ideals of our Republic as incorporated in the Constitution. Adler notes that citizenship is the most important political office in a constitutional government where citizens are the primary and permanent ruling class, and all other offices are secondary. Therefore, rather than being "subjects" of the state, as the rulers, the people elect officials to carry out the responsibilities and perform the duties of public education.

It is sometimes difficult for most Americans to fathom the vast authority they have in decisions that dictate educational opportunities for themselves and for their children. This is especially true for less-empowered, low-wealth families, and often the reason the public perceives educational legislation and school reform, as "top-down" structures. Tyack (1974) argues that from its inception, public education in America has always been the privy of local communities. Moreover, the "Nineteenth Century school belonged to the community in more than a legal sense; it was frequently the focus for people's lives outside the home" (p. 15). From this perspective, Wise (1988) points out that power control of education has shifted from communities to what he describes as "legislated learning" by educators and policymakers through a bureaucratic network; also, that control ebbs and flows among the three branches of government.

A pivotal point in the shift in power control of education was the period surrounding the 1957 Russian launch of Sputnik; and the 1958 National Defense Education Act (NDEA) that laid the ground for subsequent federal legislation and involvement in education. President Johnson's Great Society program addressing poverty and ignorance during the mid 1960's led to a series of federal legislation, including the first major aid to public schools by Title I of the Elementary and Secondary Education Act of 1965 (ESEA). Other legislation followed the 1983 report, "A Nation at Risk," that precipitated federal and state legislation requiring standardized testing and higher educational standards. Goals 2000, the reauthorization of ESEA that required standardized curriculums, was the forerunner *No Child Left Behind Act of 2001* (NCLB). This brings us to the current period of federal legislation; and the ongoing debates of high stakes testing mandates of NCLB (Ramirez, 1999; Gratz, 2002; Stiggins, 2002; Shepard, et al., 2005; Fullan, 2007; Rebell & Wolff, 2009); and current considerations for the Reauthorization of NCLB (Koretz, 2008). NCLB is currently the latest legislative efforts to "fix" the structure of education; yet questions remain unanswered or ignored on the negative impact of "legislated learning," particularly regarding the very students who are the target of these reforms—the urban children who are still being undereducated and "left behind" (Kluger, 1977; Kimmelman, 2006).

Wise (1988) contends that much of the reform has not happened due to two conflicting trends: efforts by states to increase control over local school districts and local education; and power control by educators and policymakers, who reflect a conservative political view that decisions should be made at the local level, closest to the people served. Wise argues that the advantage of "legislated learning" is that *mandates* more readily address issues of equal educational opportunity, which may be difficult to resolve at the local level due to competing self-interest groups; but the disadvantage is that *quality* cannot be legislated. Therefore, Wise contends, we're right back to a point where we started.

Similarly, French (1998) observed that with school reforms, state and district education agencies have increased their control over schools as pressures mount for increased academic performance and uniformity. The issue addressed is whether or not increased authority and uniformity accrue to the benefit of all students. French agrees that standards are necessary because the absence "guarantees that educational opportunities will be stratified according to where one lives and what one's background is . . ." (p. 186); most especially, where there is racial and economic stratification. However, he argues, standards have been replaced by standardization. Thus reforms of "legislated learning" continue the public perception that American education is a "top-down" system, because through federal mandates, state statues, and local school policies, the governmental structure of education imposes requirements and promotes standards for all students to walk in lock-step for accountability; and evaluations of school and student progress take the form of "one" measure only—high-stakes testing.

Control and Decisions in Education

The previous section discussed issues of who has the power to influence school policies; that public education no longer rests with the local community. Adler (1987) noted an issue often overlooked; which is the public's misconceptions regarding control of education, and advises contemplation of the beginning words of the Preamble to the Constitution: "*We the people, in order to form a more perfect union, do ordain . . .*" The emphasis should be placed on the words, *"We the people,"* which are often summarily dismissed or misunderstood in regards to education; primarily due to unequal empowerment among a public that is stratified by wealth. However, Adler believes that control of education still rests with local communities. He observes that "most Americans do not realize that citizenship is the primary political office under a constitutional form of government" (p. 271). Thus, the general public does not think of itself as the ruling class; and perhaps need persuasion to be better informed.

Throughout its history, the American education system has reflected continued inequities—in perception and reality—which have been addressed through decades of legislation; the most significant and defining point being the 1954 *Brown vs. Board of Education of Topeka* (Kluger, 1977; Ancheta, 2006). However, it has been pointed out, that the educational system appears to be standing still in terms of equity for all children. Clincky (2001) proposes a new Civil Rights Movement for equity in public education, contending that since states are responsible for providing education, it should be distributed on equal terms for all children; and therefore, education is a *civil right*. Moreover, federal and state legislated policies have reversed much of the good-faith efforts to attain equity through school integration; declaring race-based policies in school assignments unconstitutional.

Consequently inequities that were never resolved in urban communities and schools have grown worse, and the children are blamed for school failures. Clincky believes that a return to the mandates of *Brown* for equity in urban schools would address issues of quality staffing, class size, and outdated resources. Such a movement would also address the impact of economic disparities in student expenditures that are available according to the location of schools in particular communities.

So then, who makes decisions for equity? Clincky found that decisions are made almost exclusively by "self-appointed experts—primarily state and local politicians . . . state legislators and state departments of education . . . (and by) local districts and teacher groups . . ." (p. 497). These findings undergird Clincky's argument for a new Civil Rights Movement for equity in education to overrule the "state's power to impose a single standardized curriculum and a single high stakes testing system on all children . . ." (Ibid.).

There appears to be no acceptable answer to the questions: *Who's in control? Who wields the authority for education?* Unfortunately, it is obvious that control in education has been wrenched from the hands of *"we the people"*—except for the legislative policymakers, special interest groups, and the most influential high-wealth parents who often determine what takes place in the schools their children attend. Consequently, the urban poor—typically significant numbers of African American and other marginalized children—remain in places where they are expected to learn and perform as though they have attained equality of educational opportunity. In fact, the context of their schooling as described by Maeroff (1998) remains dismal panoramas in schools that Kozol (2005) has referred to over three decades as *the shame of America.*

The Purpose of Schooling for
African American Children: Historical
and Contemporary Perspectives

The literature is replete with data that identify and illuminate the plethora of factors that have historically framed the context of schooling for African American children. Similar to Kozol, Watkins (2001a) describes the contexts of schooling for African American children as barrier-filled conditions among social, political, economic disparities, racial subservience; and segregation that supposedly was to end with the 1954 *Brown* decision. However, as Watkins and others have observed, at the beginning of the 21st Century, African American children are still being "mis-educated." Thus from a historical perspective, the education of African Americans has followed sociopolitical changes with minor benefits accruing only through overt struggles, as the 1960's Civil Rights Movement for social and racial equality; yet current questions remain of whether or not the continuing struggles can change schools.

In response to what it may take for change to occur, Lewis (2001) finds that reforms that have attempted to answer equity questions do not provide a framework for educational programming that meets the needs of all students, particularly children from diverse cultural backgrounds. Lewis argues that answers may be found in reframing the context of education for African American children. He asserts:

128

> . . . (T)he best chance for significant improvement in the performance of low-achieving African American students lies in . . . replacing constructs rooted in past white hegemony and its current vestiges and building educational programs and communities consistent with children's ethnic, cultural, social and developmental needs (p. 2).

Hilliard (2001) agrees with the position that a transition from a race orientation to an ethnic orientation is essential to improve the academic achievement of African American children. Hilliard argues that schools must align African American children's experiences in other contexts to nurture their historical backgrounds. In his discussion of what should be known about effectively educating African American children, Hilliard advises, "We must know the history, purposes, consequences and structure of the racial paradigm, and dismantle the paradigm brick by brick" (p. 7). Hilliard believes it is necessary to study the problems of human relations that create stereotypes and prejudices, because vocabulary simply trivializes the hegemonic problems. For example, to "capitalize" *black*, makes African Americans a people described by an adjective rather than a noun. Further, use of the word, "race" is often associated with intellectual capacity and inequality. Therefore, African American traditions must be understood from a historical perspective from slavery and the subsequent conditions that attempted to use educational structures to impose a consciousness of African American inferiority, and European superiority. In current schooling these structures take the form of in-school segregation and tracking. It is thus no mystery about how to provide equitable high-quality education for African American children. Hilliard concluded: the problem is not technical, but rather "a matter of will."

A cursory review of the development and purpose of education for African Americans reveals that black education has always been tied to sociopolitical issues (Anderson, 1988; King, 1994; Kretovics & Nussel, 1994; Tyack & Cuban, 1995; Aptheker, 2001; Watkins, 2001a; Watkins, et al., 2001; Fleming, 2003). Watkins (2001a) posits that the premise of early black education was carefully "sponsored" knowledge for the purpose of "obedience, subservience, and political docility" (p. 40); and from the beginning black education was and continues to be political in nature. From the Civil War through Reconstruction and beyond, the power brokers determined "what to do with the Negro," and the consensus was that citizenship would be granted "without disturbing the racial and social traditions of the South" (p. 41).

Structures of African American Schooling

The original intent of American education system evolved from an informal system designed to serve children of the early settlers of the English Colonies; and public schools were not envisioned (Rippa, 1992). "The Scriptures underscored the family as the main social unit . . ." (thus) the delay of public education was due to the rigid class structure of society, especially in the Southern Colonies (p. 23). The structure of African American education during the pre-Civil War era provided a modicum of education by Missionary Schools for the purpose of understanding the bible, and obedience to societal laws; and pre-Civil War black education was never intended to free blacks from slavery, but rather to uplift them in their miserable state. "The Freedmen's Bureau created by Congress in 1865 . . . the Boston Educational Commission, and the American Missionary Association," attempted to implement education for recently freed slaves; but faced stanch resistance from former slaveholders (p. 120).

Ironically, one of the first southern legislated policies regarding African American education was, "no education." In the period of 1800 to 1835 many states in the South passed legislation making it illegal to teach enslaved children to read and write. However, records reveal that blacks were taught to read and write by whites and other literate blacks. After Emancipation in 1865, freed blacks enjoyed a temporary period of first class citizenship between the late 1860's and 1870's; engaged in Republican government; and as voters and free wage laborers in a new social system. By the late 1870's the rights of blacks had eroded through disenfranchisement by statues of southern law and extralegal tactics that fixed their status as second-class citizens, and "trapped" them in social, political and economic subordination. These were the ideologically deliberate and logical conditions that structured the context that incubated black education (Anderson, 1988).

Watkins (2001a & 2001b) points out that contrary to popular belief that the debates of the 19th Century between Washington and DuBois set the agenda for the development of black education, that they were minor players. Instead, it was the power brokers who were the true "architects of black education" in America. Watkins argues (2001a): from the defeat of Reconstruction to WWI, the focus "for" black education was simply reading, writing and arithmetic—the simplicity that reflected southern colonialism and subjugation; and blacks would have to adjust themselves to this existing racial and social order in the South (Ibid., pp. 40-44). The defining moment that shaped black education was in 1890 and 1891 during the "Lake Mohonk Conferences in New York (in which the power brokers and other influential men of wealth) . . . solidified the question of what structure black education was to take." Education was to be: (1) primary grade training by the states; (2) schools were to provide teachers and preachers; (3) curriculum of English studies and the English bible; and (4) emphasis was to be on "industrial education" (Ibid., pp. 43-44).

During the period of the Mohonk Conferences, however, black leaders demanded self-determination and a curriculum modeled on European middle-class liberal and classical education. They insisted that their education should be training for vocations, for teachers, leaders, managers, and skilled tradesmen, with the opportunity of "promised participation in the social life in the New America" (Ibid., 2001a, p. 41).

Anderson (1988) lamented the situation and ideologies that structured black education in America. His disillusion was that there still is a *struggle* between democratic rights and political oppression; but he recognized the reality that there had always been two traditions of education for American schooling: one kind of schooling for democratic citizenship; and another for second-class citizenship—not by accident, but by design. Anderson concluded that these two traditions were fostered by the same government, embraced by the same leaders, occupied the same time and space, and still exist and impact the current state of American education.

Contemporary Structures of Black Education in Urban Communities

Anderson's (1988) observation of the purposeful structuring of black education in America during the late 19th and early 20th Centuries that enabled two separate traditions, are recognizable in current structures of black education, as evidenced by unequal schooling based on economic wealth or lack of wealth. This dilemma continues as one of the greatest challenges in providing educational equity for African American and marginalized children. Tyack (1974) presents a compelling argument that the political process and the social system of schooling make victimization predictable and regular. He points out that when one considers "the history of education there is a hidden dynamic because the same reality may appear quite different for diverse groups . . ."(p. 4). Further, there has not been "one best system" for all people, especially those who are victimized by poverty, color or cultural differences. Therefore the social consequences of urban poverty currently affecting black schooling are often ignored or seldom addressed, except to blame those locked in poverty for their situations. Tyack concludes:

> . . . (T)o say that institutionalized racism, or unequal treatment of the poor, or cultural chauvinism were unconscious, or unintentional does not erase the effects on children (Ibid.).

Social and economic disparities among poor and ethnic group families in America are tied inextricably to the availability and access to jobs, and equitable opportunities to increase the quality of their lives (Wilson 1996). Persistent disparity among these families is also tied to the relations between race, economic status, and the lack of empowerment to influence the nature of their educational systems as well. These factors are part and parcel of the structure of black education in urban communities. Wilson (Ibid.) makes a distinction between being poor and having a job and being poor and jobless. He maintains that when there is no work for urban families the resulting hopelessness and problems—crime, welfare, and family dissolution—are assigned, specifically, to the families rather than understanding the complexities of economic distress. There is a tendency of the public to use ideological arguments of cultural problems and lack of motivation that keep these families trapped in poverty. Similarly, Darity, et al. (1998) observed:

> . . . (E)conomic fortunes of blacks are linked to the degree of economic distress felt by whites . . . When whites feel no economic threat from racial minorities there is little opposition to "diversity", "affirmative action", and similar efforts to promote the interests of the minority. When whites are threatened, as they are now with shrinking middle class and loss of working-class jobs, there is every reason to believe that policies designed to remedy racial inequality will be targeted for elimination (p. 11).

Kretovics and Nussel (1994) link this understanding directly to inequalities in education. The authors argue that schools do not exist in a vacuum; rather, are a part of other tangible and intangible factors that influence what happens in classrooms. The social, economic and political problems of society affect what takes place in schools where inequality of life continues to create a sense of powerlessness, alienation and frustration; and the problems of poverty, neglect and racism are brought into the classrooms. Thus, urban children are blamed for the poverty they are born into (Freire, 2002); and underserved by a system that claims to be the vehicle of hope and mobility; that instead, is a system that is structured—intentionally or unintentionally—to ensure that they fail.

Kozol (1967, 1991, 1995 & 2005) observed the structure of black education in urban communities and wrote of devastation and debilitating conditions that had not shown any discernible changes over a thirty-year span, from the 1960's to the late 1990's. Across the country, disparities in education persist for African American children who attend urban schools—from Mississippi to Illinois; from the Deep South to the 7th richest congressional district in the South Bronx of New York. The response by the power brokers has been perplexity, annoyance, or unconcern; concluding that these conditions do not result from injustice, and no longer merit continued national attention. Kozol (1991) contends that in America, "east of anywhere . . . (are) communities where poor blacks live and send their children to school in (dismal) . . . school conditions" (p. 4). Moreover, social policy

136

that supposedly addresses these problems has turned black schooling back one hundred years to 1896; the period of Plessey v. Ferguson. He argues that reconstruction has been ". . . little more than moving the same old furniture around in the house of poverty" (Ibid.).

Urban vs. Suburban Schools: Similarities and Differences

A first impression one gathers of contemporary schooling in American society is the extent to which schools reflect the social status of the community in which an individual school is situated. There is no argument with Kozol (Ibid.) that schools situated in the eastern part of cities, those "across the tracks" in poor neighborhoods, reflect joblessness, social isolation, political alienation, and economic inequalities—schools of the urban poor and ethnic minority children. In the western part of American cities are the schools that serve mainly the dominant group, and middle-class children. Glenn (1987) finds that "the most exclusive schools in America today are not private schools but public schools in affluent suburbs" (p. 291). Further, that since Americans expect to choose where they live and how they live, this includes what schools their children will attend. Unfortunately, families of the urban poor and ethnic minority groups seldom have a choice about where they live, and "have correspondingly little influence on where their children will go to school" (Ibid.). Therefore, it appears that geography determines the types of schooling children receive.

One method of comparing urban and suburban schools is to itemize specific conditions, or factors regarding schooling within urban schools, such as limited fiscal support, facilities, and instructional resources; the poor quality of staffing; unchallenging curriculum; and poor student achievement. Further, to simply state that the "exact opposite" of each of these conditions or factors exists in suburban schools. This approach only states the obvious—glaringly apparent and understood; though ignored or dismissed by educators and the general public—especially in the assessment-driven, standardized-student-progress environments that compare student performance in the context of vastly dissimilar types of schooling. However, it is both instructive and worth reflection to question why 21st Century schooling in America still represents what Anderson (1988) identifies as a dual tradition of purpose; and Hacker (1992) describes as two systems "one black, one white—separate and unequal." We briefly discussed some of the tangible and intangible factors that influence learning in urban schools; including legislated policies, empowerment, and control of education. The following discussions will analyze other factors that influence learning by comparing schooling in urban and suburban schools; and consider other issues regarding why and how different school patterns evolved.

Urban Schools

The obvious results, if not the intended purpose of the system of schooling for second-class citizenship for African Americans, aptly describes current structures of urban schools. A comparison of urban and suburban schools reveals that the dual system of inequitable schooling still exists. Glenn's (1987) observations of "exclusive affluent schools" would never be confused with descriptions of schools in urban communities, as well documented by Jonathan Kozol (1991, 1995, 2005); an iconic educational critic of urban school conditions. Tyack (1974) takes issue with some of Kozol's observations, but the general consensus among authors, researchers, and many educators is that little can be added to, or should be distracted from Kozol's descriptions of schooling for urban children.

Because urban schools are part of communities, the school buildings—old, outdated, hot-in-summer, cold-in-winter, broken-windowed structures—reflect the same physical conditions of the neighborhoods. Throughout urban communities there are blocks and blocks of vacated boarded up and decaying skeletal buildings—some abandoned, some occupied; and many people live in easily flooded low land areas. Children play outdoors in garbage and chemical-filled air, witness crimes and are often the victims. Railroad tracks run adjacent to neighborhoods transporting hazardous chemicals; and Interstate highways wrap around urban communities where cars discharge gasoline fumes day and night. Student populations reflect a return to the segregated state of pre-Brown years; and the children are thought to be inferior, or in some cases, dangerous. The overall view is that urban schools are little more than custodial institutions with unhappy students and teachers where little in-depth learning takes place; and one questions when is a school a school? These are the places where people "die within" long before physical death. These are the communities that "supposedly" educate urban children; the communities that people avoid, or hardly notice as they pass on their way to somewhere else (Tyack, 1974; Kozol, 1991; & 2005; Wilson, 1996; Maeroff, 1988; Morris, 1999; Haberman, 2000).

Inside the schools, there are limited instructional resources, student textbooks or computer labs; inadequate classrooms and limited space that translate into overcrowded classes; and students score at the lowest levels on statewide and standardized tests. These issues are tied directly to the levels of per pupil expenditures that often range from $4,000 to $9,000 less than in more affluent schools. High percentages of teachers are not certified; teach outside their subject disciplines; have negative assumptions about the students; and the rates of absenteeism among teachers would not be tolerated in middle-class schools. Extended day and after school programs are inadequate or unavailable, mainly because when the dismissal bell rings at the end of the day, most of the staff are driving off the parking lot before the students board school busses for home. This is the dismal panorama that elucidates the fact that second-class ghetto education in urban communities is a permanent American reality (Ibid). These are the conditions to be compared when analyzing the differences between low-wealth urban schools and middle-class suburban schools.

Paradoxically, the *only* factor that could be identified as a similarity between urban and suburban schools can be summed up in one thought. When the aggregated data among all schools are evaluated, children who attend urban schools are expected to have performed comparatively as well as their suburban peers. Urban students are expected to demonstrate the same levels of academic interest, motivation, and knowledge attainment, as defined by a standardized curriculum; and to have demonstrated acceptable or exemplary subject matter proficiencies, as measured by the mandated standardized tests. Essentially, such a comparison is the "equal assessment" of "unequally educated" children (Pierre-Pipkin, 2008).

Suburban Schools

Previously we noted that there is a choice in comparing urban and suburban schools, either by stating the obvious— that the schools in two settings are exact opposites; or by factor analysis. We extend the explanation by comparing several factors. Suburban schools operate with adequate funding, state-of-the-arts facilities and resources; and sufficient numbers of qualified permanent staffs with low absenteeism. Teachers hold high expectations for students; the student population represents the dominant, mainly middle-class culture. Parents are empowered and have significant influence regarding what will or will not be taught to their children. Students learn subject knowledge content that reflects their lifestyles, culture, and discourse; and the majority of students perform successfully on standardized tests.

From a historical perspective, suburban schools are relatively recent within educational delivery systems. Urban schools were originally predominantly white; and factors that undergirded the demise of the once "majority white" middle-class urban schools, included the development of suburbs, and the subsequent construction of schools in those middle-class communities. Other factors in the development of suburban schools were shifts in student demographics, growing enrollment, increasing expenditures, expanded curriculums, and the transfer of power from local communities to professionals (Tyack, 1974). Also, Interstate highway systems provided ease in transportation that enhanced housing construction in suburban areas; and the subsequent shift in urban student populations to significant numbers of ethnic minority groups who remained in the urban school communities. Thus, white flight from cities to the suburbs left urban poor and minority groups to be schooled in inner city urban schools, and unfortunately, the rest is history.

Educational theorists generally concede that the nature and function of public education in the context of the broader social, economic, political, and cultural interests reflect views of the dominant group. Further, because the dominant group wields the most influence on educational issues, their visions of what schools should be, have always, and continue to shape reforms regarding content, teaching strategies, and modes of evaluation (Hodgkinson, 1988; Steele, 1992; Kretovics & Nussel, 1994; Knapp & Woolverton, 1995; Delpit, 1996; Tatum, 1996; Goycochea, 1998; Kohn, 1998; Mosteller, et al., 1998; Crosby, 1999; Hilliard, 2001; Delpit & Downy 2002; Swartz, 2009). This influence occurs almost exclusively in suburban schools, because the power of high-wealth parents and groups is substantial; and in many suburban schools parents are concerned with educational benefits "only" for their children. Kohn (1998) finds that many affluent parents would rather not have "those other people's children" in the same college-bound tracks as their children; and where "those other children" are on the academic performance ladder is somebody else's problem (p. 57). Further any attempt of school reform not geared to benefit their children is often sabotaged.

Simply and sadly from any perspective, fundamental *similarities* between urban and suburban schools do not exist. Therefore, the shorter explanation of a comparison is: suburban schooling is the exact opposite of schooling in urban community schools.

School Expectations for Urban School Children

The topics in this text focus on *how people learn*—cognitively; through experiences; mediated though instruction; and influenced by culture. Other intangible related conditions, such as school and classroom climates, also impact student learning—particularly African American and other marginalized children who attend urban schools. Further, teacher expectations and modeling behaviors are critical factors of learning in classroom settings. Findings reveal that either low or high teacher expectations are often related to the social class of students. Knapp & Woolverton (1995) contend: "In a pluralistic democratic society . . . there are multiple competing purposes for education . . . (because parents have) . . . differences in power and the ability to advocate their interests . . ." (p. 550). This fact does not go unnoticed by school personnel and is acted upon by teachers in their varying presumptions and treatments of different socioeconomic classes of students. Consequently, there is a long history of teacher expectations being a "self-fulfilling prophecy" in American public schools; and low expectations have detrimental effects on equity and quality in schooling for African American and other marginalized children.

Rist (2000) examined the relationship between two variables: the caste system of the classrooms, and the caste system of the greater society. He found that the *caste* system in classrooms mirrors the "*social class*" system of the greater society, and teacher attitudes and presumptions about the capabilities of students are tied directly to students' economic status. Rist also examined the dynamics and the variables of teacher-student relationships to determine if the teacher's initial expectations of a student's academic performance may have a strong influence on the actual performance of the student. The initial assumptions of teachers centered on comparing their students to children of the dominant group in society. Teachers compared students on qualities of their interaction with adults; whether they spoke *Standard English*; whether or not they exhibited abilities of leadership; whether students were neat and clean in appearance; also, whether their parents lived together, were employed, educated, and interested in their children.

Rist identified classroom variations in teacher perceptions ranging from ". . . success or failure; praise or ridicule; freedom or control, creativity or docility, comprehension or mystification . . ." (p. 276). In one classroom case, beginning in kindergarten, seating arrangements for children reflected that children perceived as more likely to succeed were seated closer to the teacher, and children perceived as less capable were ascribed low status and described as 'failures' by the teacher. Fast learners typically received more instructional time, rewards and attention; while slower children were subjected to control-oriented behaviors, and little attention from the teacher. Thus, the teacher's perceptions and expectations became the basis for differentiated treatment of the children; and "her expectations continued to be fulfilled; and though low-performing students had accumulated knowledge, they did not have the opportunity to verbalize it and subsequently, the teacher could not know what they had learned" (p. 294).

Kunjufu (2002) makes a similar argument, that much of the achievement gap between Black and White students can be explained by analyzing how Black students are taught; especially whether they are challenged. This addresses the teaching skills of their teachers; and whether teachers model affirming attitudes toward diverse students. Further, the author points out that these inquiries are not limited to White teachers; but rather, a critical examination is warranted for middle-class Black teachers, as well.

In addition to individual teacher presumptions, the nomenclature of schools adds to the perceptions (and misconceptions) about children; particularly children of low-wealth families. Jackson (1999) argues that the term, "at-risk" when referring to African American and other urban children increases the chances that these children will fail. The author admonishes that the term, "at-risk" is debilitating and is correlated with other types of negative behaviors and treatment of children. Jackson found that the statistical data regarding children categorized as "at-risk" reflect higher rates of corporeal punishment, expulsions, referrals to special education; and lower rates assigned to gifted classes. Similar to Rist's findings, Jackson also found that teachers make pre-mature judgments of African American children in early grades, and this has a subsequent negative effect on their performance throughout their school careers.

It is important to consider the following question: *What is the most significant factor in classroom learning?* All probable responses would include the dynamics between the teacher and students. Essentially, this means whether or not teachers model confidence in students that keeps them interested, eagerly and actively engaged, challenged, and free to question content knowledge and concepts; or whether teacher behaviors—both verbal and nonverbal—reflect disappointment, disgust, disapproval, annoyance and impatience with students. Therefore, regarding cultural competence and transformative responsive practices, the following questions should be considered:

- Are teachers of culturally diverse students encouraging and supportive?
- Do teachers model positive attitudes for students' success?
- Do teachers create classroom climates that create positive communities of practice that incorporate cultural themes and activities?
- Do teachers model behaviors that are critical and unsupportive?
- Do teachers ignore or devalue the cultural experiences of students; and send messages of low expectations that students may not have the capacity to be successful?"

Teacher expectations, more than any other classroom factor, must not be a confounding classroom variable among conditions that negate or limit learning. Teachers must be continually aware of attitudes they have toward students. In order to advance opportunities and conditions for the highest levels of student performance, teachers' attitudes must be positive and accepting—free of stereotypical presumptions about students' intellectual capacities; clearly articulated and modeled in a manner that values students' cultures and the funds of knowledge and experiences they bring to the classroom. Teachers must have a sincere desire for the success of *all* students. Therefore, this text argues that an evaluative element in the definition of a *highly qualified teacher* must give significant weight to teachers' knowledge of students; and their expectations for student success. This *requires* teachers to "have" and "demonstrate" high expectations for all students at all times.

__Jean Pierre-Pipkin

CHAPTER FOUR

Standardized Tests and the Teaching-Learning Process

American education focused on assessment-driven instruction, leaves schools flooded in rivers of requirements. Addressing the dilemma created for poor and ethnic minority students drowning in floods of assessments pivots on whether to lower the water or raise the bridge.

INTRODUCTION

In chapter three we discussed the states' roles in legislated educational policies that impact school learning, especially factors of equity in schooling for African American and other marginalized urban children. Mandatory statewide standardized testing appears to be the most significant factor having a negative impact on what urban children will or will not learn. The voluminous literature on the merits of this three-decade focus on standards-driven reform captures arguments for and against standardized testing; and overwhelmingly, data reflect that single-measure-indicator results of student performance on norm-referenced or standards-referenced tests have been *major* determining factors in decision-making; and subsequently, whether equity and effective instruction accrue to the benefit of African American and other marginalized children (Popham, 1998, 2000; Stiggins, 1988, 1999, 2002; Marzano & Costa, 1988; Neil & Medina, 1989; Maeroff, 1991; Darling-Hammond, 1995; Sirotnik & Kimball, 1999; Hess & Bringham, 2000; Guskey, 2001; Kohn, 2001; Olson, 2001, 2006; Trevisan,

2002; Gratz, 2002; Boaler, 2003; Kohnhaber, 2004; Davis, 2006a, & 2006b; Hilliard, 1990 & 1996; Sunderman, 2008).

As previously stated, the purpose of this text attempts to illuminate *how children learn*, in general; and in specific, the conditions that create optimal opportunities for urban children to receive high quality, effective instruction. Research on mandatory standardized testing as it impacts achievement of this population is currently limited regarding the positive influences (Shepard, et al., 2005); however, the general consensus among most critics is that large-scale testing negatively influences teaching and learning. Many of the debates center on whether standardized test results present *accurate data* on achievement when factors that skew the results include: student anxieties and the pressures of mandatory testing, especially among cultural and socio-economically diverse students; primarily testing de-contextualized, factually memorized information; and the inequities in the quality of instruction across schools, districts, and within states. It is evident that mass standardized testing, itself, has created a contradictory condition that negatively and disproportionately impacts African American and ethnic minority groups (Johnson, 1989; Kohn, 1999a, 1999b & 2001; Lomax, et al., 1995; Hess & Brigham, 2000).

Because there is no significant body of empirical data that validates a positive impact of widespread standards-driven reforms, interpretations of student achievement data tend to be skewed toward a deficit view of what low-performing students *cannot do.* This dilemma negates the purpose and existence of reforms put in place to raise the achievement levels of this population; and to adequately determine the overall student achievement purportedly measured by such tests. Further, it is asserted, that despite the lack of such evidentiary research data, mandatory standardized testing in its present form adds to inequities of educational opportunity for urban children. Moreover, little attention is given to restructuring the educational delivery systems regarding under-funding for implementing federal mandates; unequal instructional programs and resources; tracking; inequities in physical facilities; and teacher quality and competence in urban community schools (Wilson, 1968; Maeroff, 1988 & 1998; Darling-Hammond, 1995 & 1997b; Sirotnik & Kimball, 1999; Kozol, 2005; Ladson-Billings & Tate, 2006; Kohn, 1999a; Kohnhaber, 2008; Koretz, 2008).

Knowing *how children learn* predicates an understanding of what factors influence learning; and how to determine *what* children know and *when* they know. This is the essence of what it means to design effective curriculum; provide appropriate instructional activities; and to guide and assess what children *know* in classroom settings—e.g., the purpose of the teaching-learning process. Teachers generally understand and would agree with this premise. Unfortunately, however, in public schools across the American panorama, teaching has become narrowly focused on accomplishing the goals of state standards through assessment-driven instruction (Bracey, 1987; Stiggins, 2002; Marzano & Costa, 1988; Ramirez, 1999; Lee, J. O, 2003). This begs the question many teachers might pose: *What good does it do if, as a teacher, I'm well-versed in "how" children learn; and how research "informs" that learning extends beyond simple rote skills of recognition of facts, if most of my instruction is restricted to simply "raising test scores" on upcoming state tests?* A good question—one that needs to be addressed when schools consider the significant negative impact of standardized tests on low-performing student populations that these tests are designed to help. To reiterate the point, this is the *contradictory dilemma* of assessment-driven reforms. Therefore, there is much empathy for the *Catch-22* situation confronting teachers: *i.e.,* understanding what effective, quality instruction entails; but being in the awkward position of teaching in a manner that determines whether or not their schools meet state standards. Simply put, is it logical to expect someone to do something, if his salary and job depend on his *not* doing? (Gratz, 2002) But a more important question is: *What happens to the children and the price they pay for this teaching inertia?* Simply answered, *they are left behind.*

We must be clear, high standards and accountability are critical and necessary elements of the educational system, including the public's right to know the effectiveness or ineffectiveness of schooling. However, the position of this text focuses on the *use of* standardized tests and the impact on schooling for African American and other urban children who fall disproportionately among low-scoring populations—in most cases *compose* this demographic; and the subsequent consequences of punitive decisions made regarding their educational placement based solely on paper-pencil assessments. Moreover, it is argued that effective external assessments must be designed to consider the specific conditions for learning in urban schools. There must be a shift from a deficit view of student performance, to interpretations and evaluations based on multiple forms of assessment that illuminate what students *can do*; thus, common areas of performance strengths and weaknesses across various measures would yield a broader perspective of individual student capabilities and grade level performance to guide the direction of corrective instruction (Pierre-Pipkin, 2007). Restructuring assessments would positively inform and enhance decision-making; and thereby yield significantly higher levels of educational equity for urban school children.

High-Stakes Standardized Testing:
The *Equal Assessment of Unequally*
Educated Children

Several Factors often overlooked or not considered in discussions of standards-based high-stakes assessment is that the original intent of previous assessment reforms was not the exclusive use of assessment as an end in itself; that curriculum and instruction would be distorted to ensure high performance test scores; or that test results would structure inequalities or limit access to knowledge. Testing and written exams were originally instituted for very different reasons: to sort children into grade levels to teach all in a group alike; and as noted by Haney & Madaus, (1989), to replace grading systems of teachers that were found to be unreliable, especially regarding how letter grades affected college entrance. Further, considering the time it took visiting committees in 19th Century Boston high schools to listen to student recitations, standardized tests were to be alternatives of those practices (Darling-Hammond, 1997b; Haertel, 1999; McNeil 2000; Kornhaber, 2004).

Legislated Assessment Reforms

A review of the language of recent legislated school reforms focused on improving student achievement, reflects common concepts that specify the content knowledge students are expected to learn; the levels of acceptable student performance, as measured through assessment; the means of evaluating student outcomes; the degree of school effectiveness; and the types of decisions that should result—including decisions that may negatively impact individual student's current and future education. Beginning with *The Elementary and Secondary*

Education Act of 1965 (ESEA) that established the foundation for subsequent and current school reforms, the intent of the legislation was grounded on the premise that America's current and future standings in a globally competitive world depend on the strength of a highly educated citizenry; and this goal is to be ensured through public schooling (Kluger, 1977; Ohanian, 2000; Kimmelman, 2006).

The following diagram presents a comparison of a decade of reforms—four decades beyond *Brown*: *Goals 2000,* and *No Child Left Behind* (NCLB)—along with The 1989 President's *Summit of Governors' Agreement.* The language on the chart reflects the objectives for framing reforms, and includes a similar conceptual focus and common language that stress specific educational goals (Ibid.). The language also emphasizes concepts presented by the actual legislation; and the governors' consensus on standards that should be the intent of state policies. However, nowhere in the language of federal legislation; as well as in how states and local school districts implement federal educational requirements, is there a specific attempt to address student diversity, or is attention given to the impact of changing student demographics in setting standards through policy making. This reflects significant incongruence among research, policy and practice; and is one of the major reasons most reforms fail. The list compares conceptual language used to define standards.

National and State Standards   *Recent Legislation*

CONCEPTUAL LANGUAGE	Governors' Agreement	Goals 2000	NCLB
Accountability	☆	☆	☆
State-by-state effort	☆	☆	☆
Annually reported progress	☆	☆	☆
School readiness	☆	☆	☆
Increase high school graduation/ Dropout reduction	☆	☆	☆
Improvement of academic/ subject content performance	☆	☆	☆
Rigorous measurable standards	☆	☆	☆
Demonstrated academic competence	☆	☆	☆
Professional staff development	☆	☆	☆
Propelling the US in achievement	☆	☆	☆
All adult Americans to be literate	☆	☆	☆
Decreasing the achievement gap/ increasing minority achievement	☆	☆	☆
Safe school environments	☆	☆	☆
Increased parental involvement	☆	☆	☆

What is strikingly revealing among the ideals and standards that purportedly should or will create a highly educated citizenry is the omission of language that articulates goals to address issues of *equity in educational opportunities*— specifically accountability for the unequal distribution of resources and funds in support of inner city, urban and rural school districts, and students. These issues are ignored or dismissed as not directly related to, or having significance in *setting* educational standards. Educational standards are thought of in basic terms of determining what "ideally" core principles represent the direction of efforts or goals to be achieved through public schooling; and how to evaluate outcomes and measurable gains. Thus, in setting standards the question is simply: *How do we get there, from here?* To *get there,* the answer is mass standardized testing; a measure for the "equal assessment" of "unequally educated" children (Pierre-Pipkin, 2008).

Moreover, the legislation that articulates a major goal of enhancing educational opportunities for minority and marginalized children has not reflected the foresight or hindsight to grapple with the consequences of how "one-size-fits-all" assessments have created further inequities and learning barriers for the target groups of low-scoring students (Gratz, 2002). Since schools do not function in isolation or apart from a sociopolitical context, the same inequities in the general society are evident within schools, and the educational delivery system (Tyack, 1974; Kornhaber, 2004; Kozol, 2005). Thus, to dismiss socially related inequities as only a *tangentially* important issue in setting educational standards undermines the whole premise of improving achievement for all students. This is so because where adequate progress is not occurring; regardless of inequality in schooling; the *carrots-and-sticks, rewards-and-sanctions* accountability system negatively and disportionately impact African American and other urban students. Consequently, it is folly and illusionary to believe that standardized tests in a "high-stakes" accountability system will motivate schools and students to meet what are perceived as unrealistic standards for low-scoring populations (Haertel, 1999; Ramirez, 1999; Hess & Bringham, 2000).

Another assumption for mass standards-based assessments was the belief that students and teachers were unmotivated; thus, the pressure of a standards-based accountability system that carried sanctions, would improve instructional efforts and student achievement (Ramirez, 1999). Based on the premise that public education is the backbone of America's strength in the world, policymakers intended to restructure public education through accountability and standards for all levels of education from pre-school to college. However, the focus of NCLB did not consider leveling the playing field among diverse student populations by considering the differing starting points of each group. Therefore, the requirements not only imposed standards, but also *standardized* education based on middle-class norms. It was simply assumed that *all* students should demonstrate mastery of a specific body of *norm-referenced* content knowledge that would be taught and measured through standardized tests (Neil & Medina, 1989; Hess & Bringham, 2000; Lee, 2003).

Legislated Learning: What Should Standardized Tests Do?

Shepard and colleagues (2005) contend that national, state, and district level tests "are used to collect data to answer the questions of policymakers," most of whom are far removed from classrooms; and "ideally, the data is to be used for the purpose of monitoring trends of student achievement" (p. 306). In this sense standardized tests are supposed to serve a specific educational purpose: in general, to assess the effectiveness of schooling; and in specific, to measure the extent to which students are learning academic content (Wiggins, 1989; Colarci, 2002; Gratz, 2002; Lee, 2003). Gratz (Ibid.) concluded that reforms tend to serve political purposes, rather than educational purposes; and seldom deliver because standards over promise on goals that can be realistically accomplished. Further, Gratz and others find that little attention is given to the plethora of consequences: narrowing of curriculum; piling on homework; eliminating elementary school recess; cheating, retention; denying secondary diplomas; blaming students and teachers for low test performance; and the negative stigmas placed on low performing students who are predominantly minority or from low wealth families (Neil & Medina, 1989; Ramirez, 1999; Stiggins, 1999; Hurwitz & Hurwitz, 2002; Kohn, 2001).

These factors, along with issues of equity in funding, facilities, and personnel quality all determine if the quantitative data generated from standardized tests reflect qualitative accuracy of instructional effectiveness and the degree of student learning. This is especially relevant when mass assessment results are generalized for comparisons across all school settings, and among various student populations, rather than being used for *within* school comparisons. Many assessment critics believe we have been lulled into thinking that high test scores equate to high achievement (Ramirez, 1999; Hess & Bringham, 2000; Valencia, 2001).

It is therefore essential to consider whether standardized tests are true measures of what individual students know and have learned. Marzano and Costa (1988) addressed this issue considering whether standardized tests measure general cognitive skills as purported by high-stakes test designers. The authors define cognitive abilities as "mental processes used in academic tasks that intersect more than one discipline" (p. 66).

For example, the process of division is specific to mathematics and therefore is not a *general cognitive process* skill; but skills that require comparing and contrasting can be applied across disciplines, thus require mental cognitive processing. The authors analyzed 6,942 test items from the Comprehensive Test of Basic Skills (CTBS) and the Stanford Achievement Test (SAT), and found that the majority of test items are primarily measures of *factual* or *declarative* information. Their analysis of the 6,942 test items for 22 different general categories of cognitive operations revealed only 9 of the categories on the CTBS and the SAT required cognitive mental abilities.

A general consensus of what standardized tests actually do, beyond measuring factual knowledge as argued by Marzano and Costa, is often contrary to the intended purposes of accurately ascertaining what individual and specific groups of students know. Proponents of standardized tests argue the objectivity of multiple-choice test designs as the most-efficient and best methods of enforcing accountability and improving performance (Popham, 1987). However, there is lack of agreement among proponents of assessment-driven instruction, policymakers, and educators, regarding the merits of multi-choice assessment formats. Among the various views that advocate standardized testing, performance-based testing is argued as having substantially more merit over selected—response formats. While there is substantial concern for

162

whether the data generated by current multiple-choice tests are the *most accurate* measures of what students know; there is as much reluctance to push for alternative assessment formats because it is unknown whether alternatives would yield valid and reliable data (Eisner, 1999; Haertel, 1999).

Eisner (Ibid.) argues that performance assessment is a closer measure of students' abilities than conventional forms of standardized tests that reflect a four-decade focus on de-contextualized information and selecting a single correct answer among four to five distracters. The author finds that standardized multiple-choice assessment is predicated on uniformity and homogeneity. Further, though uniformity has value; significant constraints are placed on how data are generated and analyzed. Addressing what tests are *supposed to do*, Eisner posits that tests should measure what students need to know and do outside of school. This includes skills that frame problems, formulate plans, consider relationships; and how to use knowledge for different and various purposes to access multiple outcomes.

Haertel (Ibid.) sees the value of performance assessment over traditional assessments, but cautions that if large-scale performance-driven assessment is employed as an accountability system, it is likely to fail. He contends that testing has become an end in itself; because improving the education system has become synonymous with improving test

163

scores. The author finds that the use of wide-scale performance assessment is merely a return to past mistakes. Thus the issue is not whether one test design is better than another; "(I)nstead, the accountability testing argument, itself, must be examined and reconsidered" (p. 663). Haertel concludes that performance assessment is best used in classrooms; and a mix of several formats for testing would yield more accurately reliable data. Similarly, Tyack and Cuban (1995) agree that change is not the same as progress; that typically, reform is gradual and incremental. It takes *tinkering* of a system in moving toward real change. This means, " . . . preserving what is valuable, and reworking what is not" (p. 5).

Alternative Assessments and Diagnostic Use of Standardized Tests

This discussion reiterates the purpose of understanding *how children learn,* and factors that influence classroom learning for African American and other urban children. It is noted that effective instruction for any demographic student population includes the appropriate use of classroom assessments; and understanding the importance of employing various means and multiple formats to measure student performance. Just as alternative pedagogies address specific learning styles of African American and other diverse learners; similarly, consideration should be given to providing a wide range of assessment measures so that diverse learners will not be permanently relegated to low-performing status throughout their school years as the results of decisions made solely on scores from standardized tests (Haertel, 1999; Shepard, et al., 2005; Pierre-Pipkin, 2007).

It is critical to understand that despite the controversy regarding external assessments in the overall evaluation of *what* students know, *when* they know, and the *degree of* grade level knowledge and *mastery* of academic content; standardized tests are useful tools in assessing the effectiveness of schooling in general, and classroom instruction in specific. External assessments ensure that an accountability system is in place for school districts, administrators and teachers. However, this text argues that a distinction should be made between the *merits* of standardized tests, and the *use* of tests. Moreover, standardized testing is only one factor among various evaluative measures in an accountability system. The totality of all measures, carefully coordinated and analyzed, should be used diagnostically to determine student performance and school effectiveness. Given that the purpose of assessment is to improve instruction and student learning, assessment results should never be used as a single indicator for decision-making; such as rewards; or used in punitive ways that single out, or elevate high-performing students as *better;* while stigmatizing low-performing groups as *failures.* This text argues that the *manner* or *how* external assessments are used is pivotal to understanding the impact of assessment on learning conditions for African American and other marginalized children. Moreover, combining external assessment results with district level and in-class performance-based evaluations in an analytical framework provides a broader perspective that is an equitable and appropriate approach to quality evaluation of all students. Diagnostic use of alternative, authentic formative tests in the following discussions explore the benefits of this practice.

Alternative Authentic Assessment

There is consistent and continual criticism regarding large-scale standardized testing and the subsequent problems created by assessment-driven accountability systems. Much of the criticism centers on the negative impacts on curriculum and instruction that have evolved into a limited focus on teaching and testing low skill information; and on inequities created for low-wealth, mostly minority students (Conner, et al., 1985; Darling-Hammond & Wise, 1985; Bracey, 1987; Haney & Madaus, 1989; Wiggins, 1989; Maeroff, 1991; Kohn, 1999b; Ohanian 2001; Colarci, 2002; Lee, 2003; Kornhaber, 2004).

Haney and Madaus (Ibid.) describe controversies surrounding standardized tests as the *Achilles heel* of the education system; especially when tests are used exclusively for accountability and decision-making. They argue the necessity of alternative forms of tests because, among many negative factors, test results give false information of the status of the nation's schools; there is bias in testing; and because there is growing criticism for the elimination of group standardized tests. They suggest consideration of reliance on the professional judgments of teachers; portfolio samples of students' work; and criterion-referenced tests as alternative forms of assessing students' performance. Similarly, Wiggins (1989) posits that standardized testing itself has become a problem in schooling. The author views authentic assessment as an equitable form for accurately and more precisely yielding true and realistic information of what students know and can do. He notes the many arguments against performance assessments: related costs and the extensive time for mass assessment; how teachers have been molded into a mindset that testing is something to be done as quickly as possible after teaching in order to assign a final grade; and the problems of reliability. The author concludes that as long as tests are thought of only in terms of accountability, real reform will not come about. Further, it is not a matter of completely replacing traditional assessments, but a need to build on what works. Some positive aspects of authentic assessment include: contextualized complex information that challenges, and is not fragmented or static bits of factual knowledge, or tasks; application of content knowledge that is not restricted to recall or guessing; and assessments that exist in harmony with school aims and students' learning styles.

Diagnostic Use of Standardized Assessment

If policymakers and educators could agree on the need to reconsider *how to use* standardized tests more effectively in an accountability system, perhaps there could be the condition Wiggins (1989) describes as moving "beyond lamenting . . . problems, because we have failed to ask some essential questions: Just what are tests meant to do . . . (and) whose purpose should they serve? . . . Is there a way to assess student performance . . . that might actually aid learning?" (p. 703). These, and questions not cited here, are critical elements of the premise of this text. It is argued that more effective utilization of standardized testing would guide curriculum and instruction beyond teaching and testing for declarative facts and information; and subsequently yield accurate informative data to monitor achievement trends. Darling-Hammond (1995) posits: "The outcomes of the current . . . assessment reforms will depend in large measure on the extent to which assessment developers and users use assessment in ways . . . to inform more skillful and adaptive teaching and learning for all students . . ." (p. 478).

This text recognizes the merits and value of standardized testing, but recommends that large-scale testing has significance only when used diagnostically in combination with multiple forms of in-district and in-class formative assessment systems; for monitoring and guiding instruction; and when the *high-stakes* associated with state mandated standardized test results have been eliminated.

While the negative factors identified in the literature substantially outweigh the positive elements of large-scale standardized testing in accountability systems, alternative systems have not received significant acceptance. Maeroff (1991) notes that it is much easier to articulate and propose such reforms, than to implement alternatives to traditional testing systems. This is so because of several obvious factors: time constraints; building alternative models— even based on those in existence—remain problematic; and there is no assurance that teachers would readily shift to alternative models. Colarci's (2002) definition of an effective assessment system appears to be one that does not necessitate dramatic shifts by teachers or districts. The positions of this text agree with his definition of an effective system. Such an accountability system would be one of coordinated plans among several measures: ". . . (A) constellation of measures that, together yield data that document progress toward student mastery of announced learning targets;" and must be a system of demonstrable valid reliability (p. 773).

Some critics of alternative assessment argue that for reliable data comparisons, test scores must be generated from instruments that are standardized for validity and reliability. Also, because of prohibitive costs associated with large-scale performance-based assessment, and time constraints for administering large-scale performance tests, accountability systems are better served by traditional multiple-choice formats (Popham, 1987). Critics contend that this situation is the unfortunate trade off for validity and reliability of data for cross-site comparisons.

These arguments are well founded, but this author contends that the premise is based on well-intended misconceptions that traditional standardized tests are the only means to generate meaningful and useful performance data. Employing a combination of state, district, and classroom assessments would afford multiple measures for cross-referencing what students actually know and can do. The use of multiple-measure accountability systems would also lessen the stigmas associated with one-measure-generated low performance that occurs mainly within African American and other urban poor student groups. A first step in transforming assessment for both quality and equity is comparing *within group* and *within site* factor, and domain analyses of knowledge and skill performance of multiple assessments to obtain broader and accurate evaluations. This explanation is elaborated and discussed in detail in the companion instructional text previously referenced. The in-class assessment practices recommended by both texts are performance-based, and an adaptation of Mager's (1975) constructs of evaluating instruction and learner performance through criterion-referenced objectives.

Criterion Referenced Instruction and Assessment

An effective pedagogy for increasing student performance and eliminating "achievement guesswork" is through *Criterion-Referenced Instruction (CRI)* to guide teaching; and *Criterion-Reference Assessment (CRA)* to evaluate student performance. *CRI and CRA* do not leave student progress and achievement to chance as in traditional lecture formats where learning and assessment place the major responsibility for success on students. The teaching-learning practice in most classrooms is essentially "teaching-to-test." Consequently, regardless of whether the instructor is effective in delivering clear and relevant content, students are expected to "somehow grasp" subject knowledge, which may or may not be thoroughly understood; has no contextual relevance for how students process information; or has no contextual meaning beyond the textbooks. Also, students are expected to memorize facts, and subsequently recognize de-contextualized concepts in lesson cycle and subject exit assessments.

171

In many instances, students and teachers "discover" after weeks of instruction or at reporting periods, how little progress students have made; how little in-depth content students understand; or the levels of skill mastery they have achieved. This is often reflected in testing situations, when students can repeat information in a class discussion, recognize the information in the exact context in which the content was delivered; but cannot recognize the same content or knowledge in different contexts; for example: students do not recognize alternative forms of subject content or concepts on standardized tests.

In contrast, the practice of *CRI* has a "built-in" design for benchmark formative assessment. The pedagogy begins with an objective statement clearly articulated to students, prior to the lesson, of what *content* will be delivered for each lesson; a statement that defines the *context* of the instruction (*i.e.,* the givens or stated conditions); and what students *are expected to* understand, articulate, demonstrate or apply *immediately* after the content is modeled by the teacher. In-class objective, measurable performance-based formative and summative assessments determine students' mastery of the content on an individual basis through daily and short-term feedback. Students bear responsibilities of focusing, attending, and active engagement during instruction, in individual subject related activities, and in outside work. However, *CRI places* the *major responsibility* for student success on the teacher to provide opportunities for active, reciprocal student participation in classroom activities; and in structuring conditions for students to learn with understanding. For each concept or unit taught in *CRI,* the teacher uses three basic steps:

- Ensures that students know what they are to learn (content);

- States the conditions and timeframes for the instruction, including materials to be used (context); and

- Specifies the expected outcomes for students (criteria for summative student performance).

Criterion Referenced Instruction is not a new instructional practice. Robert Mager (Ibid.) developed *CRI* as programmed training modules; and though not as widely practiced, some forms or adaptations are in current classroom use. Mager used *CRI* as a comprehensive set of instructional methods designed for:

- Identification of what is to be learned—the *goal;*

- Performance objectives or specification of the outcomes—the *criteria;*

- Criterion referenced testing—how learner objectives were to be evaluated; and

- Development of learning modules tied to specific objectives.

Criterion Referenced Assessment (CRA) is an in-class performance-based assessment structure recommended by this text. It is an approach similar to the instructional delivery; in fact, formative assessment should be an intricate element of ongoing instruction. Just as *CRI* formats specify measurable content objectives; assessment objectives should be explicit in stating expected levels of student performance. *Criterion-Referenced Assessment (CRA)* formats begin with clearly defined and precisely stated objectives for both mastery of content by students; and correspondingly, the effectiveness of instruction. Student levels of expected performances are stated for benchmark points in a lesson cycle for formative assessment; and the expected levels of student performance at the conclusion of a lesson cycle through summative assessments. This design or format of evaluation establishes *unity of efforts* between the instructor and students; provides opportunities for students to co-share responsibility in understanding knowledge; and determining the degree of individual and group success. Employing practices of *unity of efforts* is more likely to promote active student engagement in accomplishing the short term and long term goals of instruction. Students also remain actively engaged in documenting progress in student portfolios. Teachers use a master portfolio to track group progress during lessons cycles and subject units throughout the course or semester. The percent of all learners who obtain

174

levels of mastery of the content under discussion determines the effectiveness of instruction (Pierre-Pipkin, 2007).

CRI and CRA in Culturally Responsive Practices

Criterion Referenced Instruction and *Criterion Referenced Assessment* formats provide wide latitude for teachers to include *cultural themes* and *contexts* in instructional delivery as scaffolding to teach for understanding; especially when introducing new concepts. Culturally relevant contexts are teacher-designed classroom activities that allow students to incorporate subject concepts in individual demonstrations and small group projects; including opportunities for culturally diverse students to use learner-created activities to model concept understanding in formative assessments. Students are allowed to challenge, judge, or question subject concepts. These activities create a nexus between students' lived experiences and academic content when content is *situated* in familiar contexts, used as references; and permit students to see relationships between in-school and out-of-school knowledge. Additionally, students are provided opportunities to participate in establishing situational culturally related contexts to demonstrate their levels of comprehension of subject concepts. By co-designing learning objectives for content mastery, students have autonomy as co-owners, of what knowledge is delivered; as co-evaluators in assessing progress; and judging whether subject content is thoroughly understood and standards are being met. The rationale for this approach to teaching and learning is for teachers to provide many and various "relevantly contextualized" activities and opportunities for students to gain complete "insight" of subject concepts to *learn with understanding.* Teachers must ensure that students *understand* content before they are expected to demonstrate knowledge and skills in lesson cycle summative assessment; or through standardized test assessments.

To be clear, effective education and schooling extend far beyond the lived experiences and cultures of all learners. Utilizing cultural contextual formats in classroom activities *(CRI-CRA)* expands students' ability to understand academic content in two basis ways: First, the use of prior knowledge or experiences that are familiar to learners creates a critical nexus between in-school and their out-of-school learning. This nexus, or scaffold, augments the instructional process; and establishes a foundation for students to understand new concepts and knowledge that might otherwise be elusive. Secondly, because many urban learners have limited direct or wide social experiences beyond their immediate neighborhoods or communities, learning school subjects in a *CRI* format, does not penalize these students as a consequence of their economic status. Each lesson, concept or unit presented in criterion-reference context incorporates all necessary elements essential for students to learn the information. CRI provides opportunities for vicarious experiences that expand students' understanding of knowledge beyond their immediate environments. Further, by using situational cultural contexts to explain subject concepts, teachers increase the chances that students will gain insight and understanding needed to master knowledge and skills.

EXAMPLE

Ordinarily, few low-wealth urban students are familiar with the New York Stock Exchange (*NYSE*), beyond perhaps hearing references in the media, especially on TV. Thus, the *NYSE* would not be part of conversation heard in their daily out-of-school lives. Let's suppose a mathematics problem being discussed involves concepts related to the *NYSE;* and requires students to compute the percentage of a person's life savings that was lost by investing in stock of a company registered for public trading. Most students would perhaps not have difficulty in doing the mathematical computations; but some students may be unable to solve the complete problem, because all the *unknown* concepts regarding the *NYSE* may be confusing. This is an example, of "not being able to see the individual trees because of the forest!"

Q: How could *culturally responsive* classroom activities create a nexus that makes the concepts relevant?

One solution:
   a) Define all terms and concepts during introduction of the knowledge and skills to be learned.
   b) Provide opportunities for students to engage in reciprocal discussions of unknown concepts.
   c) If cable TV is available in the classroom; view a *few minutes* of the actual *NYSE* to make concepts "concrete."
   d) Allow students to create a "company" during the discussions with a *product* that is familiar to their daily lives (for instance, breakfast cereal) to be sold, purchased, etc.
   e) Use poker chips or paper money to be saved in a "classroom bank;" and subsequently withdrawn (or electronically transferred to an investor via computer activities), and invested at an actual physical location within the classroom—*i.e.,* with an investment agent.
   f) Allow students to act out simple roles of the processes involved in investing, and losing money.

Note: This activity should not consume but a portion of one class period. However, the possible extensions for concepts and activities can be related to other content; and across subject disciplines (Pierre-Pipkin, 2007; See *In Theater* activities in the companion text, previously referenced).

The use of *CRI* for relevant contextualized content benefits the instructor, as well as the students. *CRI* allows the instructor to evaluate and know immediately, whether students can articulate or demonstrate knowledge, paraphrase a level of understanding, transfer knowledge to new situations, or use information to make applications. The instructor can immediately assess how effective his/her instruction was for a specific concept or lesson—which should be a basic tenet of all classroom instruction. Using culturally relevant themes and contexts, respects the culture, language, and out-of-school learning experiences of diverse student groups. The advantages for teaching and learning in *CRI* and *CRA* instructional formats include:

- Opportunities and activities that compensate for sociocultural limitations;

- Immediate feedback through criterion-referenced evaluations; and

- Authentic assessment alternatives to multiple-choice formats.

Further, *criterion-referenced assessment* used in authentic in-class assessment of performance yields accurate data in evaluating what students actually know and can do. *CRA* can be used to complement data obtained through standardized testing by incorporating in-class CRA in a district level multiple-measures system to lessen the bias and inequities of one-measure standardized tests, particularly for culturally diverse students.

NCLB: The Good; The Bad; and The Ineffective

Currently, student teachers, pre-service teachers, school in-service teachers, and other educators are extremely familiar with the acronym, NCLB. Few, if anyone in the general public concerned with, or even slightly aware of what takes place in education—particularly in schools, have not had the opportunity to discuss, or know of the Act; specifically the well-known phrase *"No Child Left Behind."* Beyond policy makers and school personnel, other persons in the educational arena most familiar with the legislation include: state agency personnel responsible for budgeting and monitoring accountability of the Act; educational researchers; and parents of school age children.

The struggle to finally get American education right has continued for more than five decades; especially since the 1954 *Brown* decision, and the 1965 Elementary and Secondary Education Act (ESEA), including the current reauthorization of ESEA that is NCLB. The most recent quest extends beyond simple oversight of merely *looking over the shoulders of educators*. The intent of NCLB is to hold states and school districts accountable for what is wrong with education; and to set standards that will eventually solve problems of underachievement in public schools. Thus and *perhaps* society will finally be straight. Albeit, schools are microcosmic reflections of *society, as a whole*; educational problems are viewed in isolation, as distinctly separate from social contexts; and attributable solely to what happens within schools. Moreover, social responsibilities never intended, or should have been delegated to educational institutions are now part and parcel of schooling (*i.e. food programs; health, drugs, etc.)*; despite the fact that many socially related responsibilities are far beyond educators' ability to adequately address; and/or still deliver effective education.

The *No Child Left Behind Act of 2001* attempts to fix education through a trajectory, beginning at the federal level that established standards and timelines for accomplishing goals; to state level agencies that are to make decisions of *how* the standards of the Act will be implemented; to district level agencies that are required to measure and report school and student progress according to the pre-determined standards and target dates.

Using the phrase of Ross Perot, who advocated *no pass, no play*; this seems to be *"pretty simple stuff."* Has the reform been simple? On the contrary; NCLB seems to have created far more educational problems than it attempts to resolve

(Pierre-Pipkin, 2004; Shepard, et al., 2005; Sunderman, et al., 2005; Rebell & Wolff, 2008). Both critics and supporters of NCLB have begun to question the expanded role of the federal government in public education—what is *supposedly* a state responsibility.

As previously discussed, for the reason that the *General Welfare Clause* of the Constitution permits Congress to tax and spend for education, and subsequently the power of control in the interests of citizens in addressing the "general welfare" exemplified by NCLB; this well-intended policy, as with all federal interventions in public education, is legislated to promote that welfare purpose (Garber & Edwards, 1970; Reutter, Jr., & Hamilton, 1976; 1979; Zirkel, 1978).

The original purpose of Title I of ESEA was based on an awareness that states were not investing adequate amounts of money in schools populated by low-wealth and minority students; thus, the supplemental 1965 Title I funds were to address that inequity (Suderman, Kim, & Orfield, 2005). NCLB goes a step further in addressing the "general welfare" contained in equal educational opportunities by requiring states to employ uniform standardized testing in an accountability system to document student achievement. Despite the well-intentions of educational policies to promote a "general welfare" purpose; federal legislation designed to motivate state and local efforts to raise student achievement and close achievement gaps through sanctions, is not always easy, or even possible, as reflected by the strong resistance to reforms NCLB has engendered; and the unforeseen problems, as those resulting from mandated wide-scale standardized testing. Consequently, implementation of NCLB has raised major concerns among supporters and critics in how this is being played out through pre-determined standards; target timelines; and the probabilities of doing so.

This is so for several reasons: First, because the various states have plenary powers to determine *how* NCLB is implemented within individual states, a plethora of different accountability systems exist across the states. It is argued that this wide variance is due, in part, because different states determine the definition of *proficiency;* and the lack of common meaning undermines the concept of universal proficiency (Linn, R. L., 2008). For example, a particular state may need to increase student performance by 60% or more to reach the 100% standard by 2014; while other states may have to increase student performance by only 25% or less because each state starts from a different baseline of student performance; and thereby determines what percent within that state establishes *proficiency.* This discrepancy undermines the intent of the Act, and therefore makes accuracy of national achievement data fallible. Next, research informs that the greatest harm through sanctions is accrued by urban school districts and schools because the populations of subgroups that typically represent low-scoring students are concentrated in those districts with schools that are most vulnerable in not meeting NCLB benchmark standards. Moreover, both proponents and critics alike, consider *universal proficiency* by 2014 unrealistic (Suderman, et al., 2005).

Space and the specific focus of this text do not permit an extensive examination or lengthy discussions of NCLB. The discussions are limited to cursory highlights of several factors that relate to the postulates of *classroom learning;* and issues of whether or not in-depth learning is occurring in classrooms for diverse learners. The specific focus is on the *learning conditions,* including teaching and learning influenced by the implementation of NCLB; and the negative impact on academic performance of African American and other urban children. The discussions to follow will analyze several conditions created by the implementation of NCLB, noted as *the good, the bad,* and *the ineffective*:

- *The good* are elements of NCLB considered *propelling* or *positive driving forces* and opportunities for in-depth classroom learning.

- *The bad* are elements considered *barriers* that prevent in-depth classroom learning; and structure further inequities.

- *The ineffective* are elements considered *restraining forces* that inhibit learning; but could be modified to enhance learning.

It is argued that implementation of NCLB has created opportunities conducive to advancing achievement of African American and other urban children; for example, the requirement that all children will have highly qualified teachers. On the other hand, factors such as punitive decisions based on one-measure standardized test scores present *barriers;* and defeat the purpose of providing equity of educational opportunities for this population. Finally, despite the requirement for *highly qualified teachers*—if some teachers and schools continue to have low expectations for diverse children; and the same social stigmas in the general public are modeled in schools, thereby creating negative and unchallenging classroom climates; more money, higher standards, highly-degreed teachers; or teaching-to-test will not advance in-depth learning opportunities. Such conditions *restrain* and *inhibit* instruction; and make standards of equity and accuracy of score results moot. Under these *learning conditions,* poor and minority students are not achieving as expected; and will not meet the standards envisioned in NCLB by 2014; or beyond that time.

What Does NCLB Require?

No Child Left Behind is described as the most aggressive intervention in public education by the federal government since *Brown;* and is also "a landmark" piece of legislative reform to improve student achievement; close the achievement gap between various student groups; and provide an accountability system that will monitor student performance to ensure that progress is measured and reported annually by local school districts and state agencies (Valencia, 2001; Thomas & Gainbridge, 2002a, & 2000b; U. S. Government Department of Education, 2004; Linn, 2008; Kimmelman, 2006; Koretz, 2008; Sunderman, 2008). The major difference between *Brown* and *NCLB* is the intent: the former was a focus on civil rights; the latter on accountability.

NCLB is designed to improve achievement through an accountability system that requires states to have every child functioning at grade level, as measured by state level standardized tests, by the 2013-2014 school year (Ibid.). Briefly, the means of achieving this goal include the following requirements:

- States were to assess all students through state level standardized tests to determine levels of student performance beginning in 2002-2003 with reading, language arts, and mathematics, and science in 2007-2008

- States must gather student performance data (aggregate); separate performance data by subgroups—(*i.e., racial/ ethnic; economically disadvantaged; special education students;* and *students in English language classes*— disaggregate); and publicly report results of all students' performance by each demographic group within a state on an annual basis.

- Accountability systems must be designed to state standards of assessments; proficiency definitions; teacher qualifications; and adequate yearly progress.

- Each year individual schools are to increase student performance by a pre-determined percent, referred to as *Adequate Yearly Progress* (AYP). Schools not meeting AYP standards for two consecutive years will be identified as *In Need of Improvement.* (Note: According to NCLB, such schools *are not* identified as *failing*; but rather, schools that *need to improve* to meet standards.) Schools so identified must report school status to parents, and allow parental choice of transferring students to other schools that have met the AYP standards.

- Schools *in need of improvement* must deliver curriculum and instruction built on scientifically based research that will strengthen learning in core subject areas; and at least 10% of Title I funds must be spent for staff development; parental involvement; and teacher mentoring.

The Influence of NCLB Requirements on Classroom Learning

Based on NCLB requirements cited, the discussions will highlight several factors that influence the contexts and *conditions* of classroom learning for African American and other urban children:

- Accountability through standardized testing;
- Scientifically based curriculum and instruction;
- Flexibility of state control in assessment designs; and
- Highly Qualified Teacher.

Accountability through standardized testing has been the most visible and controversial issue regarding the implementation of NCLB requirements. An issue previously discussed and reiterated is the position of Haney and Madaus (1989), that testing is the *Achilles' heel* of the education system. This text agrees, and adds that the negative impact of standardized testing on African American and other poor urban children is significantly more severe than for any other student groups assessed through large scale testing. This is so because there is a deficit view of student performance data that focuses mainly on what students *cannot do;* rather than using performance data as an opportunity for diagnostic analysis to inform instruction of where concentrated efforts are needed to improve underperformance (Heartel, 1999).

Moreover, the particular subgroups of *low-scoring* students are primarily minority and poor students, who continue to bear the blame and engender stigmas for schools not meeting AYP standards. This reflects another issue previously discussed: the *contradictory conditions* created by assessment-driven school practices. The merit of standards and assessment, as critical elements in advancing student achievement is not the issue argued; but rather, *how* assessment is obtained, and *how* data are used. First, wide-scale assessment designs are mainly measures of factual information that capture basic, rote-level knowledge on multiple-choice formats, that can be *hit-or-miss* measures of what students know; and the formats limit emphasis on thinking skills. Next, test results are used in punitive ways that undercut the ideals of NCLB: to advance learning and increase equity. Instead, low-performing students can be retained in grades; denied high school diplomas; and trapped in schools the public views as failures; regardless of the percent of students in those schools or subgroups who do perform on grade level. The focus on attaining high scores neglects attention to the degree of student achievement gains within the year. Finally, there is the issue of tracking based on test scores. Tracking decisions typically begin in elementary schools and disportionately assign minority students to special education or non-college bound courses; with few referrals to advanced or college-bound tracts (Darling-Hammond, 1995; Shepard, et al., 2005; Suderman, Kim & Orfield, 2005).

Another requirement of NCLB, and a major postulate of this text, is to ensure that curriculum and instruction are predicated on *scientifically based* theories of learning; with particular emphasis on theory-based teaching practices that create *learning conditions* to advance achievement of diverse student groups. Attention is called to the fact that despite researched-based curriculum designs and instruction having maintained long-standing educational benefits, little attention has been devoted, specifically, to scientifically based research of *culturally-influenced theories* related to instruction and learning for diverse students in meeting this requirement of NCLB (Goodnow, Miller, & Kessel, 1995; Hollis, 1996; Gay, 2000; Villegas & Lucas, 2002; Hale, 2001a & 2001b; Irvine, 2002 & 2003; Nieto, 1999).

Irvine (2003) pointed out that in 2001, 40% of the nation's student population was students of color, and this population continues to increase primarily due to the growing numbers of Latino immigrant students. Currently, 50% or more students of color populate the nation's largest cities and metropolitan area schools; and by the year 2025, the nation's overall population is expected to be 47% nonwhite. The nation's leading educational demographer, Harold Hodgkinson, warns that public education systems that ignore the changing demographic nature of school populations do so at their peril (*See* Goldberg, 2002). Hodgkinson contends that a first issue to consider regarding changing demographics of school populations is not simply the numbers; but rather, what the numbers mean. For example, an increasing population of poor families accounts, in part, for lack of financial support for many schools. He points out the predictive value of data and the relationship to several educational factors including: student populations most likely to do poorly on standardized tests; household incomes and the educational levels of parents related to student achievement; and why uniformity of educational standards may not be the best solution in addressing educational issues among the plethora of diverse student populations. Hodgkinson also links the necessity of attending demographic data to implications for classroom instruction, noting the importance of students' seeing themselves as world citizens. He argues that while the skills of academic subjects should be standard; the content should be highly diversified.

Gay (2002) articulated a general consensus among many educational researchers of the benefits of culturally influenced teaching and learning. She examined teacher practices of using culturally responsive instruction and concluded that " . . . teachers (have begun to) stop blaming and trying to 'fix' the students and (have begun) . . . to validate their worth and cultural heritage" (p. 211). Current and growing diversity in school demographics, require curriculum and instruction that *create conditions* to enhance and extend opportunities for culturally diverse learners to make relevant connections to subject content; to be involved in in-depth challenging learning activities; and for standardized tests to be used diagnostically to augment instruction.

Culturally responsive learning theory should be given strong consideration regarding compliance of this NCLB requirement; along with considering the advantages of employing culturally-responsive teaching activities to elevate low-scoring minority and poor students to grade level proficiency (Kohnhaber, 2004).

State control and flexibility in assessment designs is a provision within the NCLB requirement for state standardized assessment. Some of the previous discussions looked at the language of the *Tenth Amendment* that delegates plenary powers to state governments for control of public education; the shift in community control of education to policy makers, educators, and influential groups; and how the federal government addresses the *General Welfare Clause* of the Constitution in legislating educational policy. There are many *coulda, shoulda, woulda* debates of what NCLB is doing or failing to do regarding public education. The pros and cons seem to boil down to a string of sentiments: NCLB "could have" demanded more, or demanded less, to better address achievement and the achievement gap; NCLB legislation "should have" followed through with more money to fund the costs associated with implementation; and the states "would have" been better served to be allowed to maintain their prior accountability systems that did not have sanctions attached by AYP, since state assessments seemed to be working rather well before NCLB. A serious question to be answered regarding equity in schooling is: *Will all of these issues be resolved by 2014?* The response is: *When the question, itself, is the problem; perhaps the answer will not be the right solution.*

In this regard, there are two critical elements to consider. First, NCLB is here is stay, perhaps with modifications, but will be a mainstay of educational accountability for the foreseeable future. Second, states maintain plenary powers of control over education; and to a great extent, the power to decide how NCLB is carried out in individual states. A point often overlooked is that NCLB provides for states to maintain significant flexibility in *how* the requirements are implemented; including the design of performance assessments. Though statewide-standardized tests are mandated, the requirements for meeting proficiency through assessment, do not *exclude* states' combining multiple other forms of assessment (Lewis, 2002; Mathis, 2003; U.S. Department of Education, Retrieved 10/24/2004 from: www. ed.gov/orubt.teachers/nclbguide/toolkit.hlml).

The final issue highlighted is the NCLB requirement for all students to have *highly qualified teachers*. Individual states define standards for teacher qualifications; and the deadline for meeting this provision was the end of 2005-2006. Minimum teacher qualifications are: a four-year degree; full state certification; and demonstration of subject matter competency for each subject taught. The following discussions are limited to qualifications for teachers of regular education classes.

Teacher Qualifications
- New elementary teachers must pass a rigorous state standards test to demonstrate subject knowledge competency in reading, language arts, writing, and mathematics; and other areas of curriculum in basic elementary subjects.

- New middle school and high school teachers have two paths for meeting the requirement: passing a rigorous test in each subject they teach; or by obtaining a major or equivalent coursework, advanced degree or advanced certification or credentials.

- All experienced teachers also have several options. They may meet the requirement for new teachers by passing a rigorous test; or demonstrate competence by meeting the requirements of state standards evaluation, termed HOUSSE *(High Objective Uniform State Standard of Evaluation)*.

HOUSSE requirements of individual states allow extensive flexibility in what defines teacher quality standards; however, some HOUSSE systems have been criticized as being nothing more than rubber-stamping the *status quo* (Sunderman, et al., 2008; Rebell & Wolff, 2008). Other criticisms of NCLB requirements for *highly qualified teacher* include the department's exclusive focus on credentials and content knowledge; with little attention to teachers' effectiveness, and the ability to transmit knowledge to students; especially poor and minority students from diverse backgrounds. Further, only in recent years has attention been given to enforcement of the provisions; because the greatest focus has been on raising test scores. Critics argue that poor and minority students are still disproportionately taught by under-qualified or out-of-field teachers. Also, NCLB oversight has come late in addressing teacher quality by sending monitoring teams to each state to assess their progress. It was not until 2006 did the department focus on the gap between teacher *quality* of persons who teach in different socio-economic schools by requiring states to submit plans that define progress toward compliance (Rebell & Wolff, 2008; Sunderman, et al., 2008).

Rebell and Wolff (Ibid.) pose a re-definition of the concept of *highly qualified teacher*. Instead of the definition, as defined by NCLB, the authors recommend having a definition that centers on effectiveness. Further, there should be at least three descriptions that more precisely define the level of teacher quality:

- *Provisionally qualified*, for pre-service or alternatively certified teachers;

- *Qualified*, for teachers who hold a degree, and state certification; and

- *Highly effective*, for teachers who "demonstrate" in-depth subject-matter knowledge, as well as the ability to impart subject knowledge to students from diverse backgrounds.

This text agrees with the position that a *highly qualified teacher* is not necessarily synonymous with being a *highly effective teacher*. Moreover, to be effective, it is posited that teachers should demonstrate at least two other capabilities:

- Teachers must demonstrate abilities in formative student assessment; and an in-depth understanding of the strengths and weaknesses of standardized tests; including the ability to do test-item and domain analysis.

- Effective teachers must be *culturally competent.* This means teachers of African American, poor and other marginalized students should recognize and understand the import of culture on in-school learning; and be familiar with the out-of-school experiences of their students. Further, teachers must demonstrate abilities in designing and delivering culturally responsive pedagogies to advance student learning.

NCLB and *Conditions of Learning* in Urban Classrooms

NCLB: The Good

If we were to itemize requirements of NCLB considered *good* in positively influencing classroom learning for African American and other urban students; despite the comprehensiveness of the Act, the list would be relatively short. Therefore this discussion looks at several previously mentioned elements considered *driving forces* that are currently propelling, or that have possibilities for enhancing equity of educational opportunities; for in-depth classroom learning; and fairness and accuracy of assessments for this student population.

Highly Qualified Teachers: This requirement is considered the most significant of all possible factors for providing educational equity. When the focus moves beyond merely credentials, and poorly defined and implemented standards for teacher *quality*; and incorporates and centers on *effectiveness* in "teaching and reaching" all students, the intent of the requirement will be realized. Much applause should be given this requirement ensuring that poor and ethnic minority students will not be taught by uncertified or out-of-field teachers. However, we're not there yet—but moving in the right direction. Whether or not students are provided opportunities to engage in in-depth classroom learning is predicated on their teachers' abilities to transmit high quality, challenging content; to teach for understanding; and the ability to effectively teach diverse students.

Assessment: Despite the debates and controversy, assessment is considered a positive driving force; and though there are different purposes and different forms of assessment to enhance knowledge and skills, there is a "positive intent" (Kornhabler, 2004). Used appropriately, and in combination with multiple measures, assessment can produce a broader perspective and higher levels of accuracy of student performance (Linn, 2008; Hurwitz, & Hurwitz, 2000). Further, there is evidence that testing has spurred states, districts, and schools to more closely align instruction with states' curriculum standards (Davis, 2006a). Kornhaber (2008) notes that used correctly, standardized tests can be an asset and ". . . an efficient tool for collecting large and broad amounts of data quickly and cheaply; and for data comparisons across students, schools, districts, and states" (p. 46).

Adequate Yearly Progress (AYP): There is no question that an accountability system that requires states, districts, and schools to document and report student progress is considered a positive requirement. Currently, however, a significant number of barriers need to be addressed or removed for AYP to be considered a driving force in *specifically* advancing in-depth classroom learning. The major drawback is that rewards tend to accrue to upper and middle-income schools and students; and consistently, punishment is suffered by low-income schools, and correspondingly, students in those schools as evidenced by *tracking placements.*

Scientifically-based Research: The focus on "ensuring that teaching is reaching African American and other urban students" (Pierre-Pipkin, 2008) predicates the purpose of this text; and is congruent with a positive NCLB requirement for enhancing high quality education for poor and minority children. The intent is that pedagogy for low-scoring students is grounded in empirically accepted theories of teaching and learning. This text adds that teachers must also have a thorough understanding of *how children learn*; and *how* learning theory is linked to effective classroom practices. Further, effectively educating this population of children "requires an understanding of . . . basic elements . . . (including understanding teaching practices that apply specifically) to African American children . . . and how they learn from their cultures . . . (Pierre-Pipkin, 2006 & 2008). While this NCLB requirement does not specifically address *culturally related* research-based instruction, it is argued that this issue should be given significant attention. The importance is based on data that reflect the current and growing numbers of predominantly poor and ethnic minority students in public schools; particularly where various demographic subgroups represent the greatest numbers of low-scoring students. Goldberg (2000) relates Harold Hodgkinson's observations of the importance of demographics; and strengthens the argument that much attention should be given to diversity in classroom teaching and learning. The argument centers on the growing diversity of ethnic, racial, and second-language speaking groups of students; and suggests that teachers must have extensive knowledge of students of diverse backgrounds in order to address learning needs associated with various cognitive differences and abilities (Banks, et al., 1971; Banks, 1988 & 2003).

NCLB: The Bad

In a children's game of *good guys—bad guys,* the losers are called the *bad guys* who are taunted by the winners (the *good guys)*, with the chant: *Too bad, so sad, we're glad you're mad!* In a previous discussion it was pointed out that some proponents of *standardized testing* argue, among other issues, that the current multiple-choice design of large-scale assessment is a necessary "trade-off" to ensure reliability and validity in comparing student performance across state, district, and schools. While there is a consistent, though weak, trend toward alternative and authentic forms of wide-scale assessment and use of multiple measures; for the moment this practice has not been widely accepted or realized. Consequently, similar to the children's game, opponents of large-scale standardized multiple-choice tests are receivers of the chant: *too bad, so sad, some folks must adjust to being mad!*

Kornhaber (2008) pointed out the strengths of testing; but concluded that strengths are often overshadowed by weaknesses that include: "assessment of facts and rote skills, and few problem solving skills; results infer valid representations of actual performance; and delay in feedback time for results" (p. 46). Thus, the NCLB requirement of large-scale *standardized testing,* in its present design and punitive uses, is identified as the greatest barrier negatively influencing classroom learning for poor and minority students. While testing is the greatest weakness of education for a plethora of reasons, we mention only two here as *barriers* specifically for African-American and other marginalized students.

- First, because this population represents, or forms the greatest number of students in subgroups of low-scoring students tested; they correspondingly receive the greatest number of sanctions related to state, district, or school accountability; and punitive decisions made at district and school levels disproportionately identify these subgroups for tracking placements, retention or assignments to special education; particularly African American males, where their current and future chances of having high quality education are severely limited (Welner, 1998; Hilliard, 1990 & 1996; Porter, 1997; Mosteller, et al., 1998; Pierre-Pipkin, 2004; Swartz, 2009).

- Secondly, as Shepard, et al. (2005), and others note, wide-scale assessment has had profound effects on what takes place inside classrooms, including: structuring curriculum and instruction for learners to focus primarily on factual, declarative content, with little emphasis on higher order processing; and teaching for testing, that requires memorization skills of segmented, bits of information. Thus, assessment-driven instruction dismantles the intent of decreasing inequities in education, and restricts opportunities for high quality, in-depth classroom learning.

In many instances, some schools have made cuts in social studies, and non-academic subjects as music and art; and have eliminated recess in elementary schools to provide more time for reading and mathematics. Scores that tell students what they *cannot do* stigmatize and assign them to lower track classes, where they have less qualified, and out-of-field teachers who are more likely to focus on behavioral criticisms; especially for poor and minority students. These differences explain much of the discrepancy between achievement of low and high-scoring students; and between White and minority student performances. (Gougis, 1986; Johnson, 1989; Hilliard, 1990; Fordham, 1991a; Irvine, 1991; Darling-Hammond, 1995; Singham, 1998; Kunjufu, 2002; Boaler, 2003; Kornhaber, 2004; Lynch 2006).

The NCLB requirement for *standardized testing* seems to be the most significant, unforeseen—perhaps single— underlying cause of other problems regarding compliance; because many other provisions hinge on the specific manner of implementation of mandated standardized tests. Wide-scale, high-stakes assessment creates a domino effect that touches every other requirement of the Act as it impacts documentation of improvement and quality schooling: from the varying and incompatible state plans that define AYP; to subsequent inequalities in special assignment classrooms. Regardless of how well-intended the focus to address the issues of under-achievement of subgroups, and closing multiple group achievement gaps; NCLB is doing more damage than has been realized by not addressing the socio-political causes that have historically relegated African-American children, in particular, to second-class education. This population continues to bear the major negative impact of how NCLB is being implemented.

While we cannot get stuck in past history that only explains how we arrived where we are; we have to find a new formula of social and economic transformative processes to rebuild an educational system that works *for,* rather than *against* poor and minority students. Thus far, the fragility of NCLB, in its present form, has not been the answer (Kohn, 1999b; Singham, 1998; Lynch, 2006).

NCLB: The Ineffective

A work-study conference was held between a school placement counselor and a local business owner, who cooperated with high schools to train students for employment. When asked whether a particular student had made any progress in work skills since the previous conference, the business owner responded: *Absolutely!* Then he made a clarifying statement. He said: *He (the student) has not advanced in learning higher level work skills, but he is doing better within the work tasks that he already knows how to do.*

We use this anecdote as a contextual reference for analyzing four NCLB requirements considered *ineffective* in substantially enhancing quality classroom learning for African American and other urban children; and requirements that fail to reduce inequities in education. When considering the extent to which NCLB has addressed these issues; and how districts and schools are moving toward universal proficiency by 2013-2014, we want to contextualize the following: Whether districts and schools are moving vertically to higher levels of implementation to advance the quality of education and equity for all groups; or whether schools are doing better in teaching students something they already know how to do—taking tests—either well or poorly; consequently, whether schools are merely moving horizontally and doing better in teaching students how to score higher on standardized tests. We will explore four requirements considered ineffective:

- Highly Qualified Teacher
- Accountability by Assessment;
- Sanctions; and
- Universal Proficiency.

Highly Qualified Teachers

The requirement for highly qualified teachers begins with a positive intent by identifying the essential credentials, competencies and abilities *all* teachers must have for teaching *all* students: a four-year degree; state certification; and demonstrated competency in core subject assignments. The major concern is whether simply meeting these basic requirements translates into effective teaching; and as important, what specifically represents *demonstrated*

204

competence? For beginning teachers, NCLB requires passing a highly rigorous test as evidence of competence; and for in-service teachers, either meeting standards of a state designed system (HOUSSE); or passing the test designed for beginning teachers represents competence. The fact that beginning teachers have acceptable levels of content knowledge establishes a critical foundation for becoming an effective teacher; but still leaves much to chance opportunities that credentials, alone, translate into being highly skilled in teaching abilities. The position of Rebell and Wolff (2008), presents a convincing argument that there should be various categories for teacher quality; because neophyte teachers are unlikely to *demonstrate* highly qualified competence in the first year, or perhaps well past the first few years of teaching. Also, the provision that defines *highly qualified teacher* presents problems that affect experienced teachers, as well. For example, Sunderman, et al. (2005) point out that under this NCLB requirement, many well-prepared, experienced, and highly skilled teachers of multiple subjects may not be deemed *highly qualified* because they do not have a major in every subject area taught; or may not pass a test in each of the subject areas.

The most significant issue regarding *ineffectiveness* of the highly qualified teacher provision, and where the rubber meets the road, is the impact of the requirement on classroom learning. As stated, this requirement begins with a positive intent, but then ends at that point. In most schools, the manner of implementation is that these *highly qualified teachers* ensure that they focus on having their students pass the states' standardized tests. Kutz and Roskelly (1991) contend that in the typical classroom, teachers have little impact on making real change because inhibitive school structures:

> . . . (Prevent) them from creating, rather than simply replicating a classroom. Sometimes unwillingly, sometimes gratefully, they turn to prepared curriculum guides, discussion sections at the end of textbooks, and fill-in-the-blank worksheets. They stand at the front of the room, behind a desk, maintaining a long-held tradition of education, emphasizing transfer of information from teacher to students, with the teacher at the active center, students on the passive margin of the work of the classroom (p. 7).

Thus, all teachers at all levels concentrate mainly on teaching-to-test—a practice that has distorted and restricted effective classroom instruction. Shepard, et al, (2005) note that teachers tailor instruction to what will be tested; and this distortion does not represent learning. They further contend that it is important to understand that ". . . raising test scores is not always the same thing as improving learning" (p. 311).

Another issue is that of "tracking," but not necessarily the tracking of students; but rather, *tracking of teachers*. In most states, beginning teachers; the least prepared; the least skilled; or out-of-field teachers are typically assigned to low-wealth schools, or classes of low-performing and subgroup students. Many of these teachers tend to have low expectations for diverse students directly related to race, culture, language, and socioeconomic status (Kornhaber, 2004; Banks, et al, 2005). The most qualified and skilled teachers are conversely assigned to upper-tracked classes. Further, the inequities of resources available to highly qualified, and less qualified teachers are similarly apparent. Low-tracked teachers have limited textbooks, instructional supplies, and computers; while adequate resources are made available to teachers of high-tracked classes. The discrepancies that impact instructional delivery by low-tracked teachers extend beyond resources. Many low-tracked teachers are less motivating and supportive of their students; and are less academically oriented. Many low-tracked teachers lack teaching expertise; and significant numbers simply leave, thus increasing turnover rates (Banks, et al., 2005).

Expertise in classroom assessment; and competence in implementing culturally responsive instruction are other issues not considered in defining *highly qualified* teachers. Stiggins (1988; 1999; 2002) posits that more attention should be paid to the day-to-day assessment that takes place in classrooms that informs instruction and leads to learning and student motivation. He finds that teachers have not been trained in pre-service programs because programs devote limited time to the topic of classroom assessment, except to stress paper-pencil type testing. Further, in-service teachers do not receive technical assistance to ensure the quality and appropriate use of daily classroom assessment of student progress. Moreover, states' standards for certification do not require competence in student assessment, except for particular special education personnel, who generally specialize in standardized, norm-reference tests. Stiggins (1999) argues: *"Ineffectiveness* in schools most often arises not from lack of effort, but from lack of expertise, time, and resources needed to increase student achievement" (italics added, p. 197).

The topic of culturally relevant pedagogy has been discussed at length in other sections of this text; and the position agrees with a general consensus found in the literature, that teacher effectiveness includes the ability to teach culturally diverse students. It is posited that a redefinition of *highly qualified teacher* should include the ability to enhance the quality of instruction to provide equity for African American and other marginalized students through *demonstrated* knowledge of diverse student populations; to teach for understanding, rather than for testing. Further, culturally responsive pedagogy should predicate all instruction for diverse student populations. Effective teaching requires creating a *nexus* between in-school and out-of-school learning that can be mediated through culturally relevant instructional practices.

Although instruction has become skewed toward teaching what's to be tested; it is obvious that schools and teachers have begun to give more attention to the cultural learning styles of African American and other marginalized students. This is considered only a slight upward move toward quality and equity; and the advantage for classroom learning is barely discernible, if indeed any enhancement can be gleaned. This is so because of the *manner* of instructional delivery by most *teachers*: Instruction is standards and assessment-driven; with an interpretation of effective teaching based on the ability to produce high student test scores.

Accountability through Assessment

Considering whether this requirement is advancing classroom learning, or simply doing better in maintaining the *status quo* could be summed up in one statement: The intent that the current accountability system will motivate teachers to improve the quality of classroom instruction; and all students will be provided equitable educational opportunities is a vertical move *downward.* Rather than propelling quality classroom learning and equity, the current *punitive* and standards-driven uses of accountability by large-scale assessment has diminished quality education, where instruction is distorted by teaching-to-test; and successful learning is interpreted to be synonymous with high test scores.

The plethora of disadvantages placed on African American and other urban children through large-scale assessment are far more numerous than explored in this text. The concern here concentrates on the *use of* test data generated by states' large-scale, high-stakes assessment and the punitive consequences suffered disproportionately by the specific students who are most in need of equity and assistance through federal oversight. The way this provision is being implemented negates its intent; because students can be retained in grades, tracked into less challenging classes and programs; and denied graduation diplomas. It is therefore argued that this requirement is not advancing, nor will it advance quality classroom learning and equity for any students (Kohn, 2001; Stiggins, 1988, 1999 & 2002; Shepard, et al., 2005; Linn, R., 2008; Koretz, D. 2008; Sunderman, 2008).

The *ineffectiveness* of the *wide-scale assessment* requirement can be reversed if educational systems modify the credentials for teachers to include having competence in understanding and designing effective evaluative tools for diverse learners to demonstrate subject competence through authentic formative in-class assessments; and teachers demonstrate abilities of analysis and use of multiple assessment measures in evaluating student performance.

Further, effectiveness can be attained if classroom and in-district assessments are combined with standardized tests data in a multi-evaluation diagnostic system to better inform and guide instruction; and to obtain the actual levels of student knowledge and performance

Sanctions for Schools in Need of Improvement

This requirement is a vertical move that continues to spiral downward; but the move is also *backward,* because African American and other urban students still bear the full burden of sanctions; similar to past historical inequities, though for different reasons. Past injustices through discrepancies in educational quality and inequities stemmed, in large part, from segregated schools and lack of sociopolitical commitments to equality of educational opportunity. This NCLB provision of rewards and sanctions assumes higher standards with the intent of improving achievement, rather than focusing on competence by educators to deliver effective schooling. Stiggins (2002) argues that this is a "flawed vision" because many students are overwhelmed by tougher standards in a system where they are already failing, and simply give up. Further, while many students who pass standardized tests with ease, approach assessment metaphorically as coming to "slay the dragon;" others expect to be "devoured" by the dragon. Consequently, high-wealth schools that typically produce high scores, continue to be rewarded and applauded for what they already are "good" at doing—producing "high scores" on standardized tests; while low-scoring schools continue to be sanctioned for doing what they "already do poorly"—attaining *high test scores*. This provision is interpreted as *ineffective* because it returns educational quality and equity for African American and other urban students to pre-*Brown* years for the reasons identified in the previous discussion on the punitive decisions of tracking; and the subsequent stigmas associated with low-scoring students and subgroups based solely on test scores. This author posits:

> It is myth to conclude that African American (and other urban) children will necessarily advance upward on the educational ladder simply because school districts are required to . . . assess all children by the same measuring criteria. In reality, African American (and other urban) children will be those *'left behind'* because they do not see themselves in America's educational system. They are *devalued* in urban schools; *invisible* and *outcasts* in many suburban schools; and have *wounded spirits* . . . (connected) directly to the educational (system). How do we *reclaim* . . . (these) *children,* knowing that there is no legislative prosthetic for *amputated spirits?* (Pierre-Pipkin, 2004)

Thus, nothing seems to propel this population of students forward; they simply stand still or move backwards, being pushed by an agenda set in motion by policymakers for higher standards in a race where they are already five-decade laps behind. Moreover, the sociopolitical issues of neglect and disparities of second-class schooling of poor and minority students that created these conditions have not been addressed; continue to abate equity of opportunity; and continue the cycle that penalizes these students based on race, ethnicity, language, and socio-economic status. The sanction provision for schools *in need of improvement*—intended to motivate schools to improve—simply does not enhance classroom learning for African American and other marginalized children. There is no reasonable modification of this requirement that could be interpreted as *"propelling."*

Universal Proficiency

This requirement is no move in any direction given the present structure of educational delivery of teaching-to-test; however, it is not as *unrealistic* as it appears on the surface. The problem that makes this requirement *ineffective* in advancing quality and equity is that districts and schools are "forcing a fit" of square pegs into round holes; or trying to implement the requirement based on erroneous interpretations of the NCLB requirement, and making implementation *unrealistic*. NCLB never intended that students with severe learning problems; or all English-language learners would be able to perform, academically, at grade level commensurate with content subject standards by 2013-2014; or indeed at all—*that would be unrealistic* (Thomas & Gainbridge, 2002; U. S. Government Department of Education, *No Child Left Behind: A Toolkit for Teachers.* Retrieved 10/23/2004: www.NoChildLeftBehind. gov).

It is inaccurate to interpret the intent of the requirement as ignoring problems of various students with learning disabilities. However, despite the historically tiered education that has always been unequal between White and minority students; or education that currently divides, and subdivides schooling—inside schools, and outside of schools; by wealth and class; urban and suburban; fully-funded and under-funded; low-performers and high performers—universal proficiency *is possible* for all students, who are intellectually capable of functioning at grade level. Moreover, this standard should be the focus of implementation.

There is much debate regarding either eliminating or modifying NCLB; but the general consensus is that NCLB is here to stay (Koretz, 2008). Therefore it is incumbent on educators to deal with all the elements—*the good, the bad,* and *the ineffective.* Educators know what's *good,* but could be better implemented; for example, avoiding teaching-to-test in classroom instruction. Many educators know what elements are especially *bad* for poor and ethnic minority students; but are often prohibited from having autonomy in practicing critical theory pedagogy. Often educators do not agree on the specific ways the barriers can be removed; or how approaches can be done differently; for example, re-designing multiple-choice assessments. Thus, schooling becomes a matter of determining what works for *some* students, and not for *all* students; and most importantly, not considering what is *effective* to increase equity in instruction and assessment for all student populations. Finally, in dealing with what is considered *ineffective*; such as, defining highly qualified teachers; and evaluating students' standardized test performance; educators must cease viewing schooling through the prism created by the sociopolitical structure of general society that perpetuates inequalities for African American and other marginalized cultural groups. School districts must provide well-prepared highly skilled, culturally sensitive teachers for all students; and use assessment data appropriately for curriculum design and teaching practices, rather than creating more inequalities for culturally diverse learners.

CHAPTER FIVE

<table>
<tr><td>

The Impact of School and Classroom Climates on African American Student Achievement

</td><td>

Until the lions have their own historian, tales of the hunt will always favor the hunter.

__ An African Proverb

</td></tr>
</table>

INTRODUCTION

The literature on theories of learning reflects evolving interpretations of cognition from concepts that individual intelligence is biologically-based cognitive abilities represented by behaviors that can be measured and numerically quantified; to an emphasis that attempts to explain cognition as neurologically developmental, dynamic, mediated, and influenced by the external environment (Lohnman, 1989; Shade, 1992; Bransford, et al., 2000). There is general agreement among traditional and contemporary views that the external environment influences cognition, and *how people learn*; however, the old chicken-egg debate has not disappeared. Viewpoints that stress the biological nature of cognition defend the position that an anatomical neurological structure determines, to a greater degree, the extent to which an individual will learn. Other theorists concede that anatomical and neurological readiness are critical elements, but are only foundational for cognitive development; that specific *conditions for learning,* and interaction with the external environment

216

are the fundamental requisites for cognition, higher order thinking, and learning (Gagne, 1967; Critchley, 1975; Byrnes, 2001; Bransford, et al., 2005).

Bransford, et al. (Ibid.) addressed the role of learning theories related to teaching. They identified four components teachers should understand, learn to balance, and integrate these components to teach effectively: *what is to be taught*; *who learns,* and *how;* the *kinds of classroom environments* that enhance learning; and the *kinds of evidence* that reflect that learning is occurring (Italics added; p. 41).

In recent years teacher education programs have become more focused on coordinating pre-service education courses and clinical work to reinforce and better reflect key ideas and aspects that emphasize deeper understanding of teaching and learning; grounded in both theory and practice. This is a shift from previous programs that were mainly a collection of "unrelated courses without a common conception of teaching and learning . . . (and were) criticized for being overly theoretical, having little connections to practice . . ." (Darling-Hammond, et al., 2005, pp. 391-392). It is critical for prospective teachers to have a sound understanding of learning theory regarding child development. Therefore, teacher education should include in-depth study and coursework on *how people learn* as foundational components of pre-service training programs.

Teacher education programs usually include at least one required course in human growth and development, or developmental child psychology; however, despite the substantial amount of literature that supports culturally responsive teaching practices; training programs typically do not place extensive emphasis on pre-service courses regarding *how people learn* in social contexts (Irvine, 2003; Darling-Hammond, et al., 2005, Ares, 2006). Darling-Hammond and colleagues posit that teachers must know how theories of learning apply to classroom instruction regarding the import of different cultures, language, community influences and prior schooling. Similarly, Rogoff (2003), Nieto (2004), and others write extensively on learning as a cultural process of socially sanctioned knowledge, a concept prominently reflected in the literature; taking center stage especially with Vygotsky's theory of culturally mediated learning, and his concept of the *zone of proximal development*.

Previous discussions in this text argued that classroom learning would be enhanced for African American and other urban children if curriculum and pedagogies placed more emphasis on creating a nexus between the contexts of in-school learning and out-of-school contexts that form *how children learn* in everyday life. We also attempted to establish a foundation for the discussions of this chapter that include issues of school and classroom environments; social conditions that influence cognition of African American and other urban children; the link between research and culturally responsive teaching practices; and the impact of uncaring school climates, poor instruction, and teacher attitudes on achievement of culturally diverse students.

School and Classroom Climates: Factors and Conditions of Learning

A large body of literature on classroom learning reveals that among many factors that influence in-school learning, school and classroom climates are found to have significant impacts on student achievement (Castenelle, 1984; Fordham, 1996; Pollard, 1989; Hoy & Miskell, 1996; Hoy & Tarter, 1997; Hoy, & Hannum, 1997; Singham, 1998; Pierre-Pipkin, 2001; Rapp, 2002; Wood, 2002). The impact of classroom environments on achievement is especially true and apparent for African American and other marginalized urban students, where significant numbers of these students find schools hostile environments; because they are *devalued* by attitudes related directly to race, ethnicity, language, socio-economic status; and in many cases, by their school performances, when found to be lower than their middle-class peers.

A distinction is made between the terms, *school culture* and *school climate* found in the literature; and are often thought to be synonymous. Discussions of *school culture* will not be addressed in this text; except to make this distinction. *School culture* refers to observable behaviors that create "norms" among school personnel, and reflect "the way we do things around here." For example, school personnel may take pride in celebrating special occasions by teachers and other staff wearing clothing with the school's logo; or having a student "dress up day" for special occasions. Some schools may have "zero tolerance" in a disciplinary system; while other schools may use "peer-review panels" that assist in a discipline system. *School culture,* similar to other types of cultures; relates to overall forms of school practices and behaviors that reflect school wide traditions.

School and *classroom climates* refer to *perceptions* of the school and classroom environments by teachers, administrators, students, parents, and other stakeholders. For decades, surveys and studies have shown that in-school environments that are perceived as hostile, distant, and uninviting, have a correspondingly negative impact on student achievement; while classrooms perceived as warm, emotionally supportive; and reflect friendly teacher-student relations, are correlated with positive influences on student achievement.

The impact of classroom environments on learning are explained in studies using the Organizational Climate Descriptive Questionnaire (OCDQ) that analyzes and determines if school climates are *open, closed, engaged* or *disengaged.* Findings from many OCDQ surveys support hypotheses that school climates described as *open* (friendly, warm, inviting, caring) create positive conditions conducive to high levels of student performance (Brookover, 1978; Hoy and Tarter, 1997; Sabo, 1995). *Open school* climates include a high degree of authenticity and congeniality among staff; a positive atmosphere, commitment to students, and advancing school goals (Hoy & Feldman, 1987; Hoy and Tarter, 1997; Hoy & Hannum, 1997).

Sabo (Ibid.) used the OCDQ to examine the quality of student life in middle schools. He theorized that open school climates resulted in student satisfaction regarding commitment to school work, and teacher-student relations. He reasoned that satisfaction would positively impact student achievement; and findings of his research supported his hypothesis. Similarly, in a study of performance among eighth-grade students in six middle schools, Pierre-Pipkin (2001) used the OCDQ to determine the influence of specific demographic and school variables on the achievement of African American students. Demographic variables were socioeconomic status of each school's community (Low income, Middle income, Upper income). School variables were ethnicity of the schools' principal (black, and white); and each school's climate (open, closed, engaged, and disengaged). Two null hypotheses stated that there would be no significant differences in the mean score performances among the middle school students in reading, and in mathematics, as measured by the state's standardized test regarding each variable.

Results revealed various differences in mean scores among the six schools: a 15—17 point mean difference between African American and White students when upper and lower income communities were compared; but little to no variances between mean scores of African American and White students in lower income communities. Data analysis revealed that neither the ethnicity of the principal nor socioeconomic status of the schools' communities was found to be statistically significant in student achievement. For the climate variables (*open, closed, engaged, disengaged*), a statistical difference was found between the four climate groups; *open school climate* was statistically significant with an alpha level of .05; and "school climate" was reflected as the most significant factor that impacted student achievement. In both, reading and mathematics, school climate had a significant and an independent effect on student achievement. While not statistically significant, the socioeconomic status of the schools' communities also, appeared to be a strong indicator of achievement. In higher income schools, student achievement was correlated with higher student performance for African American students, even though they represented 25% or less of the student populations.

Slaughter-Defoe & Garlson (1996) sought to examine perceptions of school climate from primary grade students' perspectives. Their two-year research focused on perceptions of African American and Hispanic students enrolled in James Comer Model School Development Programs (SDP); and students enrolled in non-Comer Model schools. It was hypothesized that students enrolled in Comer schools would report more positive perceptions of school climate, in part because teachers would have less negative attitudes and perceive students more favorably. Their findings determined that African American and Hispanic students appeared to differ in perceptions of teacher treatments. African American students' perceptions indicated teacher-child relationship is an important element in school perceptions; and by contrast, Hispanic students stressed teacher fairness, caring, and praise for their efforts. In the first year, the comparisons in perceptions of students in Comer and non-Comer schools were not found to differ. However, in year two, there were differences in perceptions; with non-Comer students reflecting more favorable responses. The differences were attributed to a multiplicity of external factors that affected both groups of students' perceptions of school climate. The authors suggest that findings should be suggestive, rather than definitive.

While the overall climate of a school is typically reflected throughout an individual school, teachers have considerable autonomy in establishing the climate within individual classrooms (Anderson, 1982; McLaughlin, et al., 1990; Stokes, 2001). *Classroom climate* describes the specific environment within individual classrooms; and is regarded as a major factor in determining whether or not students learn; the degree of content mastery and levels of student performance; and the quality of classroom learning. Different scholars refer to classroom climate by various terms (*personalized classrooms; learner-centered classrooms; personalized environments; learner-friendly classrooms, etc.*); however, the focus is generally on the *conditions for learning* and the affects on student achievement.

Keefe and Jenkins (2002) focused on personalized instruction as the dominant factor in creating effective learning environments. They contend that learning environments should be organized to consider individual student characteristics and needs through flexible instructional practices. Further, classroom activities should be learner-centered and flexible in time, space, and authentic performance-based assessment of student progress. The authors suggest that teachers should create thoughtful environments that provoke information processing; and objectives should be clearly articulated to students. McLaughlin, et al. (1990) employ the definition "personalized school environment;" contending that such environments create an "ethic of caring" that extends beyond formal classroom roles. Schools and classrooms that *personalize* learning environments promote high levels of student commitment and engagement in learning. Further, such environments provide scaffolding from what students know to what they need to know.

Fagarty (1998) discussed classroom climate as a factor to consider in student learning specifically related to instructional delivery; and explained how "intelligence friendly classrooms" bridge theory and practice. He identified several theories of learning, and the implication and application in structuring classrooms environments where all students feel emotionally secure, safe and valued. He argued that learning theories are connected to instructional practice when teachers provide rich learning environments; challenge students; and provide activities for students to transfer knowledge in relevant learning activities. Wubbels, Levy & Brekelmans (1997) presented a different view that complements a methods approach in creating positive classroom climates. Rather than analyzing teacher techniques, they emphasized interpersonal relations between teachers and students as the essential factors in creating positive classroom climates. The authors concluded that effective teachers are perceived as friendlier, and more understanding. They identified two types of teachers: dominant teachers, who are fair and produce high achievers;

and student-oriented teachers, who create warm, shared, affective classroom environments.

Connor, et al. (2009) reported the results of an extensive study involving classroom observation to obtain a picture of the classroom environment at the level of the individual student. The authors used a multidimensional program of videotaping and detailed field notes. They used the *Individualizing Student Instrument* (ISI) system to document that children in the same classroom have very different learning opportunities; that instruction occurs through interactions between teachers and students; and effective instruction depends on knowledge of children's language and literacy skills. They found that effective patterns of instruction and classroom environments depend, specifically, on entry-level skills children bring to the classroom in language, literacy, and self-regulation; and skills differ along a continuum. Thus, effective teachers adjust instruction to accommodate individual differences. Further, direct observations of what takes place in classrooms can better elucidate the important elements of classroom environments that affect student learning and development; thereby results can assist the "design of more effective instructional environments for all children" (p. 95).

Rapp (2002) goes a step further than simply explaining whether *classroom* environments are positive or negative and points to external factors that often *determine* the climate.

For example, Rapp argues that "high-stakes" testing is a significant factor that actually creates stressful classroom climates that have subsequent negative impacts on student achievement. In a Likert-Scale survey he administered to teachers that included items related to classroom climate, 191 board certified teachers in Ohio responded to nine items related to the extent they believed their practices and classroom climates were affected by state education policy. Teachers overwhelmingly believed that high-stakes tests had negatively affected students' "love for learning;" had diminished the quality of education; and had a negative impact on classroom climate.

An essential element in teacher competence centers on two critical factors: knowing and recognizing *conditions for learning;* and the ability to create classroom environments conducive for maximal learning to occur. In fact, the skills and responsibility for doing so cannot, and should not, be viewed as separate and apart from qualifications and effectiveness. Creating positive classroom climates establishes conditions for delivering effective instruction, and ensuring enhanced student learning. Further, it is argued that critical, deliberately specific attention must be given to creating positive learning environments through scaffolding activities of culturally relevant and culturally responsive pedagogy for African American and other urban children; because teachers' perceptions of students undergird the quality of instruction. This is particularly at issue related to students' ethnicity, class, and social status. Teacher behaviors as influencing factors in classroom climates—whether consciously or unconsciously—present often ignored paradigms that either advance or limit opportunities for equity and the quality of student learning.

Educating Children Who Live "Culturally" in Marginalized Communities

The sociopolitical, geopolitical, and socioeconomic structures of American society have substantial flaws and discrepancies; but despite the stratified, typically polarized configurations, the average American, and great majority of Americans, cling wholeheartedly to the lyrics: *My country 'tis of thee, sweet land of liberty.* As Americans, we pledge allegiance to our 21st Century imperfect nation in the mist of continuing racial, economic, and educational inequalities that reflect "persistent disparities" (Darity & Meyers, 1998); a nation that is figuratively defined by Hacker (1992) as "two nations:" one black, one white; hostile, separate and unequal. The good news is that as Americans, we are free to come and go, dwell and work generally, as we please. The bad news is that while there is *freedom* to do pretty much as we desire; a significant number of Americans *technically* do not have choices to live, work or to be educated *pretty much as they perhaps desire.*

This is so because empowerment, or lack of empowerment in social, economic, educational, and political arenas pretty much determines that certain people live, work, and are educated in "marginalized spaces" in American society.

Therefore, since schools are microcosmic representations of the society at large, significant numbers of children—predominantly African American, poor and other ethnic students—are educated in "marginalized places" called urban or inner-city schools. To be clear, many urban schools in America are doing magnificent jobs in educating students (Sizemore, 1989; Trueba, 1977; Reed, et al., 1995; Fine, 1997; The Cognition and Technology Group at Vanderbilt, 1997; Ancess, 2003; Fleming, 2003). However, highly successful urban and inner city schools, among all public schools, are typically the exceptions for many of the reasons previously discussed. The important point emphasized in this current discussion, is to highlight two specific issues: First, schools should be diligent in delivering quality education to all children; and avoid traps of negative attitudes, low expectations, and the misleading characterizations that are attributed to students because of their race, ethnicity, and/or socioeconomic status. Second, a part of removing the plethora of negative stigmas generally associated with diversity among students is to change the "language" used to define or describe children from diverse cultural backgrounds.

We've discussed at length the urgent need to address the inequities of educational opportunities for African American and other urban children; the poor quality of their schooling; and the repressive affects on achievement by traditional mainstream pedagogy and assessment that ignore the importance of the cultural context of learning. When we fundamentally restructure the delivery system to address these critical issues we will better educate all students by focusing on their capabilities; regardless of their ethnicity, or their social and economic statuses. Currently this is not happening. Across America, significant numbers of public schools continue to label and categorize children based mainly on presumptions derived from demographic variables.

It is essential that there is a fundamental shift away from deficit language used to discuss or describe diverse students. Terms typically used to describe students from urban and diverse backgrounds include: *culturally deprived; culturally disadvantaged; at-risk; educationally disadvantaged; economically disadvantaged; lower-class; working-class; impoverished; low-income; under-privileged;* and terms that have surfaced in recent nomenclature: *the under-class,* and *low-performers.* The major problem caused by these terms is the language is misleading; denotes that something is "lacking" in the students; and structures inequalities by the very nature of categorizing children based on comparisons with characteristics of middle-class, mainstream students; the group supposedly representative of where all children should be or strive to be.

Consider what happens, for example, when the label "at-risk" identifies a group of children. The label alone stigmatizes children; and as a consequence tells teachers, parents, and the students, themselves, that their *chances for success* may be highly unlikely, because they simply are of a different culture, live in a particular community, or come from a low-wealth family. Moreover this practice opens the door to the Pygmalion nature of schools and teachers, who may or may not have low expectations for students; but the practice is self-defeating; as well as, self-fulfilling (Cadzen, 1972; Labov, 1986; Kottkamp & Mulhern, 1987; Irvine, 1990; Delpit & Downy, 2002).

Knapp and Woolverton (1995) contend that the plethora of negative titles "have objectified the conception of learner deficit due to low social class as something real and . . . inevitable . . . (T)his objectification of learner deficit slipped in the unconscious assumptions of educators; (and) most teachers automatically assume deficiencies in the skills and abilities of (diverse) . . . students" (p. 559). In the current standards-based, assessment-driven instructional classrooms, students so identified, are pressured into learning isolated, factual, and declarative information through memorization; when their cultural ways of learning require contextual relevance. By underperforming, they fulfill the expected perceptions: that their levels of performances will be less than standard; and the schools' perceptions and subsequent demographic labeling are justified. Therefore, these specifically demographically identified students are "at-risk" of failure regardless of student efforts; opportunities to learn; or the quality of instruction. It's a vicious cycle that Sizemore (2008) calls "walking in circles;" inequity perpetuates itself; and schools need to be aware of this dilemma, and take corrective actions.

As discussed, Hilliard (1995) contends that no child is "deprived of culture;" and the term *cultural deprivation* is a misnomer. Many children may be uninformed and in-experienced in other people's culture, but they know *all of their own* culture. This discrepancy, alone, should be of great concern to educators. Since many African American and other urban children live *culturally different* in socially marginalized spaces, it is not likely that schools will change the nature of their cultural ways of living, knowing, and learning. Therefore, it seems incumbent on educators to find *diverse ways* to teach school content to *diverse learners*—not from a perspective of the dominant culture—but rather, in ways that are relevant to the frame of references these students bring to school.

One term particularly oxymoronic is *educationally disadvantaged*. Why? Because a pre-school child entering kindergarten from an ethnic minority or low-wealth family could be labeled *educationally disadvantaged* before she spends one week in a public school classroom. Thus, by the end of the first year who bears the responsibility if the child is not ready to enter first grade? If she is not, has the school *created* the "educational disadvantage" by failing to teach the child the requisite level of knowledge and skills needed for first grade; or is the child still blamed for being ethnic-minority or poor? The multiplicity of terms listed above implies that students somehow bear the responsibilities for their oppressed, marginalized social and economic statuses (Freire, 2002); and subsequently, their concomitant school labels. These children are expected to bring a particular level or "kind of" social exposure and readiness in order to "fit" into a pre-determined school schema.

Children come to school from different cultures and social backgrounds, and with varying degrees of readiness for academic work; this is a given that educators have been aware of for centuries. Therefore, educators must endeavor to meet students at their entry knowledge levels, and create school environments that are conducive to moving them along a continuum of age-grade expectancies in knowledge and skills; not by consistently pointing out *what they do not know*; which is why schools are created, and why parents send their children to school. Thus, the job of educators is to teach students the information "they do not know;" and to do so without penalizing them for living in *socially marginalized* cultures and circumstances that neither schools nor the students can control. Teachers must render children secure in their abilities to tackle the unknown; and ensure that they receive the emotional and guided support needed to be successful. This can best be accomplished in positively caring, challenging, encouraging learner-centered; and culturally responsive classroom environments.

What Should Teachers Know About the Cultural Nature of "Knowing"?

Every culture has its own history that tells how it arrived at its current social and political state of existence. Its history shaped the ways of living; of what's important to the well being of its members; and the meanings of what is important. Whether or not persons external to the culture agree on what is or is not important to that culture or what *should* be important is a matter of perspective; but each culture tells its own historical story demonstrably in lifestyles, languages, and patterns of knowing. Children from various cultures, who populate schools, unknowingly and perhaps unconsciously, bring with them their historically developed ways of knowing and learning. However, when children from diverse backgrounds walk through most schoolhouse doors, in order to be successful, they must relinquish their patterns of learning, if *how they learn* is incongruent with the teaching and learning styles of most schools. Consequently, until educational systems take seriously, the plethora of literature that "tales" (pun intended) what *should* be important in addressing the particular ways of knowing of diverse children; school success will always favor those for whom current curriculum is written and pedagogy is practiced.

There is general agreement among traditional and contemporary learning theorists that culture plays a role in shaping cognitive development. While theorists may differ on the degree of influence culture has on learning, there is no argument that the immediate environment, and an individual's interaction with others within a culture, form the context for patterns of *how people begin to know,* and how they learn (Hale, 1986, 2001a; Giglioli, 1986; Labov, 1986; Knapp & Woolverton, 1995; Tatum, 1997; Bernstein, 1986; Rogoff & Lave, 1999; Greenfield, 1999; Irvine, 2002; Nieto, 2004; Heath, 2006). Mehler and colleagues (1995) find that although a body of social knowledge is generally available to most adults within a society; any variances in how people express the same body of knowledge can be attributed to cultural differences.

The question then is "What specifically explains cognitive development in social contexts?" First we must define what it means to be *culturally socialized.* Bernstein (1986) contends that "(S)ocialization refers to the process whereby the biological is transformed into a specific cultural being" (p. 162). This means that agents of socialization are family, peer groups, school, work and community. The implication regarding cognitive development related to "knowing" is that learning is an intricate part of being socialized; thus children learn and are socialized in the contextualized environments into which they are born and live their daily lives. Rogoff and Lave (1999) explain that context plays a significant role in socially developed cognition; that cognitive activity is socially defined, interpreted, and supported by interactions among people; and is guided by social norms. Further, in order to understand thought processes, one must attend to both the content and context of intellectual activity. For instance, a child may have difficulty solving in-school tasks that are spontaneously accomplished in everyday contexts; e.g., the child may find difficulty in dividing the number 8 by the number 2, presented in a paper-pencil task; but can easily and spontaneously divide 8 play items so he and his playmate each have 4 items.

Rogoff and Lave caution, however, that it should not be assumed that *real* cognitive abilities are only found in natural environments; nor can it be assumed that the *context* of an activity does not affect the activity, itself. They conclude that cognition develops in the social orchestration between culture and context; and that content of any activity can be "aided," as well as "constrained" by context. Therefore, teachers should understand that learners must be able to generalize some aspects of knowledge and skills to new situations.

Hale (1986) supports the concept of socially influenced cognition. She argues that awareness and attention should be given to the *content* and the *context* of intellectual activity in order to understand thought processes. She posits that teachers must gain insight into the ways Black children learn; and have an understanding of relations between culture and thinking. Also, teachers must develop an appropriate psychological theory of learning that encompasses knowledge of the social, historical, and cultural forces that affect the learning styles shaped by the Black community. One means of providing culturally responsive instruction is to "recast" content that reflects the local world-and-life views of these children.

Knapp and Woolverton (1995) addressed the cultural nature of knowing from a social class perspective. They contend that regardless of formal schooling, children learn language and behaviors that eventually allow participation in adult roles of their specific communities; that "class-based conditions offer varying degrees of material security which influence children's physical reality and attendant anxiety or contentment; (thus) . . . in the broadest sense, children are taught by the culture of family and community how to think, behave, and communicate" (p. 558). They conclude:

> Students walking through a classroom door are entering a well-established culture complete with linguistic codes, behavioral expectations, and assumptions about the nature of teaching and learning. (Further,) most of these communications and behavioral codes reflect the values, power dynamics, and knowledge base of mainstream middle- or upper-class cultures . . . The degree to which learners' linguistic and behavioral codes and expectations differ from those of the mainstream determine the degree of incongruity and the probability that these students will do poorly in mainstream schools (Ibid.).

Cultural Relevance in Practice

What is culture; and why is it important to focus on culture in school learning? The concept of culture is explained through various social and Socio-Historical theories that are congruent, overlap, or diverge. Some theorists think of culture in terms of being descriptive rather than something that lends itself to definition. Others find definition in contending that social practices among various culture groups delineate behaviors, customs and traditions, beliefs, and influences that are definitive in explaining culture.

Geertz (1973) addressed culture making several points: the nature of culture; the role culture plays in social life; and how culture should be studied. He posits, ". . . The concept of culture is essentially a semiotic one (as Max Weber believes):

> . . . man is an animal suspended in webs of significance he himself has spun. . . . (Further,) culture is one of those webs, and the analysis of it therefore, not to be an experimental science in search of law but an interpretative one in search of meaning (p. 5).

Gay (2000) states: "Culture, like any other social or biological organism, is multidimensional and continually changing . . . (As) manifested in expressive behaviors, culture is influenced by a wide variety of factors, including time, setting, age, economic and social circumstances . . ."(p. 10). Rogoff (2003) contends that the concept of culture can be explained though human development in cultural contexts. She maintains that human development is a cultural process, and "people develop as participants in cultural communities . . . (understood) in light of cultural practices and circumstances of (their) communities . . ." (pp. 3-4).

Giroux (1997) makes the case for the construction of meaning in cultural forms; and finds that: "Human agents always mediate the representations and material practices that constitute their lived experiences through their own histories and their cross- and gender-related subjectivities; (and this) is true within the parameters defined by school, the family, the workplace, or any other social site" (p. 87). Giroux argues, also, that marginalized students are socially positioned, because of the power structures in society. Similarly, Greenfield and Cocking (1996) consider the material or ecological/ economic side of culture being the conditions; that "the need to create meaning intrinsic to all human culture means that these different adaptations are reflected in different value orientations, the symbolic side of culture" (p. 4). Also, that the key to understanding culture is that it is intergenerational and transmitted through the socialization process. Thus in the broadest sense, "socialization process includes informal education in the family as well as formal education" (p. 4). Hollis (1996) looked at culture related to school learning and reasoned that several definitions can explain the central aspects in school learning. She identified several descriptive types of related cultures: artifact and behavior; social and political relationships; and affect, behavior, and intellect.

A significant body of sciocultural theory supports the position that schools should employ practices that connect the cultural experiences of marginalized children to the discipline knowledge they are expected to learn. King and colleagues (1997) provide clarity on the cultural aspect of instruction by explaining: "Culturally relevant education is defined as a pedagogy that incorporates the language and culture of linguistic minority students into the educational process" (p. 40). Okihiro (1994) pointed this out in his examination of the margins of historical consciousness; and contended that marginalized people have drawn people of a nation together; (thus), "ethnic studies began as an alternative vision of American history and culture that was (meant to be) broadly inclusive" (p. 150).

Culturally Responsive Pedagogy

Specific issues of what teachers need to know about the social nature of cognitive development is discussed by Greenfield (1999) in positing a Vygotskian approach to closing the gap between task requirements, and the skill levels of learners. Greenfield suggests that scaffolding proposed by Vygotsky, addresses *what* teachers need to know:

- *What* a student can do, *when* they can do; and *what* *assistance* may be needed;

- *Understand* that regardless of age, culture, native language, or skill levels; when learners are aided by teacher-mediated scaffolding, all learners can advance to higher levels of knowledge and skills; and

- Scaffolding extends the range of abilities of learners, and allows them to perform tasks otherwise not individually possible.

Stated differently, students must have a "frame of reference" to connect new information and concepts to the mental images (pictures) they have stored in their minds; and understanding may not be possible apart from being interpreted, and modeled by the teacher through scaffolding activities (Pierre-Pipkin, 2008).

Similarly, Nieto (1999) suggests that teachers should see the relations between culture and learning. From a Vygotskian perspective, if culture forms and influences how a learner thinks through social mediation, then classroom conditions can be created to help most students learn. Moreover, learning cannot be separated from the context in which it takes place. The author advises that learning should not be thought of in terms of mastery of skills; i.e., the transmission of information from teachers to students. Nieto argued: "Learning develops primarily from the social relationships and actions of individual that take place within particular sociopolitical contexts" (p. 11). Consequently, it is important for teachers to be aware of the influence that social contexts have on learning to better inform how to *understand students*; how students learn in out-of-school environments; and subsequently, how to teach them.

Lee (2005b) explored the social context of learning from a historical perspective related specifically to education of African Americans. She discussed the link of the cognitive goals of schooling, with cultural and political empowerment goals; and how the state of research knowledge on learning intersects with cultural orientations of many researchers of color. She found that views of Black children in traditional research typically reflect a deficit perspective; particularly positing that African American children often have inadequate amounts of declarative knowledge and readiness for school as preschoolers; and much is blamed on parenting skills. However, the author points to studies that show, "Black infants come into the world well-equipped to learn" (p. 47). Moreover, the perspectives of Black psychologists, who advocate the significance of social contexts of learning encompassed in sociocultural theories, are not reflected in mainstream literature. The author identifies several overarching themes among sociocultural theories; and the relevance of cultural contexts in classroom practices: *learning potential; the role of prior knowledge;* and *the social contexts of learning.*

Regarding *learning potential,* Lee contends that no class or group of people has more or less capacity for learning; and the premise that cognition is determined solely by genetics is not the substantive basis for differences in test score achievement. Secondly, it is widely accepted in the research literature that *prior knowledge* influences learning. As such, teachers should provide learners with the "conceptual or mental models . . . to filter new knowledge . . . (and) when learning environments do not provide explicit opportunities . . . (often students') misconceptions of the new target knowledge . . . remain stable even after extensive teaching to the contrary" (p. 60).

The *social context for learning* can be addressed by employing sociocultural learning theory to inform effective instructional design and classroom practices. From Lee's (Ibid.) perspective, several practices are applicable:

- *scaffolding;*
- *apprenticeship;* and
- *guided participation.*

According to the author, s*caffolding* is based in Vygotskian theory of interactive learning; and Werth's concepts of cross-cultural studies of cognition in contexts. Teachers can employ cultural themes in scaffolding; and as mediating factors to provide more in-depth learning. For example, use of oral storytelling styles and topic-centered instruction.

Apprenticeship is a metaphor for the negotiated forms of social organization typically reflected in the interdependent nature of African American cultures. This refers to the structures of the extended family, networks, the Black church, and use of language in everyday practices. Lee warns that teachers should focus on "analysis of cultural behaviors;" rather than on presumed behaviors because of students' membership in a specific culture.

Guided participation involves the various roles by persons involved in learning activities. Attention is given to the interaction between a learner and other people; usually a teacher; or more knowledgeable peers. Teachers must be aware that learning does not occur in isolation by individuals; this is supported by a body of research on "social interaction in classrooms related to educating African American students" (p. 66).

The Role of Group Dynamics in Situated Teaching and Learning

Psychologist, Kurt Lewin, is known as the father of group dynamics; but the name, *Carl Rogers,* is most often associated with group dynamics in contemporary American literature. Although Rogers' attention does not focus exclusively on educational institutions specifically related to classroom dynamics, or on teacher-student groups; much of what Rogers (1970) explains of encounter group behaviors can be usefully adopted in analyzing interactions of teachers and students in classroom settings. Rogers does not define, but rather, describes what is meant by an encounter group; mainly because each *individual group* typically differs from other groups; yet certain trends are evident among groups. Thus, the description is of "observable events; . . . the way in which events seem to cluster . . . (and) certain threads which weave in and out of the pattern" of behaviors (p. 16).

Rogers explains a series of behaviors among group members that begin with initial confusion, awkwardness, silence, and polite interactions. Initially there is no structure; people do not know their purpose; and there is no commitment to other persons. As the length of time members spend together increases, medial behaviors occur that include progressing from expressing public feelings, to expressing private feelings. Concluding or exit behaviors of group members involve feelings of trust toward other group members; individual members self-acceptance; accepting feedback from others; and expressions of positive feelings and closeness "in group spirit." The following example adapted by Pierre-Pipkin describes group behaviors in an airport include the three stages of group dynamics:

- Stage I—Confusion; awkwardness; silence; politeness.
- Stage II—Expressions of public; the private feelings.
- Stage III—Feelings of trust and closeness; self acceptance and group spirit.

Group Dynamics: Implications for Classroom Discourse

A group of individuals sitting in an airport terminal, waiting to board the same airplane flight ordinarily do not know each other, yet they are a participatory group because they share an event—waiting to board the same flight. Thus, the first stage of group dynamics described by Rogers (1970) is evident; that of awkwardness, silence, and polite interactions. This scenario describes the first level of group encounter; or the *primary stage* of group dynamics.

If the time for boarding the flight is delayed—for instance—by an announcement that the departure time is extended because of weather conditions; this means that the passengers will spend more time together. During this time, people may begin conversations with each other; or may share momentary statements of frustrated feelings because of the delay. A toddler may start to cry, and someone offers the mother a cookie for the toddler. Two persons seated next to each other discover they are going to the same town; or others may find that they are going to separate graduations, weddings, or family reunions. At this point group members have begun to share public feelings and the group has evolved into what is described as a *secondary stage* of group dynamics.

The longer the group waits to board the flight, expressions may evolve into feelings of trust and group "membership;" and eventually private expressions, as the group evolves into a *tertiary stage* of group dynamics. When the announcement is heard that the flight has finally arrived and is readied for boarding, typically a "unitary" applause (or other exclamation) is heard from the group. This spontaneous behavior further represents a "common connection" because each passenger "shares" the momentary feeling of relief, or "group-spirit" that the wait is over. Had the wait for the passengers been only a very short time span, this unitary response would possibly not have happened. When passengers finally board the plane, the group reverts back into *secondary*, and then *primary stages* of interactions (Pierre-Pipkin, 2004a; 2007; 2008).

This example is the basis for a discussion of whether the process of group dynamics can be effectively applied in classroom settings. This text argues that until a tertiary level of classroom dynamics has been created, many students will not fully benefit from introductory instruction; because a "shared level," unity, or "group spirit" of communication, or receptiveness to instruction and to others is lacking.

Rogers explains both the dangers and advantages of encounter group application; but that one of the most important implications is that it helps the individual as well as institutions in adapting to change. He states: "What we need in fact is not changed institutions but a changingness built into institutional life: an instrument for continued renewal of organizational form and institutional structure and policies" (p. 178). Using his position as foundational, an argument is presented for a theoretical approach to analyzing classroom dynamics to better inform teachers of the importance of understanding students' classroom interactions; and the various stages of classroom group dynamics. Rogers points out, teachers must be able to handle interpersonal, intergroup, and interracial tensions in classrooms; conflict between students, teachers and other school personnel; and individual human feelings in everyday life (See also: Bigelow, et al., 2001; Cazden, 1972).

Classroom Dynamics

The interactions of students who compose a classroom group can be viewed as a community of practice; and group behaviors are conditioned by participation within the group. Moreover, student behaviors help to shape the group's dynamics based on past experiences and the cultural capital each student brings to the classroom. Educational researchers of the cultural nature of learning; and theorists who espouse the sociocultural nature of human behavior explain the flow of communication among individuals, and the importance of understanding the complexity that exists as various diverse groups interact in situated circumstances (King, et al., 1997; Rogoff and Lave, 1999; Gay, 2002; Comber & Simpson, 2001; Irvine, 2003; Lave and Wenger, 2003; Ares, 2006). Often the school classroom is not thought of in terms of being a community of practice; and as such, in the initial stages of classroom instruction, most teachers simply "begin instruction" with no conscious awareness of the need to allow individual student members to progress though a minimum of a secondary stage of dynamic interactions. It is therefore argued that students are not likely to be receptive to instructions, or to understand subject content until a level of comfort in group interactions and communications has been established. Moreover, in cases where this foundational dynamic has not been created, or allowed to evolve—especially for students from diverse backgrounds who need an initial transition period to establish a grounding for understanding communications from teachers, and students of different cultures—these students find themselves playing catch-up from day one; and subsequently, significant numbers never do (Boykin & Bailey, 2000; Boykin, et al., 2004). The following discussions highlight various perspectives of classroom inter-group communications, and the concept of classroom dynamics in communities of practice.

In her book: *Why Are All the Black Kids Sitting Together in the Cafeteria?* Tatum (1997a) establishes a framework for an understanding of group dynamics in classrooms. She explains a factor often avoided or ignored: group interactions in the context of race relations. She presents a compelling argument of the significance of understanding racial identity theory; and the salient nature of racial issues that impact racially-mixed classroom dynamics. The author contends that much of identity theory is confined in scholarly journals; and seldom do teachers deal with the complexities of racial or ethnic identity development because, "a psychological understanding of cross-racial interaction has been noticeable absent from public discourse" (p. xvi). Consequently, many important questions go unanswered. In response to the question contained in the title of her book about black students "clustering" as a group, she notes that seldom is a similar inquiry posed of white children who exhibit the same tendencies. Also noted, is that as students advance to higher grades, the greater and more spontaneous the tendency of their clustering in racial peer groups. Further, school practices of ability grouping and tracking where Black students are more likely than other racial groups to be grouped in lower tracked classes that are racially identifiable, send environmental and institutional cues to diverse students. Tatum posits that the need of students to explore self-identity with others who are engaged in a similar process (e.g., school and classroom activities), is manifested "informally in school corridors and cafeterias across the country" (p. 71). She argues that schools must provide adolescents with identity-affirming experiences and information about their particular cultures and experiences; and efforts or activities should be deliberate, informative cultural programs from a historical perspective.

Gay (2002) analyzed ethnic interactions and classrooms communication; cultural communicative styles; discourse dynamics of who participates, under what conditions; how patterns of participation are affected by cultural socialization; and how interactive communications influence teaching and learning in classrooms. The author found that students of color are more traditional in their communication styles related to their cultures and ethnicity; but are likely to encounter obstacles to achievement when they do not " . . . think, behave, and express themselves in ways that approximate mainstream cultural norms" (p. 78). Thus, in the absence of shared communication frames of references, teachers may not fully understand the intellectual abilities of diverse students; and will not be able to fully access, or facilitate most of what these students know and can do. This is further explained through the principle of "linguistic relativity" that the author defines as language that reflects cultural patterns, and in turn how people understand and respond to social phenomena. Gay posits: "Communication is dynamic, interactive, irreversible, and invariably contextual . . . (and) governed by rules of social and physical contexts in which it occurs" (p. 74). The author stresses the importance of understanding that the relationship of language, thought, and behavior extends beyond reporting experiences; but rather, communications through language is a "way of defining experiences, thinking and knowing . . . (because language is used to) code, analyze, categorize, and interpret experiences" (p. 80).

Communities of Practice

Everything that happens in classrooms is not always under the strict control of a teacher as pointed out by Cazden (1998), hooks (1994), and Bizzell (1994); because the discourse in communities of practice has a dynamic all its own that is created by all participants; the teacher, as well as the students. Bizzell writes of a discourse community in college composition instruction; but her discussion of academic discourse can be used to explain what it means to be a community of practice in any classroom setting. She defines a discourse community as "A group of people who share certain language-using practices" (p. 222). She explains two conventions of a discourse community. First, a stylistic convention regulates the internal and external interactions of its members. Second, language use as social behavior, conveys canonical knowledge of the world view of its members and regulates how members interpret experiences; similar to that of an "interpretive community." Thus a discourse community is bound together primarily, by its use of language; even though factors as geography, socioeconomics, and ethnicity, also unite the members. The key to understanding a discourse community is to know that whether or not members are aware that they function in a community of practice, there is a built-in dynamic that is shaped by socioeconomic and cultural inputs; and subsequently shapes individual world views. Elements identified within a discourse community include determining the stylistic convention and canonical knowledge; and identifying the appropriate pedagogy to initiate newcomers to the discourse community.

Teaching as a linguistic process in cultural settings is the focus of Cazden's (1988) treatment of classroom discourse. The goal is to seek insight by understanding social events in classrooms that impact cognition; and which students learn. The author draws attention to the differences of spoken language in social setting in public places, such as crowded subways or waiting stations; and language spoken in classroom settings.

In community public places, simultaneous conversations take place; but in classrooms, one person—usually the teacher—is responsible for controlling who talks and when. Cazden points out that classroom language is problematic because in a laboratory context, it may be least obvious that "spoken language is an important part of the identities of all participants" (p. 3); and there are many variations of language that occur in classroom communication systems. Therefore it is important to understand three communication features of classroom life: language of curriculum; language of control; and language of personal identity. These can be defined as propositional, social, and expressive functions; and thus the study of classroom language is essentially, "The study of situated language use in one social setting" (p. 3). It can be surmised that the implications for understanding classroom dynamics is to address specific questions:

- How do patterns of language use affect what counts as "knowledge" and what occurs as learning?

- How do these patterns affect equality and inequality of students' educational opportunities?

- What communicative competence do these patterns presume and/or foster? (Bullets added., pp. 3-4)

Ares (2006) uses Putney and Floriani's explanation in describing classroom dynamics: "As teachers and students work together in a dynamic way, their knowledge of academic content and patterned ways of acting are transformed as they construct a community of practice" (p. 7). The diversity of student cultures represented in classrooms—especially when diverse groups represent urban, ethnic minority and other marginalized populations—presents a challenge that increases the dynamics of teacher and student classroom communications and interactions. Therefore, unfortunately, as Vasquez (2006) points out; when diversity is perceived as a deficit factor, rather than an intricate parcel of the social unit of communities of practice; effective teaching and learning are further challenged, and often compromised.

Thus, keen awareness of diversity provides opportunities for teachers to create environments where the cultural resources students bring to the classroom can be marshaled to obtain optimal achievement in communities of practices, as well as through *unity of efforts*. First, teachers must be able to identify, interpret, and incorporate students' cultural funds of knowledge into the instructional program; and build contexts that link their experiences to classroom learning. Teachers must also understand that learning is not a benign activity, but includes conflict, tensions, and contradictions. Understanding how individual actors relate to conflicting cultural norms in the classroom, and providing opportunities for all students to confront, deal with, and resolve discontinuities as members of the community of practice, recognize the sociocultural nature of classroom dynamics among diverse learners; and structure a framework for teachers to understand, manage, and facilitate development of all students in the instructional process (Irvine, 1990; Fine, 1997; Engle, 1998; Hull and Schultz, 2001 & 2003; Gee, 2004).

What is Situational Teaching and Learning?

Previous discussions involved social practice theory posed by Lave & Wenger (2003), which explains individual learning as participation in communities of practice; the impact of culture on in-school learning; and other concepts of the influences of cultural experiences on cognition of individual learners. Lave & Wenger state: "(A) theory of social practice emphasizes the relational interdependence of agent and world, activity, meaning, cognition, learning, and knowing. It . . . emphasizes the inherently socially negotiated character of meaning and the interested, concerned character of the thought and action of persons-in-activity" (p. 50). The authors contend it is important to note that social practice or situational learning is a "circumstance," not a method or technique; but rather "an analytical viewpoint on learning; . . . (and) a way of understanding learning" (p. 40).

While the authors make a distinction between individual learning, and learning as participation in the social world; this discussion emphasizes the situatededness of learning in regards to the influence of the "classroom environment" on interdependent learning. This means that learning, thinking, and knowing that take place in a social and cultural world is an interactive process that shapes individual learning; and in turn, an individual in a particular setting is a constitutive element of the situation. Thus, classrooms are particular kinds of social contexts; and the dynamics within a classroom are mutually constituted with each element affecting all other elements in the interactions.

For the purpose of this text, the concept of situatededness in teaching and learning addresses what takes place in the classroom, and specific elements that are in play—whether spontaneously dynamic, or by instructional design—and includes:

- Classroom climate created by all actors through interactive participation;

- Learning as reciprocal knowledge sharing between students and the teacher;

- Relations between individual students and their classmates; and

- The kinds of classroom conditions and situations that provide opportunities that either enhance or restrain student learning.

Teachers must be sensitive to, and constantly aware of how classroom practices affect the interactive nature of classroom dynamics; what practices propel learning or present barriers; and strive for active, contributory participation by all students as members of a learning community.

Transformative Practices and Classroom Climate

Ares (2006) advocates implementing critical theory in teaching practices that create positive classroom dynamics. She argues that three generative processes occur in classroom communities: *autonomy, responsibility*; and *contributions* that provide opportunities for classroom practices to be connected to the goals of transformative learning. These practices can change the "learning environments to engage students in authentic practices of communities . . ." (p. 2). Further, critical theory practices provide opportunities for classroom activities to become more central for all students; allow access to legitimate participation in culturally valued activities; and opportunities for student autonomy, responsibilities; and student contributions through their cultural capital of language and experiences. Thereby, transformative practices become a general rather than an alternative pedagogy.

The difficulties in transformative practices lie in implementation because critical practices are not generally defined, accepted; or framed in mainstream cultural and political contexts. Moreover, most teachers have limited knowledge of the out-of-school lives of diverse learners upon which to build curriculum and instructional contexts. Further, transformative practices are inconsistent with teacher preparation training programs; challenges language, power, and lifestyles of the mainstream; and theorists have typically avoided or ignored critical practice theory for many of these reasons (Ibid.).

Similar to the question discussed by Tatum (1997a & 1997b) of why the Black kids tend to "cluster" in identifiable groups, the question now becomes: *What happens to the White kids when the focus turns to culturally responsive teaching?* The answer is an expansion of opportunities to learn about other cultures; as well as understanding more of the nature of their own cultures; and how classroom demographics reflect the globally diverse world in which all students will eventually negotiate. Often the perception is that culturally responsive education focuses "only" on African American students; and the word "diverse" is ignored. However, others write extensively of many cultural groups, including Hispanic, Native American, Puerto Rican, Asian, and other immigrant children; and how they are often marginalized in public schools (Flores, 1977; Sotomayor, 1991; Okihiro, 1994; Wu, 2002; Nogurera, 2006; See, also: Banks & Banks (Eds.), 1995 & 2004). Carruthers (1999) points out that the infusion of multicultural curriculum is only one aspect of bringing clarity to the importance of addressing diversity; and maintains, that "the inclusion must occur in all disciplines and grade levels of the curriculum and in the development of basic skills and cognitive thinking" (p. 87).

What is emphasized in culturally responsive teaching is articulated in the companion text previously cited: It's not a matter of "either-or" to focus exclusively on one specific cultural group at the expense of other students; but rather, for school practices and teaching to be more inclusive; not simply to *recognize*, but to seriously *address* "diversity." The goal is for education and schooling to consider the significant numbers of marginalized students within American public schools, who, historically, have not been given the attention needed to be academically successful (Pierre-Pipkin, 2004a & 2007).

Resistance to Transformative Practices

Huber, et al. (1997) comment on culturally "responsible" pedagogy and the position taken by Urbanski; that today's schools are often viewed as not being as good as schools of yesterday. They argue, however, it is not that schools are not as good; but rather, it's that schools are the "same" as they once were; with unexamined traditional delivery systems that mirror the status quo; and have not dealt with the changing demographics of school populations or with cultural diversity. Huber and colleagues make a strong case for culturally sensitive and responsible pedagogy to maximize learning; positing that "culturally responsible pedagogy is not color-bound or language-specific; but subsumes all diversities to ensure sensitivity to and responsibility for all learners" (p. 131).

Ares (2006) poses an essential question that has implications for culturally responsive instruction: *How do you move from critical thought to critical practice?* She points out that this can be done by focusing attention on social behaviors in sociocultural and situated learning theories that seek to understand classroom practices as ". . . systems that are culturally, socially and historically constructed . . ." (p. 3). She argues that teachers must have a foundation in learning theory that provides an "anchoring framework for translating thought into action" (Ibid.) Further, sociocultural and situated learning theories provide a framework for examining interdependent action in identifying processes that assist in transforming conventional classroom practices. This includes classroom dynamics among diverse students that can mirror their world experiences. It is cautioned that critical theory practice does not advocate that a prescriptive, technical, or sequential process has to replace daily teaching practices; "but rather, this can lead to an understanding of the dynamic structures that operate in classrooms that either reproduce or transform oppressive, monoculture pedagogies" (p. 5).

261

Writing from the perspective of college or university teaching, bell hooks (1994) argues that any approach to depart from traditional pedagogy is generally resisted; and historically the majority of students learn though conservative, educational practices that typically focus on the professor; with little attention to the influences that students bring to the classroom situation. She contends that there must be ongoing recognition of the dynamics that result from contributions of all participants. Further, when used constructively, the resources of student contributions create open learning communities; and enhance the likelihood that collective efforts not only create, but also sustain learning communities. Referencing Freire's "banking system" of education that is rooted in the notion that students need only consume, memorize, and store information; the author posits that learning must be dynamic with students as active participants rather than simply passive consumers of information. (H)ooks concludes that educators must combine "theory and practice" to demonstrate pedagogical practices that create new language, decentralize authority; and rewrite institutional discursive and political conditions in teaching.

Unfortunately, the same resistance to critical theory practices occurs in public schools (Simon, 1992; Ares, 2006; Johnson 1990; Wise, 1990). Teachers trained in conventional preservice college and university programs typically approach elementary and secondary classroom instruction in the manner in which they were taught; using didactic pedagogy, and a "banking system" of teaching. Little emphasis is given to theories such as *culturally responsive* practices that elucidate the negotiated roles and contribution of ideas, divisions of work functions that generate school-based cooperative learning. Ares (Ibid.) posits that simply identifying transformative practices is not sufficient to truly "understand how transformative teaching and learning are either facilitated or stymied in classrooms" (p. 5). She identifies with Ladson-Billings' definition of what constitutes culturally relevant critical theory practices: "Culturally relevant pedagogy rests on three criteria or propositions: students must experience academic success; students must develop and/or maintain cultural consciousness; and students must develop a critical consciousness through which they challenge the status quo of the current social order" (p. 6).

It is noted that sociocultural theories focus mainly on development of individuals learning in cultural contexts. Situated learning theories concentrate on the *circumstances* that explain human action with others; behavior in communities; and examine participants' evolving membership in communities of practice (Gearing & Sangree, et al. 1979; Battistich, et al, 1995; Giroux, et al., 1983; Giroux, 1997 & 1997a; Morris, 2002; Lave & Wenger, 2003; Warren, 2005).

Connecting Theory to Situated Teaching and Learning

The discussions on classroom dynamics highlight how every group—whether publically social, communally spontaneous or constructed in school settings—has its own "built-in" dynamic. Therefore, the discussions are meant to be informative, and not an attempt to prescribe specific methodologies of how individual teachers should address classroom dynamics that are spontaneously created in his or her classroom. The essential issues for teachers to be aware of include:

- First, teachers must recognize and understand that the dynamics created in classrooms are inevitable elements of group interactions;

- Second, teachers must recognize how their particular modeling behaviors, perceptions of diverse students, and teaching practices influence, and often determine, whether classroom dynamics contribute to enhanced learning or stifle student achievement; and

- Finally, teachers must focus on managing, guiding, and utilizing the "circumstances" created by classroom dynamics in a way that allows all students to be culturally affirmed; contributors to knowledge building; and members of a community of shared classroom knowledge and successes.

How this is done depends on the teacher's creativity and commitment to student success by teaching for understanding.

Teachers can *design* instruction to connect *thought to practice.* This is specifically accomplished through activities of critical transformative sociocultural and situated activities that create open, challenging, learner-centered classroom environments. Astute teachers employ the *community nature* of classroom dynamics, and student diversity to design instruction conducive to optimal learning opportunities for all students. Moreover, effective teachers know and understand what responsibilities and behaviors are critical for transformative practices. First, teachers become agents of change. They become what Gay (2002) describes as cultural *organizers, mediators*, and *orchestrators.*

According to Gay, teachers who function as *cultural organizers*, understand how culture operates in daily classroom dynamics; and have the ability to create classroom climates that radiate cultural and ethnic diversity, and enhance academic achievement for all students. A *culturally mediating* teacher provides opportunities for critical dialogue among students about conflicts in cultures through activities that analyze inconsistencies between mainstream cultural ideals/realities and those of different cultural systems; thereby culturally diverse learners can celebrate and affirm each other and work collaboratively for mutual success. Teachers, who are *cultural orchestrators* of social contexts for learning, recognize the important influence culture has on learning and make teaching processes compatible with the sociocultural contexts and frames of reference of ethnically diverse learners. Gay concludes that culturally responsive pedagogy is not set apart from ongoing instruction; but rather, develops simultaneously, "along with academic achievement, social consciousness and critique, cultural affirmation, competence, and exchange . . ." (p. 43). It incorporates legitimate, accurate cultural knowledge about different ethnic groups into all subjects and skills taught.

Rogoff & Lave (1999), and Lave & Wenger's (2003) concept of *situated* learning explains that it not a methodology, or teaching strategy; but is a way of understanding learning that focuses on "circumstances" of interaction between a learner and the environment. However, this text extends their postulate regarding situated "circumstances;" and departs from their concepts of *situational learning;* to propose that *situational teaching* and *learning* can be either spontaneous, or by design. This means that contexts can be "created or constructed circumstances" in which teaching and learning occur. Extensive discussions of this postulate are included in the companion application text. Briefly, the following points are made:

- Situational teaching and learning are addressed when teachers utilize classroom *dynamics of the moment* that are *spontaneous*, referred to as "teachable moments." This means to utilize an event, a statement, or a "circumstance," that happens during instruction that may be relevant and applicable to the content or concepts under discussion.

- Situational teaching and learning can be *by design*; either by the teacher or learner-created circumstances (group projects; demonstrations; or metaphors) in which the content is "contextualized" in various and different formats for students to articulate and demonstrate understanding of concepts and content.

- Similar to the previous bullet, students' out-of-school knowledge and experiences can create *situations* and circumstances to culturally contextualized content.

- Teachers, who are acutely aware of the various learning styles of students, provide activities and instructional formats that allow students to use their strength learning modalities to demonstrate capabilities in knowledge and skills in various contexts of extended activities. The *situational circumstance* is that different students may demonstrate abilities in activities and formats quite different from others; but all students are provided *situations* in which they are not penalized by having to conform to a "standard" method of demonstrating competences (Pierre-Pipkin, 2004a; 2007).

It is important to repeat the caution of Lee (2005a), that teachers should approach an understanding of student learning styles analytically rather than categorically; thereby presuming all students of a particular ethnic group share the same learning styles and experiences.

Hale's study (1986) points this out by showing what may be analyzed as "typical of" but not "exclusive to" a particular ethnic group. Her findings revealed that children develop culturally specific cognitive styles through the socialization they receive from families and peer groups; and identified by two types of family structures: the "formal style" and the "fluid style." Children who participate in formal structures develop analytical cognitive styles of learning; and children who live in families identified as "fluid" or "shared-functions" are more likely to utilize relational cognitive styles. She found the "shared-functions" style was typical of low-wealth communities, and is different from middle-class groups. Critical functions are periodically performed or shared by all members in a fluid-identified group. Although not exclusively confined to a particular ethnic or social group, fluidity appears to be associated more closely with African American socialization practices that include movement, episodic, mini-climaxes; and open-ended practices. Compared to Western cognitive styles, which are linear, progressive, and demand closure type practices that are "analytical;" African-American socialization practices are circular, rational, and reflect interdependent and co-responsibilities. Having an awareness of these distinctions can assist and augment teacher abilities to create classroom environments of *situational* teaching and learning that are continuously deliberate in addressing the needs, cognitive styles, and cultural capital of all students; thereby, enhancing the quality and effectiveness of instruction and subsequently, the achievement of culturally diverse students.

Ancess (2003) finds that all too often,

> (T)eachers' middle-class values, which emphasize individuals acting in their own self-interest independent of a cultural context, often leave (us) blind to the realities of (our) students' lives . . . (S)tudents are individuals who are engaging in ongoing dialogues with their communities and their families as they are trying to make sense of what is happening in their lives and plan for their future (p. 163).

It is therefore not surprising, that among the plethora of responsibilities teacher must juggle in instructional delivery, concentrating on "transformative culturally responsive" aspects of pedagogy is often thought of as optional; or an alternative practice that has no immediate or significant impact on student learning. However, the abundant sociocultural literature reveals just the opposite; that the very reason so many African American and other marginalized children continue to be "left behind" in public schools is primarily because of the lack of attention to diversity—both consciously and unconsciously; and the monoculture curriculums, pedagogy, and sociopolitical practices of public schooling.

To be change agents, teachers must be what comedians quip as *all of that and a bag of potato chips, too*. Teachers must be magicians; they must wear many hats; must juggle many things at once; and must have a bag of full "surprises" to keep students interested and engaged. Teachers must be ringmasters of three-ring circuses: they must know where all the performers are; when they are to come into the center ring, what acts they are to perform; and simultaneously, know what's going on in the two side rings. Teachers must be orchestra conductors: they must know the various instruments; how various performers are to play each instrument of the composition; must ensure that no one instrument stands out to suppress others; so that the *unity of efforts* of all performers renders a beautiful concert.

Teachers who do "all of this" on a daily basis to deliver effective instruction that reaches all students are to be applauded and supported; because students, as recipients of their efforts, are the benefactors. Teachers who are still struggling need to be supported, trained, mentored, and encouraged so that the children they teach are provided effective, quality, and equitable education.

CHAPTER SIX

Summary, Conclusions, and Recommendations

The future may be beyond our vision; but it is not completely beyond our control.
__ Senator Edward M. "Ted" Kennedy

SUMMARY

There is always the hope that what is being done can be viewed from a different, perhaps clearer perspective; can perhaps be improved; can be more than simply extended or enhanced, but rather, that what is being done is the most effective means of accomplishing a goal. Educational reforms contain this hopefulness, with goals of providing the most effective means of schooling. While most educational reforms are visionary and optimistic, often many unforeseen circumstances shift the focus; or blind us to the full range of insightfulness needed to address fundamental critical issues in accomplishing those goals. Shortfalls in current educational reforms include the failure to critically, realistically, or successfully, address issues of cultural diversity as a means of providing equality of opportunities for all students; and dealing with issues related to the negative impact "high-stakes" testing has on the specific populations that restructuring attempts to assist. Consequently, many reforms have not well-served significant numbers, in fact most, African American and other urban students who continue to populate the bottom rungs

271

of every ladder with respect to academic performance within a two-tiered educational system. This is evidenced by decades of school reform data and observations that such reforms have not addressed critical issues as under funding of programs and facilities. Moreover, despite NCLB requirements—poor teacher quality in many urban schools; tracking systems of assessment-determined placements; and the current standards-based teaching-to-test practices are factors that have direct negative impacts on learning and the quality of instruction (Bowles, 1968; Glenn, 1987; Welner, 1998; Balfanz & Legters, 2004; Kozol, 2005). The important issue to consider is that effective, high quality, culturally responsive education is possible; is within our control and ability to deliver; and is an urgent and fundamental task that must be addressed if we are truly serious about *leaving no child behind.*

This summary chapter will review points discussed in previous chapters; and will include concepts and other issues that address teaching and learning. The attempt has been to emphasize theories that support *how people learn;* and to assert that learning is a complex process. Therefore, cognition is the process of perceiving, decoding, and encoding sensory input by multi-modal associations; and integrating prior and current information in a manner that allows the *mind to see* what is *heard* through and "ear-eye" function (Kavanah & Mattingly, 1972). This hypothesis is presented to offer a re-conceptualization of classroom pedagogy. This text presents several basic concepts.

- First, to provide foundational information for understanding the importance of teacher competence in knowing learning theory and the implications for classroom pedagogy.

- Second, the discussions attempt to illuminate how school practices, classroom climates, and teacher expectations for students impact their performance and achievement.

- Discussions emphasize the importance of *cultural competence* as a criterion for teacher quality; *i.e.,* cultural competence involves understanding the cultural experiences of students in order to provide transformative culturally responsive instruction.

- It is recommended that attention is given to inequities created by the manner districts have implemented the requirements of NCLB, including teaching-to-test; and tracking placements of African American and other urban students.

- Finally, it is argued that effective diagnostic use of authentic, formative classroom and in-district assessments can remedy the ineffective use of standardized and norm-referenced assessments by combining various authentic measures in a diagnostic framework to improve instruction; and to lessen the subsequent negative impact of one-measure evaluations and the punitive decisions that affect the quality education for urban students.

The theory presented in this text augments discussions included in a companion instructional text, previously referenced. The review of theories and research is not meant to be comprehensive of the plethora of available research data in the literature; but rather, to provide a context and rationale that explain how pedagogy can be reframed to include the funds of knowledge and learning styles of culturally diverse students in addressing their educational needs. In this sense, discussions emphasize the links between *research* and *theory;* the link between *theory* and *practice;* and for educators to give serious attention to reframing traditional instruction to include critical thought, transformative, and culturally responsive practices.

Considering the issue of research-based theory, it is important to note that there is a school of thought that cautions against over reliance on, or blanket acceptance of, unexamined or unchallenged research (Standfield, II, 1993; Reese, 1998; Tanner, 1998; Ashton, 1999; McLaughlin, et al., 2002). This issue was not discussed in preceding chapters, but is highlighted here in agreement with the concern that school practices and pedagogy that attempt to address culturally responsive teaching must avoid the mindset that simply because particular reform or critical theory emanates from empirical research, that there is large-scale applicability. Tanner (1988) advises that attention should be paid to the biases that are systemic in some empirical research that may be flawed for various reasons. For instance, over representations in sampling populations often skew the results; or in some cases research is used to validate statistical data that was initially wrong. Reese (1998) found that, historically, it has not been possible to pinpoint "the influence of research on schools . . . (because few) records provide direct evidence of how research shapes practice" (p. 10). Further, the author contends it is not that specific studies, or several studies necessarily pinpoint what is the cause and what is the effect when theory is applied to practice; rather, that research illuminates or gives transparency to what does or does not work; and as important, the conditions that might propel learning or pose barriers. Therefore, theory that evolves from research should be critically examined and challenged, because it is also important to note that what works in theory, does not always work in practice; and in some instances, what appears to go against sound theory, may be effectively used in practice. Further, it's not that absolute proof of cause and effect is readily available; rather it's the "use" of what findings show "when" theory is applied to practices.

Reframing Instructional Delivery and Student Assessment in Urban Schools

This text proposes a paradigm for reframing instructional delivery within various contextual formats that include:

- First, direct links between research-base theories of *how children learn,* and all classroom instructional activities.

- Second, classroom activities of teaching and learning that are reciprocal between teachers and actively engaged students; where students have autonomy in contributing to the content knowledge through *unity of efforts.*

- Third, instructional formats of teaching and learning that include culturally affirming activities to provide scaffolding between students' out-of-school knowledge and in-school content knowledge; and scaffolding as mediating support to move students to higher levels of academic performance.

- Next, it is recommended that teachers provide a wide variety of teacher-designed and learner-created *situational contexts* and activities for students to *learn with understanding.*

- Finally, teachers are encouraged to use assessment results diagnostically to improve student performance and instructional design and delivery.

From Research to Theory

The various learning theories discussed include biological and ecological perspectives. It was pointed out that while perspectives on cognition differ, there is a common thread that runs through various perspectives; that both biological and ecological factors influence learning (Wertsch, Minick, & Arns,

1999). Moreover, it appears that a Vygotskian approach to understanding the mediated basis of learning is a perspective that exemplifies the consensus among various seemingly different views of cognitive development. A theoretical element that appears to be illusive, however, is discourse on *how* culture, *per se;* "forms" cognitive development for diverse learners; rather than simply having an influence on cognition. It's not that culturally influenced discourse is absent from theory or limited in the literature; but rather that there appears to be no concerted transformative reform efforts or school practices to address diversity with respect to curriculum design, pedagogy; and the negative impact of high-stakes assessments on culturally diverse students.

Two factors are evident in why this situation exists: First, most teacher training programs place little to no emphasis on culturally responsive pedagogy (Wise, 1990; Darling-Hammond, 2005; Bullough, 2006; Lampert, 2006). Second, there are substantial political difficulties associated with recognizing and giving credence to theories of critical thought (Ares, 2006). Most teachers approach teaching in the traditionally conservative manner in which they were trained; employing what hooks (1994) describes as Freier's "banking system" of information—imparted from teachers and stored by students. Further, in the current era of assessment-driven instruction of teaching-to-test, and memorization of factual, declarative information, attention to culturally responsive pedagogy is completely ignored or not considered a significant factor in advancing cognitive development; or for learning subject knowledge and skills (Bigelow, et. al, 2001; Shephard, et al., 2005; Bigelow & Karp, 2007).

Consequently, whether or not teachers understand the importance of how research predicates learning theories; increases the knowledge base for effective pedagogy; and elucidates implications for teaching and learning; it is not likely that any reforms will be transformative, effective, or successful in addressing the needs of diverse students if the research is ignored or neglected. Until and unless, culturally responsive theories of critical thought transform and reframe the delivery systems in urban and low-wealth schools attended by African American and other marginalized students, these students will continue to be *left behind.*

Classroom Dynamics and Reciprocal Teaching and Learning

It is important to consider group dynamics in discussions of teaching and learning because classrooms are *communities of practice;* and as such, the interactive relations and discourse establish a particular context, or learning environment that impacts student performance and achievement. Therefore, teachers must understand group behaviors and the various factors that contribute to students' anxieties, self-confidence, positive peer relations, and motivation. Further, it is critical for teachers, not only to be aware of the dynamics created in classrooms, but to be able to effectively manage conflict; and guide classroom behaviors to create positive social atmospheres. In doing so, teachers must give attention to diversity; provide opportunities for students to be responsible for their behaviors; and to be contributing members in advancing knowledge.

From preceding discussions on classroom dynamics, and the relation to classroom discourse in teaching and learning, several issues appear to be supported by the literature:

- First, at the beginning of newly formed classes, sufficient time should be provided for interactive communications to advance group relations beyond the *primary stage* of interactive communications between the teacher and students; and among classroom students. This is a period described as awkward politeness where members are unsure of their purpose; and students may feel a great deal of apprehensiveness and anxieties. This suggests that teachers must be attentively deliberate in getting to know students, individually; and establishing an atmosphere where students feel comfortable in interpersonal relations with classmates; with voicing thoughts without fear of ridicule; and eventually being receptive to instructional goals and content knowledge and skills.

- Next, by inference and by definition, learning is a dynamic process that is reciprocal between agent and environment (Vygotsky, 1978; Karpov, 2006a

& 2006b; Barab & Roth, 2006); and the nature of the interactive conditions that frame learning, in general; and classroom learning, in specific, involve changing behaviors by the agent, and the specific environment that forms the behaviors. In school settings, *agent* is the student; and *environment* is the classroom. This means that behaviors that occur in one environment may not be applicable in a different environment or under different conditions; e.g., behaviors acceptable in public social settings may not be appropriate in classrooms. For example, appropriate simultaneous conversations in small group work activities would be appropriate; but inappropriate when students are to be attentive to a lecture. The observed contradiction in classrooms, however, is that few small group or reciprocal activities are provided for students to be engaged in *communities of practice*; and they spend most of their time "listening" to the teacher (Kutz & Roskelly, 1991). It is therefore important that teachers understand how reciprocal, dynamic discourse applies to classroom learning; and to articulate, and model the differences for students. Teachers should understand the nature of culturally influenced patterns of learning of diverse students that may involve more overt interactions with others; and long stretches of "sit and listen" formats may inhibit their receptiveness to instruction.

- Effective teaching is demonstrated when teachers are able to identify and provide a context for the three basic stages of classroom dynamics:

  ➢ the initial or *primary stage;*
  ➢ the medial or *secondary stage;* and

> ➢ the final, exit, or *tertiary stage* of classroom dynamics.

A timeframe or specific point cannot be stated for exactly when classroom discourse and relations move from the *primary* to the *secondary stage*—this transition may take only one class session; or several sessions. The important point is that teachers are able to recognize the relative state of students' "receptiveness" and "preparedness" needed by time, space, and activities for the transition to occur to enhance students' confidence and performance; as well as for instructional effectiveness. It is also important that *reciprocal,* interactive relations and communications are established in the *primary* and *secondary* stages of classroom teaching and learning to foster student-teacher rapport; opportunities for students to have autonomy and to share responsibilities in individual engagement, and in *unity of efforts*; and to develop a sense of being a contributing member of a community of practice.

**Culturally Affirming and
Mediating Scaffolding**

An abundance of literature exists regarding theories and perspectives that social contexts influence, shape or condition, and situate learning. (Vygotsky, 1978; Kozulin, et al., 2006; bell hooks, 1994; Hilliard, 1995; King, et al., 1997; Gay, 2002; Rogoff & Lave, 1999; Delpit, 2002; Irvine, 2002; Lave and

Wenger, 2003). Theories and perspectives differ in regards to the degree that specific factors influence or contextualize socially constructed knowledge (Wertsch, et. al, 1999); and whether learning in social situations is context-dependent; or whether learning is context-independent. The basic postulate of this text is that learning is not an isolated, de-contextualized process; but rather dynamic and reciprocal; socially constructed, and context-dependent; either occurring spontaneously, influenced by the situation; or by design, mediated through instruction. Thus, the degree of social influence is determined by the *situatededness* of the content; and the specific conditions that create context. The degree of influence of the environment on classroom learning often depends on whether or not the content is made relevant; has meaning or purpose for the learner; and whether there is a *nexus* to prior knowledge. It is posited that scaffolding activities are opportunities for teachers to *create* conditions; or *situate* content to teach for understanding; and providing culturally responsive activities is a way of creating scaffolding, or the *nexus* that establishes this relevancy for culturally diverse students.

Bigge and Shermis (1999) describe scaffolding as ". . . the engagement of children in the interesting, culturally meaningful collaborative problem-solving activities;" and a critical element of scaffolding is *intersubjectivity*; which "means that two or more persons begin a task with different understandings but arrive at a constructive shared one" (p. 130). The most obvious means of classroom scaffolding is therefore mediated discourse.

We discussed how language plays a significant role as a mediating agent in learning in all discourse, in public social situations, as well as, in classrooms. Therefore teachers must consider the various language backgrounds that influence the learning styles and language meanings different students bring to the classroom. Students from diverse backgrounds whose language is markedly different from mainstream language have historically been perceived and educated from a deficit view of their intellectual and academic capabilities; and this practice is systemic at all levels of the educational system, especially in public schools located in urban and inner city communities (Labov, 1986; Blake, 1994; Delpit, 1995, 1996, & 2002). Consequently, it is imperative that teachers are constantly aware of the influences that have shaped students' readiness for mainstream approaches to language discourse; and the need to have a positive perspective of culturally influenced patterns of language use among diverse students. This suggests that teachers utilize the cultural capital diverse students bring to the classroom as scaffolding and mediating tools to connect out-of-school language use and meanings, to classroom knowledge and content, to teach for understanding; and to provide culturally responsive activities that affirm and value the cultural backgrounds of all students (Pierre-Pipkin, 2007).

Situational Contexts for Learning

Situated learning explained by the social learning theory of Lave and Wenger (2003), and Rogoff and Lave (1999) hypothesized learning as a *situated activity*, as opposed to being a cognitive process involved in the acquisition of knowledge. Lave and Wenger contend that learning occurs in communities of practice and learning by doing, where the initial stage of participation is peripheral, but eventually progresses to a state of full participation. Further, learning is not specifically mediated by a single person, such as a teacher; and does not depend specifically on instruction, but can occur as a result of instruction. According to the authors, the principal concept is that situated learning is not an approach or technique, but is a way of understanding the necessary conditions or situations in which learning occurs. Consequently, the more limited the contexts, the more limited the opportunities for learning.

This text departs slightly from the position of situated learning as *activity only*, and not an approach to learning. It is posited that conditions can be designed that *situate content* for learning to occur, and *situated classroom activities* can be used as mediating tools to bridge what students know, to what they need to know. *Situational context designs* are addressed in more detail in the companion text. The approach is based on Lave, Rogoff and Wenger's position of *activity* in communities of practice; but extends their thinking to include situations of teacher assigned, or student-created activities to connect content knowledge to students' prior experiences to teach for understanding. Opportunities are provided to include culturally relevant themes in teaching and learning that are *situated* in scaffolding activities.

Authentic and Diagnostic Assessment

A rationale was stated that argues the need to restructure student assessment through the use of multiple measures to gain accuracy in evaluating student performance; that using authentic assessment avoids penalizing African American and other urban children by relying solely on one "high-stakes" standardized test. In addressing the requirements of NCLB, it was noted that there is no "mandate" that "high-stakes" tests are to be the single instrument to evaluate student performance. There is a provision in NCLB that allows individual states to determine how performance is assessed; however, because of many restraining factors, most states rely on single-shot multiple-choice formatted instruments (Linn, 2008).

The difficulties pointed out in using alternative forms of authentic large-scale measures relate to the costs; the assurance of validity of test instruments, and performance data; and lack of general appeal, or reluctance in adopting alternative instruments. Proponents of current forms of assessment argue that large-scale standardized tests allow reliability of measurements; and statewide, district, and school comparisons among various groups (Popham, 1987 & 1998). The consensus among opponents of large-scale testing, in the current forms, argue that cognitive abilities are not being measured; instead, factual declarative information is assessed, much of which relies on low skills of recognition and memorization (Marzano and Costa, 1988). Kornhaber (2004) points out that proper use of standardized testing has merit, but the fallacies tend to outweigh benefits. This is the position argued in this text, that standardized tests are useful, but test results should be combined with classroom formative assessment, observations of demonstrated knowledge and skills, and anecdotal data from students' portfolios to yield broader more authentic evaluations of students' capabilities. Moreover, "high-stakes" tests should never be used to punish one group of students (albeit it punitive use is not the intended purpose for comparisons); or to elevate mainstream or high-scoring groups, as superior.

Re-defining Highly Qualified Teachers: Implications for Urban Students

The NCLB requirement that all students will have *highly qualified teachers* is viewed as a mixed blessing, because on one hand, for the first time in the schooling of African American and other urban children, attention is given to a factor that

286

has been ignored or neglected: the impact of teacher quality and capabilities on student achievement. Therefore it is more likely, that previously neglected urban students will have better qualified teachers. Secondly, the conflicting circumstance presented by the "highly qualified teacher" requirement is twofold: First, states have flexibility in defining *highly qualified teachers;* but federal oversight has not been as focused on the equity provision, compared to other requirements. For example, more emphasis has been placed on ensuring that schools meet AYP based on high-stakes assessments (Darling-Hammond, 2008). Second, the least qualified teachers are still assigned to ethnically identified schools or classes (Sunderman, et al., 2008). The postulates of this text are congruent with Rebell and Wolff's (2008) position for re-defining *highly qualified teachers;* that there are varying degrees of teacher competence. Further, it has not been established that teachers who are degreed and certified through rigorous testing are necessarily effective teachers; especially for poor and diverse students. Darling-Hammond (Ibid.) contends that NCLB ". . . *should ensure that teachers are not labeled 'highly qualified' until they have completed preparation and mastered essential teaching skills"* (p. 159). This text goes a step beyond the basic criteria of a four-year degree; state certification; and subject knowledge; or even experience; to include *cultural competence* as a needed and required criterion of teacher quality. Similarly, King

(1994) posits that teachers must have a level of self-awareness and cultural knowledge because their beliefs about students influence pedagogy. Further, teachers must understand issues ". . . regarding the matters of culture, ethnicity, educational purpose and societal injustice are all part of the *social cultural context knowledge* that should be included in the knowledge base of teaching" (p. 41). The criteria Darling-Hammond and Bransford (2005) list for *highly qualified teachers* include:

- Subject matter knowledge;
- Abilities in student assessment;
- Classroom management; and
- Understanding learning theory.

Among these and other criteria; the factor that is typically not included in state definitions of a *highly qualified teacher* is demonstration of sociocultural consciousness by understanding the social context of learning; especially regarding diverse student populations. Thus, a *re-definition* of *highly qualified* teacher to include *cultural competence* is not simply a matter of addressing an issue that has been marginal or tangentially related to pedagogical inclusiveness; it is a matter that essentially determines if African American and other marginalized students will ever be provided maximum opportunities to learn in high quality programs designed with both academic and cultural relevance. Educators must determine whether instructional programs are designed to capitalize on students' prior knowledge and learning styles; or whether students fail because instruction is essentially teaching-to-test. Further, educators must determine how to change practices that culturally diverse students perceive as hostile and unequal; and create climates that prevent these students from dropping out of school (Balfranz & Legters, 2004).

The present forms of schooling are not what African American and other marginalized students deserve; where many are disinterested, disengaged; and memorize-facts-to-test. This is the schooling that says to students, what Kohn (1999a) sees happening figuratively: "Don't do something, sit there" (p. 64). Despite NCLB, and the well-intended requirements of teacher quality; these trends of mis-education will not be reversed for culturally diverse children until teachers are required to have extensive knowledge of diverse student populations (Banks et al., 2005); and demonstrate *cultural competence* through effective, culturally responsive instruction.

Conclusions and Recommendations

Conclusions

A view of the American panorama of public education reveals a landscape of hills and green valleys; roads that twist and turn—some smooth, some bumpy. Green valleys and smoothly paved roads meander through suburban and high-wealth communities; and hills and cracking roads with potholes weave through inner cities and dead end in urban communities. Educators aware of this scene might suppose this to be unreal; that they will awake to find this educational scene in 21st Century America was just a horrible nightmare. Unfortunately, it is not. As bleak as this appears, this metaphorical description is not exaggeration; but is symbolic of the typical reality and disparate two-tier educational system; where schooling is dispersed on uneven roads, and insurmountable hills in marginalized urban places throughout America. Moreover, to add insult to injury, large-scale "high-stakes testing" is *equally* administered to *unequally* educated children with the goal of leveling access to quality education; and providing equality of educational opportunity through legislated requirements, and "other people's standards" for diverse student populations. At the same time there is no commitment to equalize funding, programs, and facilities as factors of equity. Thus, to use another metaphorical phrase— *Meanwhile, back at the ranch*—the question becomes, what is to be done in the meantime; not waiting on legislation or funding to mandate effective schooling; but to address these issues *right now?* No single educational approach, or one well-intended nationwide reform effort can do all that is needed to provide equal educational opportunities; but every educational institution; along with the best and most effective parts of reform efforts can do much to reverse the current state of inequalities in schooling.

We indeed cannot see the future, but if we reverse past mistakes that continue to "under-educate" African American and other marginalized children, we can indeed have significant control in providing more effective education and schooling. The purpose for the development of *The Pierre Pedagogy* is to offer a transformative paradigm for possibly doing this; and to address some of the discontinuities in instructional practices for African American and other marginalized children.

The aim of this text is that readers use the information as foundational; and a reference to the companion application text: *The Pierre Pedagogy: Teaching Learners to "See" What You Are "Saying"—From Theory to Practice.* Each text may be used as a stand-alone resource; but used together; the texts are designed to help the reader understand the paradigm of *The Pierre Pedagogy* that hypothesizes the *mind* has the *ability to hear;* and to *see* though an "ear-eye" function. The postulate implies that effectively teaching African American and other urban students requires teaching learners to "*see what is said.*" The metaphors represent a play on words (or the senses); but explain the need for a paradigm shift from traditional didactic forms of instruction to dynamic, reciprocal teaching and learning where in-school knowledge is connected to students' prior knowledge and experiences. This pedagogy theorizes that to be effective, teachers must teach in a manner that allows students to gain *insight* (e.g. to "see" what is "said") in order to *learn with understanding.*

Additionally, *Chapter Seven* of the application text has been published as an interactive Power Point reference for understanding the concepts of the pedagogy; or for staff development training. It is re-emphasized that this text presents several theories of learning that support the pedagogy of the two-volume publication, and is not intended to be extensively inclusive of the vast amount of available theory in the literature. The intent is that the reader connects the theories in this text, *Hearing With the Minds Eye,* to several sections of the application text: the *Levels of Teaching and Learning Master Chart (LTLMC);* the Five Constructs presented in Chapter One of that text; and the application section of Chapter Seven of the companion book previously referenced (Pierre-Pipkin, 2007).

The reader of this text (particularly pre-service teachers) should take note of the concepts presented below; and is encouraged to read extensively among the references in the bibliography to broaden conceptual knowledge, especially in the areas of learning theory that include cognitive development and critical theory regarding cultural and socially influenced cognitive development. Concepts emphasized in this text include:

- How research supports critical theory;

- The impact of classroom climate and teacher perceptions on student performance; and

- An often overlooked issue that Hodgkinson (Goldberg, 2000) stresses: that significant attention must be paid to the changing social and school demographics, in order to be informed of current and future trends and factors that impact schooling.

Any approach to restructuring schooling begins with giving serious attention to at least three basic issues. The recommendations presented emphasize each of these issues as suggestions to improve schooling for culturally diverse students:

- The state of theories on learning; and how sound research and relevant theories are linked to effective, transformative school practices;

- Schooling and instructional practices that address diversity, including the impact of "high-stakes" large-scale assessment on student performance; and

- School staffing that focuses on teacher quality; including competence in teaching culturally diverse students.

A large body of literature examines learning theories that are linked to school practices, including theories of socially influenced learning; and culturally responsive school practices. While much attention has been paid to theories from a mainstream perspective, little focus, attention, or wide-scale effort is focused on utilizing theories of culturally related and transformative critical thought in teaching and learning. Anyon (2006) finds that most educational research focuses on students, teachers, curriculum, pedagogy, various levels of education; and the relations between and among these variables. The author argues that use of the standard framework of these kinds of research focus on middle-class American schools. Thus, the traditional research framework ". . . is not equipped to capture the external social structure and public policy decision that plagues urban systems and renders them impotent to fundamentally improve the education—and life chances—of the vast majority of their students" (p. 21).

Recommendations

- It is recommended that policy makers, school administrators, and in-service teachers consider theories of culturally influenced learning to be as critical, as traditionally relied-upon research and theories currently supporting school practice and instructional delivery. Moreover, educators should be required to be knowledgeable of cultural theories of learning; to employ social and cultural theories as foundational in teaching diverse students; and incorporate such theories as essential elements of curriculum design and instruction.

- School practices that address diversity must provide effective content delivery that is inclusive, and deliberately focused on all students who populate the schools. This includes a reassessment of the negative impact of large-scale testing on student performance; and the *use of* standardized assessment results that stigmatize African American and other urban students through tracking programs that restrict these students to low quality instructional programs based on standardized test scores. It is recommended that standardized test scores are used diagnostically to analyze item and domain strengths and weaknesses, to improve instruction; and that test results are used in combination with formative district-wide and classroom assessments, and other forms of student demonstrated performance.

- This text recommends *Criterion-Referenced Instruction (CRI)* and *Criterion-Referenced Assessment (CRA)* as the formats that present challenging, dynamically directed instruction; and on-going evaluations that yield authentically determined measures of what students know; and when they know content. It is recommended that teachers use *CRA* in the normal course of instruction to complement student evaluations; and to lessen the negative impact of the skewed data results of memorized declarative information obtained from norm-referenced and standardized "high-stakes" tests. The goal is to teach students *how to learn*; so they *learn with understanding.*

- School staffing begins with emphasis on teacher quality; and must include teachers' competence in teaching culturally diverse students. It is critical that concentrated efforts focus on equitable distribution of high quality, effective teachers at all grade levels, and throughout school districts. Further, special attention should address diversity among teaching staffs. Where there is a shortage of teachers that limits diversity of teaching staffs; priority should concentrate on other personnel and support staff that can be assigned in balancing school personnel to be reflective of the ethnic demographics of the student population (Gentry, 1985; Guarino, et al., 2006). This approach is posited to be conducive in establishing school and classroom environments that promote self-esteem and self-confidence among students; and to avoid feelings of isolation by culturally diverse students. Non-teaching personnel include classroom aides; technical assistants; media specialists; counselors, and administrators who should be visible and available to students where teaching staffs mainly represent non-minority groups. This approach to staffing is not meant to substitute for teacher diversity; but as an interim situation until sufficient teachers are available for diversified staffing.

- Teacher preparation programs at the college and university levels should focus on teaching in ways ("how") teachers are expected to deliver effective instruction in elementary and secondary schools. As Ares (2006) and bell hooks (1994) noted, teachers approach elementary and secondary grade instruction with the same style in which they were trained. The focus is centered on the professor, in a "top-down" fashion of dispersing information to non-engaged students; in non-reciprocal teaching and learning structures. Novices, as well as, experienced teachers, deliver instruction in the same manner— teacher to disengaged students. To make instruction dynamically interactive and reciprocal at both, the college and district levels, activities should begin with curriculum that is designed to provide a wide variety of shared group assignments; team teaching across disciplines; and cultural themes that create a nexus between in-school, and out-of-school knowledge. Teaching should be reciprocal in open, positive classroom climates. Moreover, college level programs should include extensive preparation and training courses to develop student competence in understanding standardized tests; how to use classroom and other forms of student assessment diagnostically; and the implications of assessment for classroom teaching and learning.

- College and university programs should develop a "shared-cost" type apprentice and internship course component that is taught *on site* within school districts. Such pre-service courses would provide a "hands-on" program setting for potential teachers; and provide opportunities within a school year for teachers-in-training to explore and engage in in-depth activities within the community. This team approach would also provide *bridging* and broader communications between in-service teachers and the community; providing connections that in-service teachers typically have limited time to engage in.

- At the district level, novice teachers should be pared with experienced "effective" teachers to be mentored for a minimum of three years. Novice teachers need guidance in developing commitment to social equity; positive perspectives of student abilities; and opportunities to develop *cultural competence.*

- Much has been discussed about the positives and negatives of NCLB; the need for the requirement of "high-stakes" testing to be revised; and why it is critical to re-define *highly qualified teacher.* Discussions will not be extended to repeat the points made; except to recommend that the reader re-visit the discussions; and to read extensively among the References to augment knowledge beyond the focus of this text.

APPENDIX

Levels of Teaching and Learning Master Chart

LEVELS → Teaching and Learning

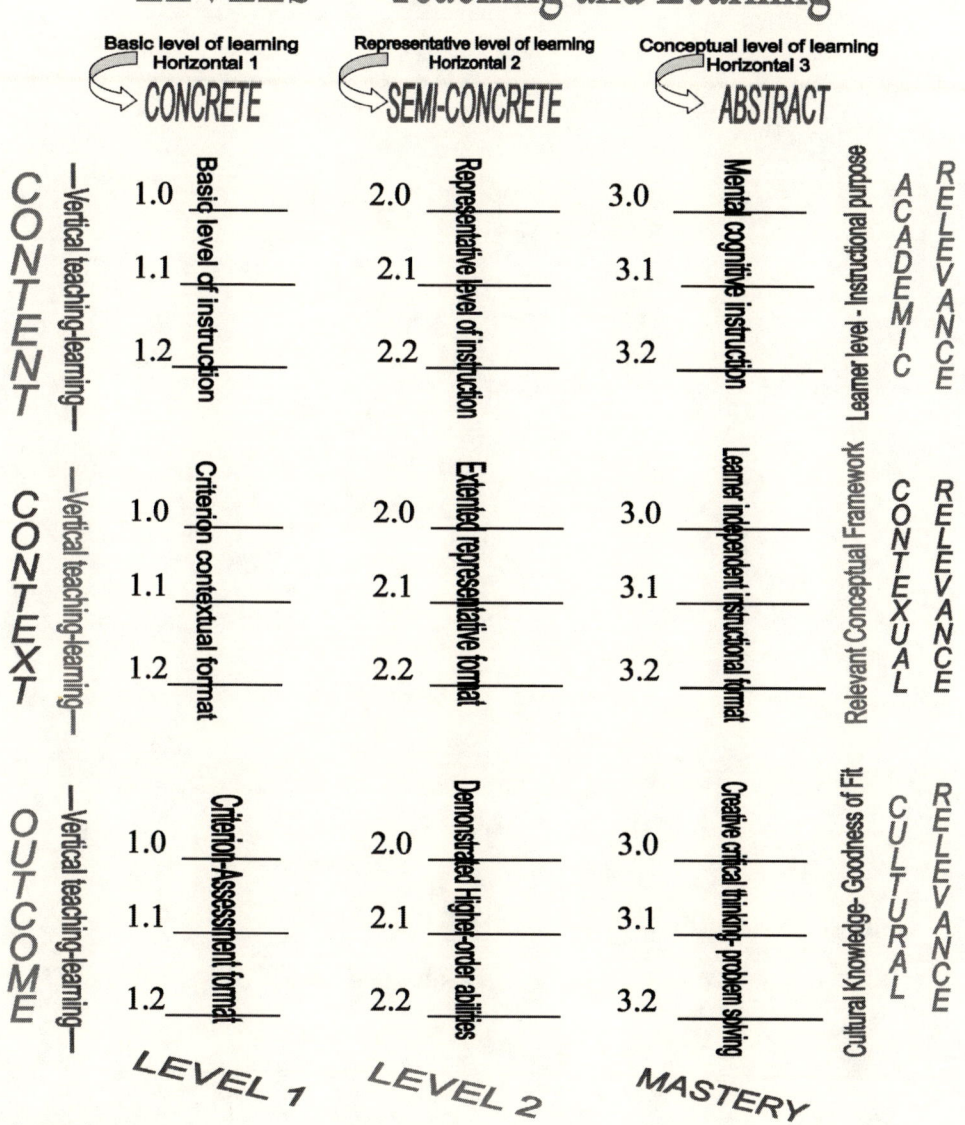

	Basic level of learning Horizontal 1 CONCRETE	Representative level of learning Horizontal 2 SEMI-CONCRETE	Conceptual level of learning Horizontal 3 ABSTRACT		
CONTENT —Vertical teaching-learning—	1.0 ——— 1.1 ——— 1.2 ——— Basic level of instruction	2.0 ——— 2.1 ——— 2.2 ——— Representative level of instruction	3.0 ——— 3.1 ——— 3.2 ——— Mental cognitive instruction	Learner level - Instructional purpose	ACADEMIC RELEVANCE
CONTEXT —Vertical teaching-learning—	1.0 ——— 1.1 ——— 1.2 ——— Criterion contextual format	2.0 ——— 2.1 ——— 2.2 ——— Extended representative format	3.0 ——— 3.1 ——— 3.2 ——— Learner independent instructional format	Relevant Conceptual Framework	CONTEXTUAL RELEVANCE
OUTCOME —Vertical teaching-learning—	1.0 ——— 1.1 ——— 1.2 ——— Criterion-Assessment format	2.0 ——— 2.1 ——— 2.2 ——— Demonstrated Higher-order abilities	3.0 ——— 3.1 ——— 3.2 ——— Creative critical thinking-problem solving	Cultural Knowledge- Goodness of Fit	CULTURAL RELEVANCE
	LEVEL 1	LEVEL 2	MASTERY		

REFERENCES

Ancheta, A. N. (2006). Civil rights, educational research and the courts. *Educational Researcher, Jan/Feb* (pp. 26-29).

Ackerman, J. (2003). The space for rhetoric in everyday life. In Nystrand, M. & Duffy, J. (Eds.), *Towards a rhetoric of everyday life: New directions in research on writing text and discourse (pp. 84-117).* Madison, WI: The University of Wisconsin Press.

Adler, M. J. (December 1987). We hold these truths. *Phi Delta Kappan, Vol.69:4* (pp. 268-274).

Ancess, J. (2003). *Beating the odds: High schools as communities of commitment.* NY: Teachers College Press.

Anderson, C. S. (Fall 1982). The search for school climate: A review of the research. *Review of Educational Research, Vol. 52:2* (pp. 368-420).

Anderson, J. D., (1988). *The education of blacks in the South 1860-1935.* NC: The University of North Carolina Press.

Anyon, J. (2006). What should count as educational research: Notes toward a new paradigm. In Ladson-Billings, G., and Tate, W. F. (Eds.), *Education research in the public Interest: Social justice, action, and policy (pp. 17-26).* NY: Teachers College Press.

Apatheker, H. (2001). DuBois: *The education of Black people: Ten Critiques, 1906-1960 W.E.B.—New Edition*. NY: Monthly Review Press.

Ares, N. (2006). Political aims and classroom dynamics: generative processes in classroom communities. Retrieved from: http://www.radicalpedagogy.capp.org/content/issue821ares.htm.

Ashton, M. C. & Esses, V. M. (Feb. 1999). Stereotype accuracy: Estimating the academic performance of ethnic groups. *Society for Personality and Social Psychological, Inc.,* Vol. *25:2* (pp. 225-256).

Au, W., Bigelow, B., & Karp, S. (Eds., 2007). *Rethinking Our Classrooms: Teaching for Equity and Justice: New Edition: Volume 1*. VT: Rethinking Schools, Ltd.

Balfanz, R. & Legters, N. (2004). Locating the dropout crisis: Which high schools produce the nation's dropouts? Where are they located? Who attends them? *Report 70:* The John Hopkins University.

Banks, J.A. & Joyce, W. W. (1971). *Teaching social studies to culturally different children*. MA: Addison-Wesley Publishing Co.

Banks, J. A. (1984). Black youths in predominantly White suburbs: An exploratory study of their attitudes and self-concepts. *Journal of Negro Education: Vol. 53:1* (pp. 3-17).

Banks, J. A. (1988). Ethnicity, class, cognitive, and motivational styles: Research and teaching implications. *Journal of Negro Education, Vol. 57:4* (pp. 452-466).

Banks, J. A., and Banks, C. A. McGee (Eds., 1995). *Handbook of research on multicultural education.* NY: McMillan Publishing USA.

Banks, J. A. (2003). *Teaching strategies for ethnic studies.* NY: Pearson Education Group, Inc.

Banks, J. A. (2004). Multicultural education: Historical development, dimensions, and practice. In Banks, J. A. and Banks, C. A. M. (Eds.), *Handbook of research on multicultural: Second Edition* (pp. 3-29). CA: Jossey-Bass.

Banks, J. A. & Banks, C. A. M. (Eds., 2004). *Handbook of research on multicultural: Second Edition.* CA: Jossey-Bass.

Banks, J. A., Cochran-Smith, M., Moll, L., Richert, A., Zeichner, K., LePage, P.

Darling-Hammond, L., Duffy, H., & McDonald, M. (2005). Teaching diverse learners. In Darling-Hammond, L. & Bransford, J. (Eds), *Preparing teachers for a changing world: What teachers should learn and be able to do* (pp. 232-274). CA: Jossey-Bass.

Barab, S. A. & Roth, W. M. (2006). Curriculum-based ecosystems: Supporting knowing from an ecological perspective. *Educational Researcher, Vol. 35:5* (pp. 30-13).

Battistich, V., Solomon, D., Dong-il, K, Watson, M & Schaps, E. (Fall 1995). Schools as communities, poverty levels of student populations, and students' attitudes, motives, and performance: A multi-level analysis. *American Educational Research Journal, Vol. 32:3* (pp. 672-658).

Beach, K. (1998). Consequential transitions: A sociological expedition beyond transfer in education. *Review of Research in Education, Vol. 24,* (pp.101-139).

Beauboeuf-Lafontant, T. & Augustine D. S. (Eds., 1996). *Facing Racism in Education.* Cambridge, MA: Reprint Series No. 28, Harvard Educational Review.

Bernstein, B. (1986). Social class, language, and socialization. In Giglioli, P. P. (Ed.) *Language and social context* (pp. 157-178). NY: Penguin Books.

Bigelow, B., Harvey, B., Karp, S. & Miller, L. (Eds., 2001). *Rethinking Our Classrooms: Teaching for Equity and Justice: Volume 2.* VT: Rethinking Schools, Ltd.

Bigge, M. L. & Shermis, S. (Eds., 1999). *Learning theories for teachers (6th Edition).* NY: Addison Wesley Longham, Inc.

Bizzell P. (1994). *Academic discourse and critical consciousness.* Pittsburg: University of Pitssburg Press.

Blake, I. K. (1994). Language development and socialization in young African-American children. In Greenfield, P. M. & Cocking, R. R. (Eds.), *Cross-cultural roots of minority child development* (pp. 167-195). NJ: Lawrence-Erlbaum Associates, Publishers. MA: Cambridge University Press.

Bloom, B. S., Englehart, M. D., Furst, E. J., Hill, W. H., & Krathwohl, D. R. (Eds., 1956). *Taxonomy of educational objectives. The classification of educational goals: The cognitive domain—Handbook I.* NY: David McKay Publishers.

Boaler, J. (March 2003). When learning no longer matters: Standardized testing and the creation of inequality. *Phi Delta Kappan:* Vol. 84:7 (pp. 502-506).

Bodrova, E. & Leong, D. (2006). Learning development of preschool children from Vygotskian perspective. In Kozulin, A.; Gindis, B; Ageyev, V. S.; Miller, S. M. (Reprint: 2006, Eds.), *Vygotsky's educational theory in cultural context, (pp. 156-176).* NY: Cambridge University Press.

Bullough, Jr., R. V. (Nov. 2006). Developing interdisciplinary researchers: Whatever happened to the humanities in education? *Educational Researcher, Vol. 35:8* (pp. 3-10).

Bower, G. (1972). A selective review of organizational factors of memory. In Tulving, E. and Donaldson, W. (Eds.), *Organization of memory* (pp. 93-137). NY: Academic Press.

Bowles, S. (Winter, 1968). Toward equality of educational opportunity. *Harvard* Educational Review: Vol. 38:1 (pp. 89-99).

Boykin, A. W. & Bailey, C. T. (2000). The role of cultural factors in school relevant cognitive functioning: Synthesis of findings on cultural contexts, cultural orientations, and individual differences. *Report No. 42 (pp. i-43).* Center for Research on the Education of Students Placed At Risk. The John Hopkins University. (CRESPAR)/USDE.

Boykin, A. W. Coleman, S. T., Lilja, A. J., & Tyler, K. M. (2004). Building on children's cultural assets in simulated classroom performance environments. _Report No. 68_ _(pp. i-32)_. Center for Research on the Education of Students Placed At Risk Baltimore, The John Hopkins University: (CRESPAR)/USDE.

Bracey, G. W. (May 1987). Measurement-driven instruction: Catchy phrase dangerous practice. _Phi Delta Kappan. Vol. 68:9 (pp. 683-686)._

Bransford, J. D. & Schwartz, D. L. (1998). Rethinking transfer: A simple proposal with multiple implications. _Review of Research in Education. Vol. 24_ (pp. 61-100).

Bransford, J. D., Brown, A. L., and Cocking, R. R. (Eds., 2000— Expanded Edition). _How people learn: Brain, mind, experiences, and school._ Washington, DC: National Academy Press.

Bransford, J. D., Brown, A. L., and Cocking, R. R. (Eds., 2002). _How people learn: Brain, mind, experience, and school._ Washington, DC: National Academy Press.

Bransford, J., Derry, S., Berliner, Hammerness, K. & Beckett, K. L. (2005). Theories of learning and their roles in teaching. In Darling-Hammond, L. & Bransford, J. D. (Eds.), _Preparing teachers for a changing world: What teachers should learn and be able to do_ (pp. 40-87). CA: Jossey-Bass.

Brookover, W. B., Schweitzer, J. H., Schneider, J. M., Beady, C. H., Flood, P. K & Wisenbaker, J. M. (Spring, 1978), Elementary school social climate and school achievement. _American Research Journal, No. 15:2_ (pp.301-318).

Brown, E. R. (2001). Comment: Human development and the social structure. In Watkins, W. H., Lewis, J. H. and Chou, V. (Eds.), *Race and education: The roles of history and society in educating African American students* (pp. 128-139). MA: Allyn and Bacon.

Bryant, P. E. (1975). Cross-Modal development and reading. In Duane, D. D. & Rawson & M. B. (Eds). *Reading, perception and language: Papers from the world congress on Dyslexia* (pp. 195-213). Baltimore, MD: York Press, Inc.

Byrnes, J. P. (2001). *Cognitive development and learning in instructional contexts.* Boston, MA: Allyn and Bacon.

Calfee, R. C. (1975). Memory and cognitive skills in reading acquisition. In Duane, D. D. & Rawson & M. B. (Eds), *Reading, perception and language: Papers from the world congress on Dyslexia* (pp.55-95). Baltimore, MD: York Press, Inc.

Carroll, J. B. & Freedle, R. O. (1972). *Language comprehension and the acquisition of knowledge.* Washington, DC: Winston and Sons, Inc.

Carruthers, J. H. (1999). *Intellectual warfare.* Chicago: Third World Press.

Castenelle, L. (1984). A cross-cultural look at achievement motivation research. *Journal of Negro Education, Vol. 53:4* (pp. 435-443).

Cazden, C. G., John, V. P. & Hymes, D. (Eds., 1972). *Functions of language in the classroom.* NY: Teachers College Press.

Cazden, C. B. (1998). *Classroom discourse: The language of teaching and learning.* NH: Heineman Educational Books, Inc.

Cazden, C. B. (2001). *Classroom discourse: The language of teaching and learning. (Second Edition)* NH: Heinemann.

Chaiklin, S. (2006). The zone of proximal development in Vygotsky's analysis of learning and instruction. In Kozulin, A.; Gindis, B; Ageyev, V. S.; Miller, S. M. (Eds.), *Reprint:* (pp. 39-64). *Vygotsky's educational theory in cultural context.* NY: Cambridge University Press

Clincky, E. (March 2001). Needed: A new educational civil rights movement. *Phi Delta* Kappan. Vol. 82:7 (pp. 493-506).

Cochran-Smith, M. (1996). Uncertain allies: Understanding the boundaries of race and teaching. In Beauboeuf-Lafontant, T. & Augustine D. S. (Eds.), *Facing Racism in Education: Reprint Series No. 28* (pp. 369-401). Cambridge, MA: Harvard Educational Review.

Cochran-Smith, M. (Summer 2000). Blind vision: Unlearning racism in teacher education. *Harvard Educational Review, Vol. 70:2* (pp. 157-190). Cambridge, MA.

Cocking, R. R. (1994). Ecologically valid frameworks of development: Accounting for continuities and discontinuities. In Greenfield, P. M. & Cocking, R. R. (Eds.), *Cross-cultural roots of minority child development* (pp. 393-409). NJ: Lawrence-Erlbaum Associates, Publishers.

Colarci, T. (June 2002). Is it a house . . . or a pile of bricks? Important features of a local assessment system. *Phi Delta Kappan, Vol. 83:10* (pp. 722-774).

Cole, M., John-Steiner, V., Scribner, S. & Souberman, E. (Eds., 1978). *L. S. Vygotsky: Mind in society: The development of higher psychological processes.* London, England: Harvard University Press.

Cole, M. (Spring, 1995). The supra-individual envelope of development: Activity and practice, situation and context. In Goodnow, J. J., Miller & Kessel, F. (Eds.), *cultural practices as contexts for development* (pp. 105-118). San Francisco: Jossey-Bass Publishers.

Comber, B. & Simpson, A. (Eds., 2001). *Negotiating critical literacies in classrooms.* NY: Routledge.

Conner, K, Hairston, J., Inez, H., Kopple, H.,. Marshall, J., Scholnick, K., and Schulman, M. (Oct. 1985). Using formative assessment at the classroom, school, and district levels. *Educational Leadership, Vol. 43:2* (pp 63-67).

Connor, C. M., Morrison, F. J., Fishman, B. J., Ponitz, C. C., Glasney, S., Underwood, P. S., Piasta, S. B. Coyne, & Schataneider, C. (March 2009). The ISI classroom observation system: Examining the literacy instruction provided individual students. *Educational Researcher: Vol. 38:2* (pp. 85-99).

Cook-Gumperz, J. (Ed., 2006). *The social construction of literacy.* NY: Cambridge University Press.

Cooper, P. M. (2002). Does race matter? A comparison of effective Black and White teachers of African American students. In Irvine, J. J. (Ed.), *In Search of wholeness: African American teachers and their culturally specific classroom practices (pp. 139-146)*. NY: Palgrave.

Critchley, M. (1975). Developmental dyslexia: Its history, nature, and prospects. In Duane, D. D. & Rawson & M. B. (Eds), *Reading, perception and language: Papers from the world congress on* Dyslexia (pp. 9-14). Baltimore, MD: York Press, Inc.

Crosby, E. A. (1999). Urban schools: Forced to fail. *Phi Delta Kappan, Vol. 81:4* (pp. 298-303).

Crowder, R. G. (1972) Visual and Auditory Memory. In Kavanagh, J. F. and Mattingly, I. G., (Eds.), *Language by ear and by eye: The relationship between speech and reading* (pp. 251-275). Cambridge, MA: MIT University Press.

Cruickshank, D. R. (1990). *Research that informs teachers and teacher educators*. Indiana: Phi Delta Kappa Educational Foundation.

Cubberley, E. P. (1920). *The history of education*. Boston, MA: Houghton-Mufflin.

Darity, Jr, W. A. and Myers, Jr., S. L. (1998). *Persistent disparity: Race and economic inequality in the United States since 1945*. Northhampton, MA: Edward Elgar.

Darling-Hammond, L. & Wise, A. E. (1985). Beyond standardization: State standards and school improvement. *The Elementary School Journal, Vol. 85:5* (pp. 315-336).

Darling-Hammond, L. (1995). Inequality and Access to Knowledge. In Banks, J. & Banks, C. M. (Eds.). *Handbook of research on multicultural education* (pp. 465-483). NY: McMillian Publishing.

Darling-Hammond, L. (1997a). *The right to learn: A blueprint for creating schools that work.* CA: Jossey-Bass.

Darling-Hammond, L. (Nov. 1997b). Using standards and assessments to support student learning. *Phi Delta Kappan, Vol. 79:3* (pp. 190-199).

Darling-Hammond, L. & Bransford, J. (Eds. 2005). *Preparing teachers for a changing world: What teachers should learn and be able to do.* CA: Jossey-Bass.

Darling-Hammond, Banks, J., Zumwalt, K, Gomez, L., Shermin, R., Griesdorn, J. & Finn, L-E. (2005). Educational goals and purposes: Developing a curricular vision for teaching. In Darling-Hammond, L. & Bransford, J. (Eds.), *Preparing teachers for a changing world: What teachers should learn and be able to do (pp. 169-200).* CA: Jossey-Bass.

Darling-Hammond, L. (2008). Improving high schools and the role of NCLB. In Sunderman, G. L. (Ed.). (2008). *Holding NCLB accountable: Achieving accountability, equity and school reform* (pp. 153-171). CA: Corwin Press.

Davis, M. (April 2006a). Study: NCLB leads to cuts for some subjects. *Education Week. Vol. 25. No. 30* (p. 5).

Davis, M. (May 2006b). NCLB panel gathers views on testing and data collection. *Education Week, Vol. 25. No. 37* (p. 25).

Delpit, L. (1995). *Other people's children: Cultural conflict in the classroom.* NY: The New York Press.

Delpit, L. (1996). The silenced dialogue: Power and pedagogy in educating other people's children. In Beauboeuf-Lafontant, T. & Augustine D. S. (Eds.), *Facing Racism in Education: Harvard Educational Review Reprint Series No. 28* (pp. 127-146). Cambridge, MA:

Delpit, L. (2002). Introduction. In Delpit, L. & Dowdy, J. K. (Eds.), *The skin that we speak: Thoughts on language and culture in the classroom* (pp. xv-xxiv). NY: The New Press.

Delpit, L. & Dowdy, J. K. (Eds. 2002). *The skin that we speak: Thoughts on language and culture in the classroom.* NY: The New Press.

Demetriou, A. & Kyriakides L. (2006). The functional and developmental organization of cognitive developmental sequences. *British Psychological Society, 76:* (pp. 209-242).

Donahoe, T. (Dec. 1993). Finding the way: Structure time, and culture in school improvement. *Phi Delta Kappan, Vol. 75:4* (pp. 298-305).

Donovan, S. M., Bransford, J. D. & Pellegrino, J. W. (2005). *How people learn: Bridging research and practice.* Washington, DC: National Academy Press.

Drake, S. M. (2007). *Creating standards-based integrated curriculum: aligning curriculum, content, assessment, and instruction. CA: Corwin Press.*

Duane, D. D. & Rawson, M. B. (1975, Eds.). *Reading, perception and language: Papers from the World Congress of Dyslexia of the Orton Society in cooperation with the Mayo Clinic.* Baltimore, MD: York Press, Inc.

Edmonds, R. (1979). Effective schools for the urban poor. *Educational Leadership,* Vol. 37 (pp. 15-24).

Edmonds, R. (1986). Characteristics of effective schools. In Neisser, U. (Ed.), *The school achievement of minority children: New perspectives* (pp. 93-143). NJ: Lawrence Erlbaum Associates, Publishers.

Eisner, E. W. (1994). *Cognition and curriculum reconsidered.* NY: Teachers College Press.

Eisner, E. W. (May 1999). The uses and limits of performance assessment. *Phi Delta Kappan, Vol. 80:9* (pp. 658-660).

Engle, B. S. (Fall 1998). *Getting to know city kids: Understanding their thinking, imagining, and socializing.* NY: Teachers College Press.

Falk. B. (1996). Teaching the way children learn. In McLaughlin, M. W. & Oberman, I. (Eds), *Teacher learning: New policies, new practices* (pp. 22-29). NY: Teachers College Press.

Fan, X., Wilson, V. L. & Knapes, J. T. (June, 1996). Ethnic group representation in test construction samples and test bias: The standardization fallacy revisited. *Educational and Psychological Measurement, Vol. 56:3* (pp. 365-381).

Fargarty. R. (May 1998). The intelligence friendly classroom: It just makes sense. *Phi Delta Kappan: Vol 79:9* (pp. 655-65).

Fine, M., Weis, L. and Powell, L. C., (Summer, 1997). Communities of difference: A critical look at desegregated spaces created for and by youth. *Harvard Educational Review, Vol. 77:2* (pp. 247-284). *Cambridge, MA.*

Fleming, D. (2003). Subjects of the inner city: Writing the people of Cabrina-Green. In Nystrand, M. and Dufy, J. (2003). *Towards a rhetoric of everyday life: New directions in research on writing, text, and discourse* (pp. 207-244). Madison, WI: Wisconsin Press.

Flores, J. (1977). Latino studies: New contexts, new concepts. *Harvard Educational Review, Vol. 77:2* (pp. 208-221). Cambridge, MA. Floyd, C. (1996). Achieving despite the odds: A study of resilience among a group of African American high school seniors. *Journal of Negro Education, Vol. 65: 2* (pp. 185-194*).*

Fordham, S. & Ogbu, J. U. (1986). Black students; school success: Coping with the "burden of 'acting White.'" *Urban Review, Vol. 18* (pp.176-106).

Fordham, S. (2001a). Why can't Sonya (and Kwame) fail math? In Watkins, W. H., Lewis, J. H. and Chou, V. (Eds.), *Race and education: The roles of history and society in educating African American students* (pp.140-158). MA: Allyn and Bacon.

Fordham, S. (2001b). Racelessness as a factor in Black students' school success: Pragmatic strategy or pyrrhic victory? In Beauboeuf-Lafontant, T. & Augustine D. S. (Eds.), *Facing Racism in Education* (pp. 209-243). Cambridge, MA: Reprint Series No. 28, Harvard Educational Review.

Freire, P. (2002). *Pedagogy of the oppressed: 30th Anniversary Edition.* NY: The Continuum International Publishing Group, Inc.

French, D. (November 1998). The states' role in shaping a progressive vision of public education. *Phi Delta Kappan, Vol. 80:3* (pp. 184-194).

Fullan, M. (2007, Fourth Edition). *The new meaning of educational change.* NY: Teachers College Press.

Furth, H. G. (1970). *Piaget for teachers.* NJ: Prentice-Hall, Inc.

Gagne, R. M. (1967). *The conditions of learning.* NY: Holt, Rinehart and Winston, Inc.

Garber, L. O. & Edwards N. (1970). *The public school in our governmental structure: School Law Casebook Series No. 1.* Danville, Ill.: The Interstate Printers and Publishers, Inc.

Gay, G. (2002). *Culturally responsive teaching: Theory, research, and practice.* NY: Teachers College Press.

Gearing, F. & Sangree, L. (Eds., 1979). *Toward a cultural theory of education and schooling.* NY: Mouton Publishing.

Gee, J. P. (2004). *Situated language and learning: A critique of traditional schooling.* NY: Routledge.

Geertz, C. (1973) *The interpretation of cultures: Selected Essays by Clifford Geertz.* NY: Basic Books.

Gentry, B. F. (1985). *Differentiated staffing for urban schools: Creative staffing of urban schools should incorporate community strengths.* Florida: Exposition Press of Florida, Inc.

Giglioli, P. P. (Editor, 1986). *Language and social context.* NY: Penguin Books.

Giroux, H. & Purpel, D. (Eds.1983). *The hidden curriculum and moral education: Deception or discovery?* CA: McCutchan Publishing Corporation.

Giroux, H. A. (1997a). *Pedagogy and politics of hope: Theory, culture and schooling—A critical reader.* CO: Westview Press.

Giroux, H. A. (Summer, 1997b). Rewriting the discourse of racial identity: Towards a pedagogy and politics of whiteness. *Harvard Educational Review, Vol. 77:2* (pp. 285-329).*Cambridge, MA.*

Glenn, C. (Dec.1987). The new common school. *Phi Delta Kappan, Vol.69:4,* (pp. 290-296).

Glick, W. H. (1985). Organizational and psychological climate: Pitfalls in multilevel research. *Academy of Management Review, Vol. 25:4* (pp. 601-616).

Goldberg, M. F., (Dec. 2000). Demographics: Ignore them at your peril: An interview with Harold Hodgkinson. *Phi Delta Kappan, Vol. 82:4* (pp. 304-306).

Goodnow, J. J., Miller, P. J & Kessel, F. (July, 1995). *Cultural practices as contexts for development.* San Francisco, CA: Jossey-Bass.

Gordon, G. L. (Dec. 1999). Teacher talent and urban schools. *Phi Delta Kappan,* Vol. 81:2 *(pp. 304-312).*

Gough, P. B. (1975). The structure of the language. In Duane, D. D. & Rawson & M. B. (Eds), *Reading, perception and language: Papers from the world congress on Dyslexia (pp. 15-37).* Baltimore, MD: York Press, Inc.

Gougis, G. A.(1986). The effects of prejudice and stress on the academic performance of Black-Americans. In Neisser, U. (Ed.), *The school achievement of minority children: New perspectives* (pp. 145-160). NJ: Lawrence Erlbaum Associates, Publishers.

Gould, S. J. (1996). *The mismeasure of man.* New York: W. W. Norton & Company.

Goycochea, B. B., (Dec., 1997/Jan., 1998). Rich school, poor school. *Educational Leadership, Vol. 55:4* (pp.30-33).

Gratz, D. B. (May 2002). High standards for whom? *Phi Delta Kappan, Vol.81:9.* (pp. 681-687).

Greenfield, P. M. (1994). Independence and interdependence as developmental scripts: Implications for theory, research and practice. In Greenfield, P. M. & Cocking, R. R. (Eds.), *Cross-cultural roots of minority child development* (pp. 1-37). NJ: Lawrence-Erlbaum Associates, Publishers.

Greenfield, P. M. & Cocking, R. R. (Eds., 1994). *Cross-cultural roots of minority child development.* NJ: Lawrence-Erlbaum Associates, Publishers.

Greenfield, P. M. (1999). A theory of the teacher in the learning activities of everyday life. In Rogoff, B. and Lave, J. (Eds.). *Everyday cognition: Development in social context* (pp. 117-138). MA: Cambridge University Press.

Guarino, C. M., Santibanez, L & Daley, G. A. (2006). Teacher recruitment and retention: A review of the recent empirical literature. *Review of Research in Education, Vol. 76* (pp. 173-208).

Guskey, T. R. (March 2001). High percentages are not the same as high standards. *Phi Delta Kappan, Vol. 82:7* (pp. 534-536).

Haberman, M. (November 2000). Urban schools: Day camps or custodial centers? *Phi Delta Kappan, Vol. 82:3* (pp. 203-208).

Hacker, A. (1992). *Two nations: Black and white, separate, hostile, unequal.* NY: Ballantine Books.

Haertel, E. H. (1999). Performance assessment and education reform. *Phi Delta Kappan,* Vol. 80:9 (pp. 662-666).

Hale, J. (1986) *Black children: Their roots, culture, and learning styles.* Baltimore, MD: Jossey-Bass.

Hale, J. E. (2001a). *Learning while black: Creating educational excellence for African American children.* Baltimore, MD: The John Hopkins University Press.

Hale, J. E. (2001b). Culturally appropriate pedagogy. In Watkins, W. H., Lewis, J. H. and Chou, V. (Eds.), *Race and education: The roles of history and society in educating African American students (pp. 173-189).* MA: Allyn and Bacon.

Haney, W. & Madaus, G. (May 1989). Searching for alternatives to standardized tests: Whys, whats, and whithers. *Phi Delta Kappan, Vol. 70:9* (pp. 683-687).

Hanks, W. F. (2003). Foreword. In Lave, J. & Wenger, E. (Eds.), *Situated learning: Legitimate peripheral participation (pp. 13-24).* NY:Cambridge University Press.

Harris, C. L. (n.d., Article 00559). Language and Cognition. Boston University, MA. Massachusetts, USA. Downloaded April 19, 2008, from http://www.bu.edu/psych/faculty/charris/papers.

Heath, S. B. (Spring, 2002). Linguistics in the study of language in education. *Harvard Educational Review, Vol. 71:1* (pp. 49-59).

Heath, S. B. (Reprint, 2006). *Ways with words: Language, life, and work in communities and classrooms.* NY: Cambridge University Press.

Helms, J. E. (Sept. 1992). Why is there no study of cultural equivalence in standardized cognitive ability testing? *American Psychologist, Vol. 47:9* (pp. 1083-110).

Hess, F. M. and Brigham, F. (Jan, 2000*).* None of the above: The promise and peril of high-stakes testing. *American School Board Journal, Vol. 187:1* (pp. 26-29).

Hess, F. M., Rotherham, A. J. & Walsh, K. (Eds., 2004). *A qualified teacher in every classroom? Appraising old answers and ideas.* Cambridge MA: Harvard Education Press.

Hilliard, III, A. G. (1990). Limitations of current academic achievement measures. In Lomotey, K. (Ed.) *Going to School: The African American Experience* (pp. 135-142). NY: University of New York Press.

Hilliard, III, A. G. (1991). Do we have the will to educate all children? *Educational Leadership, Vol. 24:3 (pp. 18-25).*

Hilliard, III, A. G. (1992). Behavioral style, culture, and teaching and learning. *Journal of Negro Education, Vol. 61:3* (pp. 370-377).

Hilliard, III, A. G. (1995). *The maroon within us: Selected essays on African American community socialization.* Baltimore, MD: Black Classic Press.

Hilliard, III, A. G. (1996). Excellence in education versus high-stakes standardized testing. *Journal of Teacher Education, Vol. 51:4* (pp. 293-304).

Hilliard, III, A. G. (2001). "Race," identity, hegemony, and education: What do we need to know now? In Watkins, W. H., Lewis, J. H. and Chou, V. (Eds.), *Race and education: The roles of history and society in educating African American students (pp. 7-23).* MA: Allyn and Bacon.

Hilliard, III, A. G. (2002). Language, culture, and assessment of African American children. In Delpit, L. & Dowdy, J.

K. (Eds.), *The skin that we speak: Thoughts on language and culture in the classroom* (pp. 87-105). NY: The New Press.

Hodgkinson, H. (Feb. 1988). The right schools for the right kids. *Educational Leadership, Vol. 45:5* (pp. 10-14).

Hollins, E. R.; King, J. E.; and Hayman, W. C. (1994). *Teaching diverse populations: Formulating a knowledge base.* NY: State University of New York Press.

Hollins, E. R., (1996). *Culture in school learning: Revealing the deep meaning.* NJ: Lawrence Erlbaum Associates Publishers.

Hollins, E. R., (1997). Directed inequity in preservice teacher education: A developmental process model. In King, J. E., Hollins, E. R. & Hayman, W. C. (Eds.), Preparing teachers for cultural diversity (pp. 97-112). NY: Teachers College Press.

hooks, b. (1994). *Teaching to transgress: Education as the practice of freedom.* NY: Routledge.

Howard, G. R. (1999b). *We can't teach what we don't know: White teachers, multiracial Images.* NY: Teachers College Press.

Hoy, W. K. & Feldman, J. (Summer 1987). Organizational health: The concept and its measure. *Journal of Research and Development in Education, Vol.20:4* (30-40).

Hoy, W. K. & Tarter, J. C. (Fall 1992). Faculty trust in colleagues: Linking the principal with school effectiveness. *Journal*

of Research and Development in Education, Vol. 26:1 (
pp. 38-45).

Hoy, W. K. & Miskell, C. G. (Fall 1996). *Educational administration: Theory, research, nd practice.* (5th Edition). USA: McGraw Hill.

Hoy, W. K. & Tarter, C. J. (1997). *The road to open and healthy schools: A handbook for change: Elementary and middle school edition.* CA: Corwin Press, Inc.

Hoy, W. K. & Hannum, J. W. (1997). Middle school climate: An empirical assessment of organizational health and student achievement. *Educational Administrative Quarterly, Vol. 33:3* (290-311).

Huber, T., Kline, F. M., Bakken, L. & Clark, F. (1997). Transforming teacher education: Including culturally responsible pedagogy. In King, J. E., Hollis, E. R. & Hayman, W. C. (Eds.), *Preparing teachers for cultural diversity* (pp. 129-145). NY: Lawrence Erlbaum Associates Publishers.

Hull, G. & Schultz, K. (Winter 2001). Literacy and learning out-of school: A review of theory and research. *Review of Educational Research, Vol. 71:4 pp. 375-611).*

Hull, G. & Schultz, K. (Eds. 2003). *School's out: Bridging out-of-school literacies with classroom practice.* NY: Teachers College Press.

Hurwitz, N. & Hurwitz, S. (Jan 2000). Tests that count: Do high-stakes assessments really improve learning. *American School Board Journal, Vol. 187:1 (*pp. 21-25).

Irvine, J. J. (1991). Research on teacher-student interaction: Effects of student race, gender, and grade level. In Irvine, J. J. (Ed.), *Black students and school failure: policies, practices, and prescriptions* (pp.63-79). CT: Praeger Publishers.

Irvine, J. J. (1991). *Black students and school failure: Policies, practices, and prescriptions.* CT: Praeger Publishers.

Irvine, J. J. (Ed., 2002a). In *Search of wholeness: African American teachers and their culturally specific classroom practices.* NY: Palgrave.

Irvine, J. J. (2002b). African American teachers' culturally specific pedagogy: The collective stories. In Irvine, J. J. (Ed.), *In Search of wholeness: African American teachers and their culturally specific classroom practices* (pp. 139-146). NY: Palgrave.

Irvine, J. J., (2003). *Educating teachers for diversity: Seeing with a cultural eye.* NY: Teachers College Press.

Jackson, J. F. (Dec. 1999). What are the real risk factors for African American children? *Phi Delta Kappan, Vol. 81:4* (pp. 308-312).

Johnson, S. T. (1989). Test fairness and bias: Measuring academic achievement among Black youth. In Smith, W. & Chunn, E. (Eds.), *Black Education: A Quest for Equity and Excellence (pp.76-92).* NJ: Transaction Publishers.

Jones, R. (April 1998). Researchers tell what schools must do to improve student achievement. *The American School Board Journal, Vol. 185:4* (pp. 28-33).

Joynt, R. J. (1975). Neuroanatomy underlying the language function. In Duane, D. D. & Rawson & M. B. (Eds), *Reading, perception and language: Papers from the world congress on Dyslexia (pp. 39-54)*. Baltimore, MD: York Press, Inc.

Kaplan, G. R. (November 2000). Friends, foes, noncombatants: Notes of public education's pressure groups. *Phi Delta Kappan, Vol. 82:3 (Special Report, K1-K12)*.

Karpov, Y. V. (2006a). Vygotsky's doctrine of scientific concepts: Its role for contemporary education. In Kozulin, A.; Gindis, B; Ageyev, V. S.; Miller, S. M. Eds,). *Vygotsky's educational theory in cultural context, Reprint:* (pp. 65-82*)*. NY: Cambridge University Press.

Karpov, Y. V. (2006b). Development through the lifespan: A Neo-Vygotskian approach. In Kozulin, A.; Gindis, B; Ageyev, V. S.; Miller, S. M. (Eds.), *Vygotsky's* educational theory in cultural context, Reprint: (pp. 138-155). NY: Cambridge University Press.

Kavanagh, J. F. and Mattingly, I. G., (Eds., 1972). *Language by ear and by eye: The relationship between speech and reading*. Cambridge, MA: MIT University Press.

Kearnes, D. T. (June 1993). Toward a new generation of American schools. *Phi Delta Kappa, Vol. 83:1* (pp. 773-776).

Keefe, J. W. & Jenkins, J. M. (Feb 2002). Personalized instruction. *Phi Delta Kappan Vol. 83:6 (pp. 440-448)*.

Kimmelman, P. L. (2006). *Implementing NCLB: Creating a knowledge framework to support school improvement*. CA: Corwin Press.

King, J. E. (1994). The purpose of schooling for African American children: Including cultural knowledge. In Hollis, E. R., King, J. E, & Hayman, W. C. (Eds), *Teaching diverse populations: Formulating a knowledge base* (pp. 25-56). New York: State University of New York Press.

King, J. E.; Hollins E. R. & Hayman, W. C. (Eds., 1997). *Preparing teachers for cultural diversity.* NY: Teachers College Press.

King, J. E. (Editor, 2005). *Black education: A transformative research and action agenda for the new century.* NJ: Lawrence Erlbaum Associates Publishers.

Kintsch, W. (1970). *Learning, memory, and conceptual processes.* NY: John Wiley and Sons, Inc.

Kluger, R. (1977). *Simple justice: The history of Brown v. Board of Education, the epochal Supreme Court decision that outlawed segregation, and of black America's century-long struggle for equality under the law.* NY: Vintage Books.

Knapp, M. S. & Woolverton, S. (1995). Social class and schooling. In Banks, J. & Banks, C. M. (Eds.), *Handbook of research on multicultural education* (pp. 548-569). NY: McMillian Publishing.

Kohl, H. (1994). *I won't learn from you: And other thoughts on creative maladjustment.* NY: The New Press.

Kohn, A. (April 1998). Only for my kid: How privileged parents undermine school reform. *Phi Delta Kappan, Vol. 79:8* (pp. 569-577).

Kohn, A. (1999a). *The schools our children deserve: Moving beyond traditional classrooms and "tougher standards."* New York: Houghton Mifflin Company.

Kohn, A. (1999b). Fighting the tests: A practical guide to rescuing our schools. *Phi Delta Kappan, Vol. 82:5* (pp. 348-357).

Kohn, A. (October 1999c). Raising the scores: Ruining the schools. *The American School Board Journal, Vol. 186:10* (pp 31-34).

Kohr, R. L., Coldiron, R., Skiffington, W., Masters, J. R. & Blust, S. (1988). The Influence of class and gender on self-esteem for fifth, eighth, and eleventh grade students in Pennsylvania schools. *Journal of Negro Education, Vol. 57:4* (pp. 467-481).

Koretz, D. (2008). The pending reauathorization of NCLB: An opportunity to rethink the basic strategy. In Sunderman, G. L. (Ed.), *Holding NCLB accountable: Achieving accountability, equity, and school reform (pp. 9-42).* CA: Corwin Press.

Kornhaber, M. L. (2004). Assessment, standards, and equity. In Banks, J. & Banks, C. M. (Eds.), *Handbook of research on multicultural education. 2ⁿᵈ Edition* (pp. 91-109). NY: McMillian Publishing.

Kornhaber, M. L. (2008). Beyond standardization in school accountability. In Sunderman, G. L. (Ed.), *Holding NCLB accountable: Achieving accountability, equity, and school reform* (pp. 43-55). CA: Corwin Press.

Kottkamp, R. B. & Mulhern, J. A. (1987). Teacher expectancy motivation, open to closed climate and pupil control ideology in high schools. *Journal of Research and Development in Education, Vol. 20:2* (pp. 9-18).

Kozol, J. (1967). *Death at an early age: The destruction of the hearts and minds of Negro children in the Boston Public Schools.* MA: Houghton-Mifflin Company Boston.

Kozol, J. (1991). *Savage inequalities: Children in America's schools.* New York: Crown Publishers, Inc.

Kozol, J. (1995). *Amazing grace: The lives of children and the conscience of a nation.* New York: Harper Perennial Publishers.

Kozol, J. (2005). *The shame of the nation: The restoration of Apartheid schooling in America.* NY: Crown Publishers.

Kozulin, A.; Gindis, B; Ageyev, V. S.; Miller, S. M. (Eds, Reprint: 2006). *Vygotsky's educational theory in cultural context.* NY: Cambridge University Press.

Kozulin, A (2006) Psychological tools and mediated learning. In Kozulin, A.; Gindis, B; Ageyev, V. S.; Miller, S. M. (Eds), *Vygotsky's educational theory in cultural context, Reprint: 2006* (pp. 1-38). NY: Cambridge University Press.

Kretovics, J. & Nussel, E. J. (1994). *Transforming urban education.* Boston, MA: Allyn and Bacon.

Kunjufu, J. (2002). *Black students, middle class teachers.* Ill: African American Images.

Kutz, E., & Roskelly, H. (1991). *An unquiet pedagogy: Transforming practice in the English classroom.* NH: Boynton/Cook Publishers.

LaBerge, D. (1972). Beyond auditory coding. In Kavanagh, J. F. and Mattingly, I. G., (Eds.), *Language by ear and by eye: The relationship between speech and reading* (pp. 241-248). Cambridge, MA: MIT University Press.

Labov, W. (1986). The logic of nonstandard English. In Giglioli, P. P. (Ed.), *Language and social context* (pp. 179-215). NY: Penguin Books.

Ladson-Billings, G. (1994). *The dreamkeepers: Successful teachers of African American children.* CA: Jossey-Bass.

Ladson-Billings, G. (Fall 1995). Toward a theory of culturally relevant pedagogy *American Educational Research Journal, Vol. 32:2* (pp. 465-491).

Ladson-Billings, G. (2001). The power of pedagogy: Does teaching matter? In Watkins, W. H., Lewis, J. H. and Chou, V. (Eds.), *Race and education: The roles of history and society in educating African American students* (pp. 73-88). MA: Allyn and Bacon.

Ladson-Billings, G. (2006). From the achievement gap to the education department: Understanding achievement in U. S. schools. *Educational Researcher, Vol. 35:7* (pp. 3-12).

Ladson-Billings, G. & Tate, W. F. (Eds. 2006). *Education research in the public Interest: Social justice, action, and policy.* NY: Teachers College Press.

Lampert, M. (2002). Knowing teaching: The intersection of research on teaching and qualitative research. *Harvard Educational Review, Vol. 71:1* (pp. 86-99).

Lasky, S. G. (2004). Toward a policy framework for analyzing educational system effects. *Report No. 71:* The John Hopkins University.

Lave, J. & Wenger, E. (2003). *Situated learning: Legitimate peripheral participation.* NY: Cambridge University Press.

Lee, C. D., Lomotey, K. & Shujaa, M. (1990). How shall we sing our sacred song in a strange land? The dilemma of double consciousness and the complexities of an African-centered pedagogy. *Journal of Education, Vol. 172* (pp. 45-61).

Lee, C. D. (2001). Comment: Unpacking culture, teaching, and learning: A response to "The power of pedagogy." In Watkins, W. H., Lewis, J. H. and Chou, V. (Eds.), *Race and education: The roles of history and society in educating African American students* (pp. 89-127). MA: Allyn and Bacon.

Lee, C. D. (2005a). Intervention research based on current views of cognition and learning. In King, J. E. (Ed.), *Black education: A transformative research and action agenda for the new century* (pp. 73-114). NJ: Lawrence Erlbaum Associates Publishers.

Lee, C. D. (2005b). The state of knowledge about education of African Americans. In King, J. E. (Ed.), *Black education: A transformative research and action agenda for the new century* (pp. 45-71). NJ: Lawrence Erlbaum Associates Publishers.

Lee, J. O. (Feb. 2003). Implementing high standards in urban schools: problems and solutions. *Phi Delta Kappan, Vol. 84:6* (pp. 449-455).

Leistyna, P., Woodrum, A. & Sherblom, S. A. (1999). *Breaking free: The transformative power of critical pedagogy.* Cambridge, MA: Harvard Educational Review Reprint No. 27.

Lewis, L., Smerdon, B. & Greene, B. (Jan 1999). Teacher quality: A report of the preparation and qualifications of public school teachers. *Statistical Analysis Report.* U. S. Department of Education. National Center for Education Statistics.

Lewis, J. H. (2001). Introduction: The search for new answers. In Watkins, W. H., Lewis, J. H. and Chou, V. (Eds.), *Race and education: The roles of history and society in educating African American students* (pp. 1-6). MA: Allyn and Bacon.

Lewis, A. C. (Nov. 2002). A horse called NCLB. *Phi Delta Kappan, Vol. 84:3 (pp. 179-180).*

Lidz, C. S. & Gindis, B. (2006). Dynamic assessment of the evolving cognitive functions in children. In Kozulin, A.; Gindis, B; Ageyev, V. S.; Miller, S. M. (Eds.), *Vygotsky's educational theory in cultural context* (Reprint: pp. 99-116). NY: Cambridge University Press.

Lindsay, P. H. and Norman, D. A. (1977). *Human information processing: An Introduction to psychology.* NY: Academic Press.

Linn, R. (2008), Toward a more effective definition of adequate yearly progress. In Sunderman, G. L. (Eds.), *Holding NCLB accountable: Achieving accountability, equity, and school reform* (pp. 27-42). CA: Corwin Press.

Lohman, D. F. (Winter 1989). Human intelligence: An introduction to advances in theory and research. *Review of Educational Review, Vol. 59* (pp. 333-373).

Lomax, R. G., West M. M., Harmon, M. C., Viator, K. A. & Madaus, G. F. (1995). The impact of mandated standardized testing on minority students. *Journal of Negro Education, Vol. 64:2 (pp. 171-105).*

Loury, G. C., (2002). *The anatomy of racial inequality.* Cambridge, MA: Harvard University Press.

Lynch, M. (2006). *Closing the racial academic achievement gap.* Chicago, Ill: African American Images.

Maeroff, G. I. (May, 1988). Withered hopes, stillborn dreams: The dismal panorama of urban schools. *Phi Delta Kappan, Vol. 69:9* (pp. 632-639).

Maeroff, G. (Dec. 1991). Assessing Alternative Assessment. *Phi Delta Kappan, Vol. 73:4* (pp. 274-281).

Maeroff, G. I. (Feb. 1998). Altered destinies: Making life better for school children in need. *Phi Delta Kappan, Vol. 79:6* (pp. 425-432).

Mager, R. F. (1975). *Preparing instructional objectives (2nd Edition).* Belmont, CA: Pitman Learning.

Maiga, H. O. (2005). When the language of culture is not the language of education. In King, J. E. (Ed.), *Black education: A transformative research and action agenda for the new century* (pp. 159-180). NJ: Lawrence Erlbaum Associates Publishers.

Marzano, R. J. & Costa A. L. (May, 1988). Question: Do standardized tests measure general cognitive skills? Answer: No. *Educational Leadership, Vol. 45:8* (pp. 66-71).

Marzano, R. J. and Kendall, J. S. (2007). *The new taxonomy of educational objectives.* CA: Corwin Press.

Mathis, W. J. (May 2003). No Child Left Behind: Costs and benefits. *Phi Delta Kappan,* Vol. 84:9 (pp. 679-686).

McLaughlin, M. W., Talbert, J., Kane, J. & Powell, J. (Nov 1990). Constructing a personalized school environment. *Phi Delta Kappan: Vol. 72:3 (pp. 230-235).*

McLaughlin, M. W. & Oberman, I. (Eds.). *Teacher learning: New policies, new practices.* NY: Teachers College Press.

McLaughlin, M. W., Watts, C. & Beard, M. (Dec. 2000). Just because it's happening doesn't mean it's working: Using action research to improve practice in middle schools. *Phi Delta Kappan, Vol. 82:4* (pp. 284-290).

McLauren, P. (2007) *Life in schools: An introduction to critical pedagogy in the foundations of education (Fifth Edition).* Boston, MA: Pearson Education, Inc.

McNeil, L. M. (June 2000). Creating new inequalities: Contradictions of reforms. *Phi Delta Kappan, Vol. 81:10* (pp. 729-734).

Mehler, J., Pallier, C. Christopher & Chistopher, A. (1995). *Language and cognition.* Rutgers University Center for Cognitive Science, New Brunswick, NJ, USA (pp.1-11); http://www.pallier.org/papers/mehler/_language_cognition.pdf.

Meier, D. (1992). *Will Standards Save Public Education?* Boston: Beacon Press.

Meier, D. (Sept. 2003). So what does it take to build a school for democracy? *Phi Delta Kappan, Vol.85:1* (pp. 15-21).

Morris, J. E., (Dec. 1999). What is the future of predominantly black urban schools?: The politics of race in urban education policy. *Phi Delta Kappan,Vol. 81:4* (pp. 316-319).

Morris, J. E. (2002). A communally bonded school for African American students, families, and a community. *Phi Delta Kappan, Vol. 84:3* (pp. 230-234).

Mosteller, F., Light, R. J. & Sachs, J. A. (1998). Sustained inquiry in education: Lessons from skill grouping and class size. In *Cool Thinking on Hot Topics: A Research Guide for Educators, Vol. 67:3* (pp. 67-113).

Murphy, J. A. (Oct. 1988). Improving the achievement of minority students. *Educational Leadership, Vol. 46:2* (pp. 41-42).

National Academy of Education (2005). *A good teacher in every classroom: Preparing the highly qualified teachers our children deserve.* CA: Jossey-Bass.

National Research Council, Center for Education (2001). *Knowing and learning mathematics for teaching: Proceedings of a workshop.* Washington, DC: National Academy Press.

Neil, M. & Medina, N. J. (May 1989). Standardized testing: Harmful to educational health. *Phi Delta Kappan, Vol. 70:9 (*pp. 688-697).

Newman, F. M., King, B. M. and Rigdon, M. (1998). Accountability and school performance: Implications from restructuring schools. In *Cool Thinking on Hot Topics: A Research Guide for Educators, Vol. 67:3* (pp. 34-66).

Nieto, S. (1999). *The light in their eyes: Creating multicultural learning communities.* NY: Teachers College Press.

Nieto, S. (2004). Puerto Ricans in U. S. schools: A troubled past and the search for a hopeful future. In Banks, J. A. and Banks, C. A. M. (Eds), *Handbook of research on multicultural education* (pp. 515-541). Second Edition. CA: Jossey-Bass.

Nogurera, P A., Wing, J. Y. (Eds., 2006). *Unfinished business: Closing the racial achievement gap in our schools.* CA: Jossey-Bass.

Norman, D. A. (1972). *The role of memory in the understanding of language.* In Kavanagh, J. F. and Mattingly, I. G.,

(Eds.), *Language by ear and by eye: The relationship between speech and reading* (pp. 278-288). Cambridge, MA: MIT University Press.

Nystrand, M. & Duffy, J. (2003). *Towards a rhetoric of everyday life: New directions in research on writing text and discourse.* Madison, WI: The University of Wisconsin Press.

Ogbu, J. U. (1994) From cultural differences in cultural frame of references. In Greenfield, P. M. & Cocking, R. R. (Eds.), *Cross-cultural roots of minority child development* (pp. 365-391). *NJ: Lawrence Erlbaum Associates, Publishers.*

Oanian, S. (Jan. 2000). Goals 2000: What's in a name? *Phi Delta Kappan, Vol. 81:5* (pp. 344-355).

Ohanian, S. (Jan. 2001). News for the test resistance trail. *Phi Delta Kappan, Vol. 82:5* (pp. 363-366). Okihiro, G. Y. (1996). *Margins and Mainstreams: Asians in American history and culture.* Seattle: University of Washington Press.

Olson, D. R. (1972). Language use for communicating, instructing, and thinking. In Carroll, J. B. and Freedle, R. O. (Eds.), *Language comprehension and the acquisition of knowledge* (pp. 139-167). Washington, DC: Winston and Sons, Inc.

Paige, R. (April 2002). *What to know & where to go: Parents' guide to No Child Left behind: A new era in education.* Washington, D.C: U.S. Department of Education.

Pierre-Pipkin, E. Jean (2001: Dissertation). *The impact of school climate on African-American student achievement in the middle schools.* Texas Southern University. MI: Proquest Publishers.

Pierre-Pipkin, J. (2003, Revised). *Learning packets for parents: Mini-Workshop I: Understanding learning problems.* Beaumont, TX: EEUCbyPierre Publisher.

Pierre-Pipkin, J. (2004a). *Context without context is pretext: Reframing the context of curriculum to ensure academic success for African American Children.* Research-based Workshop presented at the 19th Annual Conference of the Texas Alliance of Black School Educators; Houston, TX, March 2, 2004.

Pierre-Pipkin, J. (2004b). *Placing NCLB in perspective for African American children: Facts, Myths, and Realities.* Research-based Workshop presented at the 32nd Annual Conference of the National Alliance of Black School Educators; Dallas, TX, November, 2004.

Pierre-Pipkin, J. (2006). *Leave no culture behind: Ensuring that "teaching" is "reaching" African-American children.* Research-based Workshop presented at the 34th Annual Conference of the National Alliance of Black School Educators; Orlando, Fl.: November 2006.

Pierre-Pipkin, J. (2007). *Instructional application of the Pierre Pedagogy: Teaching learners "to see" what you are "saying"—From theory to practice. (Chapter 7/DVD)* Beaumont, TX: EEUCbyPierre.

Pierre-Pipkin, J. (2008). *Ensuring that "teaching" is "reaching" African-American children: Culturally relevant contexts for content.* Research-based Workshop presented at the

36th Annual Conference of the National Alliance of Black School Educators; Atlanta, GA; November 2008.

Pollard, D. S. (1989). Against the odds: A profile of academic achievers from the urban underclass. *Journal of Negro Education, Vol. 58, No. 3.* (pp.297-308).

Popham, J. W. (May 1987). The merits of measurement-driven instruction. *Phi Delta Kappan, Vol. 68:9* (pp. 679-682).

Popham, J. W. (Jan. 1998). Farewell curriculum: Confessions of an Assessment Convert. *Phi Delta Kappan, Vol. 79:5* (pp. 380-384).

Popham, J. W. (June 2000). The score-boosting game: Teachers are caught between standardized tests and a hard place. *The American School Board Journal,* Vol. 187:6 (pp. 36-39).

Porter, M. (1997). *The misdiagnosis of African American boys in American classrooms.* Chicago: African American Images.

President and Fellows of Harvard College (1998). *Cool thinking on hot topics: Research guide of educators.* Cambridge MA: Harvard Educational Review.

Ramirez, A. (Nov 1999). Assessment-driven reform: The emperor still has no clothes. Phi Delta Kappan, Vol. 81:3 (pp. 204-208).

Rapp, D. (2002). National certified teachers in Ohio give state education policy, classroom climate, and high stakes testing a grade of F. *Phi Delta Kappan, Vol. 84:3* (pp. 216-128).

Rebell, M. A. and Wolff, J. R. (2008). *Moving every child ahead: From NCLB hype to meaningful educational opportunity.* NY: Teachers College Press.

Rebell, M. A. & Wolff, J. R. (Eds. 2009). *NCLB at the crossroads: Reexamining the federal effort to close the achievement gap.* NY: Teachers College Press.

Reed, D. F., McMillan, J. H. & McBee, R. B. (September 1995). Defying the odds: Middle schoolers in high risk circumstances who succeed. *Middle School Journal* (pp. 3-10).

Reese, W. J. (1998). What history teachers about the impact of educational research on practice. *Review of Research in Education, Vol. 24 (pp. 1-19).*

Reinstein, D. (Dec., 1997/Jan., 1998). Crossing the economic divide. *Educational Leadership, Vol. 55:4* (pp.28-29).

Reutter, Jr., E. E. & Hamilton, R. R. (1976). *The law of public education.* NY: The Foundation Press, Inc.

Reutter, Jr., E. E. & Hamilton, R. R. (1979). *1979 supplement to the law of public education.* NY: The Foundation Press, Inc.

Rippa, S. A. (1992). *Education in a free society: An American history (Seventh Edition).* NY: Longman.

Rist, R. C. (Fall 2000). Student social class and teacher expectations: The self-fulfilling prophecy in ghetto education. *Harvard Educational Review, Vol. 70:3* (pp. 266-303).

Rogers, C. R. (1970). *Carl Rogers on encounter groups.* NY: Harrow Books.

Rogoff, B. and Lave, J. (Eds.). (1999). Everyday cognition: Development in social context. MA: Cambridge University Press.

Rogoff, B. (2003). *The cultural nature of human development.* NY: Oxford University Press.

Rumelhart, D. E., Lindsay, P. H. & Norman, D. A. (1972). A process model for long-term memory. In Tulving, E. and Donaldson, W. (Eds.), *Organization of memory.* NY: Academic Press.

Russell, J. F., Grandgennett, N. E.; & Lickteig, M. J., (1994). Serving the needs of at-risk students: The relationship to school personnel attitudes and efforts. *Journal of Research and Development in Education, Vol. 27:4* (pp. 215-225).

Sabo, D. (Spring, 1995). Organizational climate of middle schools and the quality of student life. *Journal of Research and Development in Education, Vol. 28:3* (pp. 150-160).

Schubert, E. D. (1975). The role of auditory perception in language processing. In Duane, D. D. & Rawson & M. B. (Eds*), Reading, perception and language: Papers from the world congress on Dyslexia (pp. 97-13*). Baltimore, MD: York Press, Inc.

Schultz, K. & Hull, G. (2002). Locating literacy in out-of-school contexts. In Hull, G. & Schultz, K. (Eds.), *School's out:*

Bridging out-of-school literacies with classroom practices (pp. 11-31). NY: Teachers College Press.

Scott, H. J. (October 2007). *The Black-White achievement gap: Blame the schools, but indict society.* NY: CAM Publishing Group, Inc.

Scribner, S. (1999) Studying working intelligence. In Rogoff, B. and Lave, J. (Eds), *Everyday cognition: Development in social context (pp. 9-40).* MA: Cambridge University Press

Shade, B. J. (Summer 1982). Afro-American cognitive style: a variable in school *success?* Review of Educational Research, Vol. 52:2 *(pp. 219-244).*

Shade, B. J. (1994). Understanding the African American learner. In Hollins, E. R.; King, J. E.; and Hayman, W. C. (Eds.), *Teaching diverse populations: Formulating a knowledge base* (pp. 176-190). NY: State University of New York Press.

Shepard., L., Hammerness, K, Darling-Hammond, L, Rust, F., Baratz, S., Gordon, E., Gutierrez, C. & Pacheo, A. (2005) Assessment. In Darling-Hammond, L. & Bransford, J. (Eds.), *Preparing teachers for a changing world: What teachers should learn and be able to do* (pp. 275-326).

Shujaa, M. J. (Ed., 1998). *Too much schooling too little education: A paradox of black life in white societies.* NJ: African World Press, Inc.

Simon, R. I. (1992). *Teaching against the grain: Tests for a pedagogy of possibility.* NY: Bergin and Garvey.

Sizemore, B. A (1985). Pitfalls and promises of effective schools research. *The Journal of Negro Education, Vol. 56:1* (pp. 3-19).

Sizemore, B. A (1989). The Madison Elementary School: A turnaround case. *The Journal of Negro Education, Vol. 57:3* (pp. 243-266).

Sizemore, B. A. (2008). *Walking in circles: The black struggle for school reform.* Chicago, IL: Third World Press.

Slaughter-Defoe & Garlson, K. G. (1996). Young African American and Latino children in high-poverty urban schools: How they perceive school climate. *Journal of Negro Education, Vol. 65:1 (pp. 60-70).*

Slavin, R. E., (Dec., 1997/Jan., 1998). Can education reduce social inequity? *Educational Leadership, Vol. 55:4* (pp. 6-9).

Sotomayor, M. (Ed., 1991). *Empowering Hispanic families: A critical issue for the 90's.* Milwaukee, Wisconsin: Family service America.

Spencer, M. B., Phillips-Swanson, D. & Cunningham, M. (1991). Ethnicity, ethnic identity, and competence formation: Adolescent transitional and culture formation. *Journal of Negro Education, Vol. 60:3* (pp. 366-397).

Spencer, M. B. (2001). Identity, achievement, orientation and race: "Lessons learned" about normative developmental experiences of African American males. In Watkins, W. H., Lewis, J. H. and Chou, V. (Eds.), *Race and education: The roles of history and society in educating*

African American students (pp. 100-127). MA: Allyn and Bacon.

Stanfield, II, J. H. (1993). Epistemological considerations. In Stanfield, II, J. H. & Dennis, R. M. (Eds.), *Race and ethnicity in research methods* (pp. 16-36). California: Sage Publications, Inc.

Steele, C. M. (April 1992). Race and the schooling of Black Americans. *The Atlantic Monthly* (pp. 68-78).

Steinberg, A. (1993). Adolescents and schools: Improving the Fit. *The Harvard Educational Letter.* Cambridge, MA: HER Reprint Series No. 1.

Steinberg, L. (1996). *Beyond the classroom: Why school reform has failed and what parents need to do.* New York: Simon & Schuster.

Steinberg, R. (Dec. 2007). Who are the bright children? The cultural context of being and acting intelligent. *Educational Researcher, Vol. 36:3* (pp. 148-155).

Singham, M. (1998). The canary in the mine: The achievement gap between Black and White students. *Phi Delta Kappan, Vol. 69:9 (pp. 9-15).*

Sirotnik, K. A. & Kimball, K. (Nov 1999). Standards for standards-based accountability systems. *Phi Delta Kappan, Vol. 81:3* (pp. 209-214).

Stiggins, R. J. (Oct 1985). Improving assessment where it means the most: In the classroom. *Educational Leadership, Vol. 42:2* (pp. 60-74).

Stiggins, R. J. (Jan 1988). Revitalizing classroom assessment: The highest instructional priority. *Phi Delta Kappan, Vol. 69:5* (pp. 363-36).

Stiggins, R. J. (Nov 1999). Assessment, student confidence, and school success. *Phi* Delta Kappan, Vol. 81:3 (pp. 191-198).

Stiggins, R. J. (June 2002). Assessment crisis: The absence of assessment for learning. *Phi Delta Kappan, Vol. 83:10* (pp. 758-765).

Stokes, A. (Spring 2001). Insights into African-American students' perceptions of classroom life. *Journal of the Research Association of Minority Professors. Vol. 5:1* (pp. 95-95-107).

Strachan, A. L. (Spring 2000). In the brain of the beholder: The neuropsychological basis of aesthetic preferences. *The Harvard Brain, Vol. 7* (pp. 1-10).

Stringfield, S. and Teddle, C. (Oct. 1988). A time to summarize: The Louisiana school effectiveness stud*y. Educational Leadership, Vol. 46:2* (pp. 44-49).

Sunderman, G. L., Kim, J. S. and Orfield, G. (2005). *NCLB meets school realities: Lessons from the field.* CA: Corwin Press.

Sunderman, G. L. (Ed., 2008). *Holding NCLB accountable: Achieving accountability, equity and school reform.* CA: Corwin Press.

Supovitz, J. A. & Brennan, R. T. (1998). "Mirror, mirror on the wall, which is the fairest test of all? An examination of the equitability of portfolio assessment relative to standardized tests." *In Cool Thinking on Hot Topics: A Research Guide for Educators, Vol.67:3* (pp. 1-33).

Swartz, E. (June 2009). Diversity: Gatekeeping knowledge and maintaining inequalities. *Review of Educational Research, Vol. 79:2* (pp. 1044-1083).

Tanner, D. (Jan. 1998). The social consequences of bad research. *Phi Delta Kappan, Vol. 69:5* (pp.344-349).

Tanner, D. (November 2000). Manufacturing problems and selling solutions: How to succeed in the education business without really educating. *Phi Delta Kappan, Vol. 82:3* (pp. 188-202).

Tatum, B. D. (1997a). *Why are all the black kids sitting together in the cafeteria?: And other conversations about race.* NY: Basic Books.

Tatum, B.D. (Dec., 1997b/Jan., 1998). Why are all the black kids sitting together? *Educational Leadership, Vol. 55:4* (pp. 12-17).

The Cognition & Technology Group at Vanderbilt (1997*). The Jasper Project: Lessons in curriculum, instruction, assessment, and professional development.* NJ: Lawrence Erlbaum Associates, Publishers.

Thomas, M. D. & Gainbridge, W. L. (June 2002a). No child left behind: Facts and failures. *Phi Delta Kappan, Vol. 83:10* (pp. 774-781).

Thomas, M. D. & Gainbridge, W. L. (2002b). *No Child Left Behind: A toolkit for* teachers. *http://www.ed.gov/orubt/nclbguide/toolkit.hlml (Retrieved October 23, 2004).*

Tomlinson, C. A. & McTighe, J. (2006). *Integrating differentiated instruction & Understanding by design: Connecting content with kids.* VA: Association for Supervision and Curriculum Development.

Trevisan, M. S. (June 2002). The states' role in ensuring assessment competence. *Phi Delta Kappan, Vol. 83:10* (pp. 766-771).

Trueba, E. H. (Moderator, 1977), Takaki, R., Munoz, V. I., Nieto, S., Anderson, M. L. & Sommer, D., Harvard Education Symposium: Ethnicity and education forum: What difference does difference make? *Harvard Educational Review, Vol. 77:2* (pp. 169-187). Cambridge, MA: HER.

Tulving, E. & Donaldson, W. (Eds. 1972). *Organization of memory.* NY: Academic Press.

Turvey, M. T. (1975). Perspectives in vision: conception or perception? In Duane, D. D. & Rawson & M. B. (Eds), *Reading, perception and language: Papers from the world congress on Dyslexia (*pp. 131-195). Baltimore, MD: York Press, Inc.

Tyack, D. B. (1974). *The one best System: A history of American urban education.* Cambridge, MA: Harvard University Press.

Tyack, D. & Hansot, E. (1992). *Learning together: A history of coeducation in American public schools.* NY: Russell Sage Foundation.

Tyack, D. B. and Cuban, L. (1995). *Tinkering toward utopia: A century of public school reform.* Cambridge, MA: Harvard University Press.

U. S. Department of Education. (n.d.) *New No Child Left Behind flexibility: Highly qualified teachers. Fact Sheet.* Retrieved Nov. 29, 2004, http//www.col-ed,org/smcnws/equity/ profile.html.

Valencia, R. R., Valenzuela, A., Sloan, K. & Foley, D. (Dec. 2001). Let's treat the cause, not the symptoms: Equity and accountability in Texas revisited. *Phi Delta Kappan, Vol. 83:4* (pp. 318-321).

Van Horn, R. (Dec. 1999). Inner-city schools: A multiple variable discussion. *Phi Delta Kappan, Vol. 81:4* (pp. 291-297).

Vasquez, O. A. (2006). Cross-national explorations of sociocultural research on learning. *Review of Research in Education, 30:33* (pp. 33-64).

Villegas, A. M. &Lucas, T. (2002). *Educating culturally responsive teachers: A coherent approach.* NY: State University of New York Press.

Voelkl, K. E. (1993). Academic achievement and expectations among African-American students. *Journal of Research and Development in Education, Vol. 27:1.* (pp. 42-52).

Vygotsky, L. S. (1978). *Mind in society: The development of higher psychological processes.* Cambridge, MA: Harvard University Press.

Warren, M. R. (2005). Communities and schools: A new view of urban education reform. *Harvard Educational Review, Vol. 75:2 (pp. 133-139).*

Watkins, W. H., Lewis, J. H. and Chou, V. (2001). *Race and education: The roles of history and society in educating African American students.* MA: Allyn and Bacon.

Watkins, W. H. (2001a). *The white architects of black education: Ideology and power in America, 1865-1954.* New York: Teachers College Press.

Watkins, W. H., (2001b). From accommodation to contestation and beyond. In Watkins, W. H., Lewis, J. H. and Chou, V. (Eds.), *Race and education: The roles of history and society in educating African American students* (pp. 40-65). MA: Allyn and Bacon.

Wells, G. (2000). *Dialogic inquiry: Towards a sociolocultural practice and theory in education.* Cambridge, Eng: Cambridge University Press.

Welner, K. G. & Oakes, J. (1998). (Li)Ability grouping: The new susceptibility of school tracking systems to legal challenges. *Cool Thinking on Hot topics: A Research Guide for Educators* (pp. 114-136). *Cambridge, MA: Harvard Educational Review.*

Wertsch, J. V., Minick, N., Arnes, F. J. (1999). The creation of context in joint problem-solving. In Rogoff, B. and Lave,

J. (Eds.), *Everyday cognition: Development in social context* (pp. 151-176). MA: Cambridge University Press.

West, C. A. (1985). Effects of school climate and school social structure on student achievement in selected urban elementary schools. *Journal of Negro Education, Vol. 54:3* (pp. 451-463).

Westheimer, J. and Kahne, J. (September 2003). Reconnecting education to democracy: Democratic dialogues. *Phi Delta Kappan, Vol. 85:1* (pp. 9-14).

White, S. H. & Siegel, A. W. (1999). Cognitive Development in time and space. In Rogoff, B. & Lave, J. (Eds.), *Everyday cognition: Development in social context.* (pp. 238-277). MA: Cambridge University Press. Wiggins, G. (May 1989). A true test: Toward a more authentic and equitable assessment. *Phi Delta Kappan, Vol. 70:9* (pp. 703-713).

Wilson, A. B. (Winter, 1968). Social class and equal opportunity. *Harvard Educational Review, Vol. 38:1* (pp. 77-88).

Wilson, S. (Nov. 1990). The secret garden of Teacher education. Phi Delta Kappan, Vol. 72:3 (pp. 204-209).

Wilson, W. J. (1996). *When work disappears: The world of the new urban poor.* New York: Vintage Press.

Winograd, T. (1980). What does it mean to understand language? In *Cognitive Science. Vol. 4* (pp. 209-241).

Wise, A. E.(January 1988). The two conflicting trends in school reform: Legislated learning revisited. *Phi Delta Kappan, Vol.69:5* (pp.328-332).

Wise, A. E. (1990). Policies for reforming teacher education. *Phi Delta Kappan,* Vol. 72:3 *(pp. 200-202).*

Wiske, M. S. (1998). What is teaching for understanding? In *Teaching for understanding: Linking research with practice* (pp. 61-86). CA: Jossey-Bass.

Wood, G. (1972). Organizational process and free recall. In Tulving, E. & Donaldson, W. (Eds.). *Organization of memory* (pp. 49-91). NY: Academic Press.

Wood, C. (March 2002). Changing the pace of schools: Slowing down the day to improve the quality of learning. *Phi Delta Kappan, Vol. 83:7* (pp. 545-550).

Woodson, C. G. (1933). *The mis-education of the Negro.* Trenton, NJ.: African World Press.

Wu, Frank H. (2002). *Yellow: Race in America beyond black and white.* New York: Basic Books.

Wubbels, T., Levy, J. & Brekelmans, M. (April 1997). Paying attention to relationships. *Educational Leadership, Vol. 54:7* (pp. 82-86).

Zirkel, Perry A. (Ed., 1978). *A digest of Supreme Court decision affecting education.* Bloomington Indiana: Phi Delta Kappan.

INDEX

nervous system 37, 39, 40, 80

networks 54, 103, 244

neuroanatomy 38

neurology 39

neuroscience, 41, 49

nexus 5, 8, 13, 18, 20, 22, 208,
218, 282, 297

No Child Left Behind Act 123,
181

norm-referenced tests 20

O

objectives 21, 22, 24, 50, 109,
110, 114, 115, 156, 171,
173, 224, 307, 333, 334

out-of-school experiences 30,
88, 196

out-of-school knowledge 22, 28,
100, 267, 276, 297

out-of-school learning 5, 109,
179, 209

P

paper-pencil assessments 23,
25, 154

paper-pencil tests 21

portfolios 23, 286

prior knowledge 8, 9, 12, 16,
18, 24, 46, 77, 87, 97, 99,
100, 243, 282, 292

psychological processes 79, 311

R

reciprocal instruction 18, 29

S

scaffolding 2, 5, 16, 20, 26, 28,
29, 30, 88, 93, 101, 225,
227, 241, 242, 244, 276,
282, 283, 285

schemata theory 10

scientific concepts 50, 96, 102,
113, 326

self-fulfilling prophecy 32, 145

sensory modality 9

situated activity 284

Situated Cognition Theory 85

Situated Learning Theory 106

situational contexts 93, 97, 276

situational learning 256, 266

situational teaching 33, 266

social class 2, 144, 145, 231,
237, 340

socialization 101, 105, 236,
240, 251, 306, 322

Social Learning Theory 103

socially marginalized 232, 234

sociocultural 7, 28, 42, 51, 52,
179, 243, 244, 249, 256,
261, 263, 265, 266, 288,
348

socio-economic 13, 19, 32, 195,
213, 219

Sociolinguistic Theory 103, 104

standardized tests 2, 33, 42,
109, 140, 141, 142, 153,
154, 155, 159, 160, 161,
162, 163, 165, 166, 168,
170, 172, 180, 186, 190,
191, 193, 196, 197, 202,
204, 211, 285, 297, 321,
334, 339, 346

standard language 52, 69, 70

suburban schools 1, 2, 20, 32,
138, 139, 141, 142, 143,
144, 212

summative assessments 23, 25,
172

symbolic referents 10

symbolic representations 92,
93, 112

synapses, 37, 39

T

teachers-in-training 297

teaching-to-test 4, 171, 185,
210, 213, 214, 272, 273,
277

technology 39

Edwards Brothers,Inc!
Thorofare, NJ 08086
17 December, 2010
BA2010351